LEAVE
THE WORLD
BEHIND

ALSO BY RUMAAN ALAM

That Kind of Mother
Rich and Pretty

LEAVE THE WORLD BEHIND

A Novel

RUMAAN ALAM

An Imprint of HarperCollins*Publishers*

This is a work of fiction. Names, characters, places, and incidents are products of the author's imagination or are used fictitiously and are not to be construed as real. Any resemblance to actual events, locales, organizations, or persons, living or dead, is entirely coincidental.

"Angela"
Written by Bill Callahan
Published by Rough Trade Publishing
By arrangement with Bank Robber Music

HarperCollins books may be purchased for educational, business, or sales promotional use. For information, please email the Special Markets Department at SPsales@harpercollins.com.

Ecco® and HarperCollins® are trademarks of HarperCollins Publishers.

FIRST EDITION

Designed by Michelle Crowe

Title page illustration by Proskurina Yuliya/Shutterstock, Inc.

Library of Congress Cataloging-in-Publication Data
Names: Alam, Rumaan, author.
Title: Leave the world behind : a novel / Rumaan Alam.
Description: First Edition. | New York, NY : Ecco, [2020] | Identifiers: LCCN 2020013947 (print) | LCCN 2020013948 (ebook) | ISBN 9780062667632 (hardback) | ISBN 9780062667656 (ebook)
Classification: LCC PS3601.L3257 L43 2020 (print) | LCC PS3601. L3257 (ebook) | DDC 813/.6—dc23

20 21 22 23 24 LSC 10 9 8 7 6 5 4 3 2 1

for Simon and for Xavier

Love goes on like birdsong,
As soon as possible after a bomb.

—Bill Callahan, "Angela"

LEAVE
THE WORLD
BEHIND

1

WELL, THE SUN WAS SHINING. THEY FELT THAT BODED WELL—
people turn any old thing into an omen. It was all just to say no
clouds were to be seen. The sun where the sun always was. The sun
persistent and indifferent.

Roads merged into one another. The traffic congealed. Their
gray car was a bell jar, a microclimate: air-conditioning, the funk
of adolescence (sweat, feet, sebum), Amanda's French shampoo, the
rustle of debris, for there always was that. The car was Clay's do-
main, and he was lax enough that it accrued the talus of oats from
granola bars bought in bulk, the unexplained tube sock, a subscrip-
tion insert from the *New Yorker*, a twisted tissue, ossified with snot,
that wisp of white plastic peeled from the back of a Band-Aid who
knew when. Kids were always needing a Band-Aid, pink skin split-
ting like summer fruit.

The sunlight on their arms was reassuring. The windows were
tinted with a protectant to keep cancer at bay. There was news of
an intensifying hurricane season, storms with fanciful names from
a preapproved list. Amanda turned down the radio. Was it sexist,
somehow, that Clay drove, and always did? Well: Amanda had no
patience for the attendant sacraments of alternate-side-of-the-street
parking and the twelve-thousand-mile checkup. Besides, Clay took

pride in that kind of thing. He was a professor, and that seemed to correlate with his relish for life's useful tasks: bundling old newspapers for recycling, scattering chemical pellets on the sidewalk when the weather turned icy, replacing lightbulbs, unclogging stopped sinks with a miniature plunger.

The car was not so new as to be luxurious nor so old as to be bohemian. A middle-class thing for middle-class people, engineered not to offend more than to appeal, purchased at a showroom with mirrored walls, some half-hearted balloons, and several more salesmen than customers, lingering in twos or threes, jingling the change in the pockets of their Men's Wearhouse slacks. Sometimes, in the parking lot, Clay would approach some other iteration of the car (it was a popular model, "graphite"), frustrated when the keyless entry system failed to engage.

Archie was fifteen. He wore misshapen sneakers the size of bread loaves. There was a scent of milk about him, as there was to young babies, and beneath that, sweat and hormone. To mitigate all this Archie sprayed a chemical into the thatch under his arms, a smell unlike any in nature, a focus group's consensus of the masculine ideal. Rose paid better attention. The shadow of a young girl in flower; a bloodhound might find the metal beneath the whiff of entry-level cosmetics, the pubescent predilection for fake apples and cherries. They smelled, everyone did, but you couldn't drive the expressway with the windows open, it was too loud. "I have to take this." Amanda held the telephone aloft, warning them, even though no one was saying anything. Archie looked at his own phone, Rose at hers, both with games and parentally preapproved social media. Archie was texting with his friend Dillon, whose two dads were atoning for their ongoing divorce by letting him spend the summer smoking pot in the uppermost floor of their Bergen Street brownstone. Rose had already posted multiple photographs of the trip, though they'd only just crossed the county line.

"Hey Jocelyn—" That telephones knew who was calling ob-

viated nicety. Amanda was account director, Jocelyn account su-
pervisor and one of her three direct reports in the parlance of the
modern office. Jocelyn, of Korean parentage, had been born in
South Carolina, and Amanda continued to feel that the woman's
mealymouthed accent was incongruous. This was so racist she could
never admit it to anyone.

"I'm so sorry to bother you—" Jocelyn's syncopated breath. It
was less that Amanda was fearsome than that power was. Amanda
had started her career in the studio of a temperamental Dane with
a haircut like a tonsure. She'd run into the man at a restaurant the
previous winter and felt queasy.

"It's not a problem." Amanda wasn't magnanimous. The call was
a relief. She wanted her colleagues to need her as God wants people
to keep praying.

Clay drummed fingers on the leather steering wheel, earning a
sideways glance from his wife. He looked at the mirror to confirm
that his children were still there, a habit forged in their infancy. The
rhythm of their breath was steady. The phones worked on them like
those bulbous flutes did on cobras.

None of them really saw the highway landscape. The brain abets
the eye; eventually your expectations of a thing supersede the thing
itself. Yellow-and-black pictographs, hillocks fading into prefab
concrete walls, the occasional glimpse of split-level, railroad crossing, baseball diamond, aboveground pool. Amanda nodded when
she took calls, not for the benefit of the person on the other end of
the phone but to prove to herself that she was engaged. Sometimes,
amid the head nodding, she forgot to listen.

"Jocelyn—" Amanda tried to find some wisdom. Jocelyn didn't
need Amanda's input as much as she did her consent. Office hierar-
chy was arbitrary, like everything. "That's fine. I think that's wise.
We're just on the expressway. You can call, don't worry about it.
But service is spotty once we get farther out. I had this problem last
summer, you remember?" She paused, and was embarrassed; why

would her underling remember Amanda's previous year's vacation plans? "We're going farther out this year!" She made it into a joke. "But call, or email, of course, it's fine. Good luck."

"Everything's okay back at the office?" Clay could never resist pronouncing "the office" with a twist of something. It was synecdoche for her profession, which he largely—but not entirely—understood. A spouse should have her own life, and Amanda's was quite apart from his. Maybe that helped explain their happiness. At least half of the couples they knew were divorced.

"It's fine." One of her most reached-for truisms was that some percentage of jobs were indistinguishable from one another, as they all involved the sending of emails assessing the job itself. A workday was several communiqués about the workday then under way, some bureaucratic politesse, seventy minutes at lunch, twenty minutes caroming around the open-plan, twenty-five minutes drinking coffee. Sometimes her part in the charade felt silly and other times it felt urgent.

The traffic was not so bad, and then, as highways narrowed into streets, it was. Akin to the final, arduous leg of a salmon's trip back home, only with lush green medians and mini malls of rain-stained stucco. The towns were either blue collar and full of Central Americans or prosperous and populated by the white demimonde of plumbers and interior designers and real estate brokers. The actual rich lived in some other realm, like Narnia. You had to happen onto it, trace speedbumpy roads to their inevitable terminus, a cul-de-sac, a shingled mansion, a view of a pond. The air was that sweet cocktail of ocean breeze and happenstance, good for tomatoes and corn, but you thought you could also catch a note of luxury cars, fine art, those soft textiles rich people leave piled on their sofas.

"Should we stop for a bite?" Clay yawned at the end of this sentence, a strangled sound.

"I'm starving." Archie's hyperbole.

"Let's go to Burger King!" Rose had spied the restaurant.

Clay could feel his wife tense up. She preferred that they eat healthily (especially Rose). He could pick up her disapproval like sonar. It was like the swell that presaged an erection. They'd been married sixteen years.

Amanda ate French fries. Archie requested a grotesque number of little briquettes of fried chicken. He dumped these into a paper bag, mixed in some French fries, dribbled in the contents of a small foil-topped container of a sweet and sticky brown sauce, and chewed contentedly.

"Gross." Rose did not approve of her brother, because he was her brother. She ate, less primly than she thought, a hamburger, mayonnaise ringing her pink lips. "Mom, Hazel dropped a pin—can you look at this and see how far her house is?"

Amanda remembered being shocked by how loud the children had been as infants at her breast. Draining and suckling like the sound of plumbing, dispassionate burps and muted flatulence like a dud firecracker, animal and unashamed. She reached behind her for the girl's phone, greasy from food and fingers, hot from overuse. "Honey, this is not going to be anywhere near us." Hazel was less a friend than one of Rose's obsessions. Rose was too young to understand, but Hazel's father was a director at Lazard; the two family's vacations would not much resemble one another.

"Just *look*. You said maybe we could drive over there."

That was the kind of thing she would suggest when half paying attention and come to rue, later, because the kids remembered her promises. Amanda looked at the phone. "It's East Hampton, honey. It's an hour at least. More than, depending on the day."

Rose leaned back in her seat, audibly disgusted. "Can I have my phone back, please?"

Amanda turned and looked at her daughter, frustrated and flushed. "I'm sorry, but I don't want to sit through two hours of summer traffic for a playdate. Not when I'm on vacation."

The girl folded her arms across her chest, a pout like a weapon. Playdate! She was insulted.

Archie chewed at his reflection in the window.

Clay ate as he drove. Amanda would be furious if they were killed in a collision because he'd been distracted by a seven-hundred-calorie sandwich.

The roads narrowed further. Farm stands—honor system: felted green pints of hairy raspberries, moldering in their juices, and a wooden box for your five-dollar bill—on some of the drives wending off the main road. Everything was so green it was frankly a little crazy. You wanted to eat it: get out of the car, get down on all fours, and bite into the earth itself.

"Let's get some air." Clay opened all of the windows, banishing the stink of his farting children. He slowed the car because the road was curvy, seductive, a hip switched back and forth. Designer mailboxes like a hobo sign: good taste and great wealth, pass on by. You couldn't see anything, the trees were that full. Signs warned of deer, idiotic and inured to the presence of humans. They strutted into the streets confidently, walleyed and therefore blind. You saw their corpses everywhere, nut brown and pneumatic with death.

They rounded a bend and confronted a vehicle. Archie at age four, would have known the word for it: *gooseneck trailer*, a huge, empty conveyance being towed by a determined tractor. The driver ignored the car at his back, the local's nonchalance for a familiar invasive species, as the trailer huffed over the road's swells. It was more than a mile before it turned off toward its home homestead, and by that point Ariadne's thread, or whatever bound them to the satellites overhead, had snapped. The GPS had no idea where they were, and they had to follow the directions that Amanda, adept planner, had thought to copy into her notebook. Left then right then left then left then another mile or so, then left again, then two more miles, then right, not quite lost but not quite not lost.

2

THE HOUSE WAS BRICK, PAINTED WHITE. THERE WAS SOME-
thing alluring about that red so transformed. The house looked old
but new. It looked solid but light. Perhaps that was a fundamen-
tally American desire, or just a modern urge, to want a house, a car,
a book, a pair of shoes, to embody these contradictions.

Amanda had found the place on Airbnb. "The Ultimate Escape," the ad proclaimed. She respected the chummy advertising-
speak of the description. *Step into our beautiful house and leave the
world behind.* She'd handed the laptop, hot enough to incubate
tumors in her abdomen, over to Clay. He nodded, said something
noncommittal.

But Amanda had insisted upon this vacation. The promotion
came with a raise. So soon, Rose would vanish into high school
disdain. For this fleeting moment, the children were still mostly
children, even if Archie approached six feet tall. Amanda could
if not conjure at least remember Archie's high girlish voice, the
chunk of Rose against her hip. An old saw, but on your deathbed
would you remember the night you took the clients to that old
steakhouse on Thirty-Sixth Street and asked after their wives, or
bobbing about in the pool with your kids, dark lashes beaded with
chlorinated water?

"This looks nice." Clay switched off the car. The kids released seat belts and pushed open doors and leaped onto the gravel, eager as Stasi.

"Don't go far," Amanda said, though this was nonsense. There was nowhere to go. Maybe the woods. She did worry about Lyme disease. This was just her maternal practice, to interject with authority. The children had long since ceased hearing her daily plaints.

The gravel made its gravelly sound under Clay's leather driving shoes. "How do we get in?"

"There's a lockbox." Amanda consulted her phone. There was no service. They weren't even on a road. She held the thing over her head, but the little bars refused to fill. She had saved this information. "The lockbox . . . on the fence by the pool heater. Code six two nine two. The key inside opens the side door."

The house was obscured by a sculpted hedgerow, someone's pride, like a snowbank, like a wall. The front yard was bound by a picket fence, white, not a trace of irony in it. There was another fence, this one wood and wire, around the pool, which made the insurance more affordable, and also the home's owners knew that sometimes deer strayed into attractive nuisances, and if you were away for a couple of weeks, the stupid thing would drown, swell, explode, a horrifying mess. Clay fetched the key. Amanda stood in the astonishing, humid afternoon, listening to that strange sound of almost quiet that she missed, or claimed she missed, because they lived in the city. You could hear the thrum of some insect or frog or maybe it was both, the wind tossing about the leaves, the sense of a plane or a lawn mower or maybe it was traffic on a highway somewhere distant that reached you just as the persistent beat of the ocean did when you were near the ocean. They were not near the ocean. No, they could not afford to be, but they could almost hear it, an act of will, of recompense.

"Here we are." Clay unlocked the door, needlessly narrating. He did that sometimes, and caught himself doing it, chastened. The house had that hush expensive houses do. Silence meant the house was plumb, solid, its organs working in happy harmony. The respiration of the central air-conditioning, the vigilance of the expensive fridge, the reliable intelligence of all those digital displays marking the time in almost-synchronicity. At a preprogrammed hour, the exterior lights would turn on. A house that barely needed people. The floors were wide-plank wood harvested from an old cotton mill in Utica, so flush there was nary a creak or complaint. The windows so clean that every month or so some common bird miscalculated, and perished broken-necked in the grass. Some efficient hands had been here, rolled up the blinds, turned down the thermostat, Windexed every surface, run the Dyson into the crevices of the sofa, picking up bits of organic blue corn tortilla chips and the errant dime. "This is nice."

Amanda took off her shoes at the door; she felt strongly about taking your shoes off at the door. "This is beautiful." The photographs on the website were a promise, and it was fulfilled: the pendant lamps hovering over the oak table, in case you wanted to do a jigsaw puzzle at night, the gray marble kitchen island where you could imagine kneading dough, the double sink beneath the window overlooking the pool, the stove with its copper faucet so you could fill up your pot without having to move it. The people who owned this house were rich enough to be thoughtful. She'd stand at that sink and soap up the dishes, while Clay stood just outside grilling, drinking a beer, a watchful eye on the children playing Marco Polo in the pool.

"I'll get the things." The subtext was clear; Clay was going to smoke a cigarette, a vice that was meant to be a secret but was not.

Amanda wandered through the place. There was a great room with a television, French doors out to the deck. There were two smallish bedrooms, color schemes of aqua and navy, Jack and Jill bath between them. There was a closet with beach towels and a stacked washer and dryer, there was a long hallway to the master bedroom, lined with inoffensive black-and-white beach scenes. Leaving aside tasteful, everything was thoughtful: a wooden box to hide the plastic bottle of laundry soap, a huge seashell cradling a cake of soap, still in its paper wrapper. The master bed was king-size, so massive it never would have rounded the stairwell to get into their third-floor apartment. The en suite bath was all white (tile, sink, towels, soap, a white dish of white seashells), that particular fantasy of purity to escape the reality of your own excrement. Extraordinary, and only $340 a day plus the cleaning fee and refundable security deposit. From the bedroom Amanda could see her children, already wiggled into their quick-drying Lycra, hurtling toward the placid blue. Archie, long limbs and acute angles, barely convex chest sprouting brown twists at the pink nipples; Rose, curvy and jiggling, downy with baby hair, her polka-dot one-piece straining just so at the legs, pudendum in relief. An anticipatory scream, then they met the water with that delicious clack. In the woods beyond, something started at the sound, fluttered up into view from the general brown of the scene: two fat turkeys, dumb and wild and annoyed at the intrusion. Amanda smiled.

3

AMANDA VOLUNTEERED TO GO TO THE GROCERY. THEY'D passed a store, and she retraced that path. She drove slowly, windows down.

The store was frigid, brightly lit, wide-aisled. She bought yogurt and blueberries. She bought sliced turkey, whole-grain bread, that pebbly mud-colored mustard, and mayonnaise. She bought potato chips and tortilla chips and jarred salsa full of cilantro, even though Archie refused to eat cilantro. She bought organic hot dogs and inexpensive buns and the same ketchup everyone bought. She bought cold, hard lemons and seltzer and Tito's vodka and two bottles of nine-dollar red wine. She bought dried spaghetti and salted butter and a head of garlic. She bought thick-cut bacon and a two-pound bag of flour and twelve-dollar maple syrup in a faceted glass bottle like a tacky perfume. She bought a pound of ground coffee, so potent she could smell it through the vacuum seal, and size 4 coffee filters made of recycled paper. If you care? She cared! She bought a three-pack of paper towels, and a spray-on sunscreen, and aloe, because the children had inherited their father's pale skin. She bought those fancy crackers you put out when there were guests, and Ritz crackers, which everyone liked best, and crumbly white cheddar cheese and extra-garlicky hummus and an unsliced hard salami and those carrots that are tumbled around until they're the size of a child's fingers. She bought packages of cookies from Pepperidge Farm and three pints of Ben & Jerry's politically virtuous ice cream and a Duncan Hines boxed mix for a yellow cake and a Duncan Hines tub of chocolate frosting with a red plastic lid, because parenthood had taught her that on a vacation's inevitable rainy day you could while away an hour by baking a boxed cake. She bought two tumescent zucchini, a bag of snap peas, a bouquet of curling kale so green it was almost black. She bought a bottle of olive oil and a box of Entenmann's crumb-topped doughnuts, a bunch of bananas and a bag of white nectarines and two plastic packages of strawberries, a dozen brown eggs, a plastic box of prewashed spinach, a plastic container of olives, some heirloom tomatoes wrapped in crinkling cellophane, marbled green and shocking orange. She bought three pounds of ground beef and two packages of hamburger buns, their bottoms dusty with flour, and a jar of locally made pickles. She bought four avocados and three limes and a sandy bundle of cilantro even though Archie refused to eat cilantro. It was more than two hundred dollars, but never mind.

"I'm going to need some help." The man placing every item into brown paper bags was maybe in high school but maybe not. He wore a yellow T-shirt and had brown hair and an overall square affect, like he'd been carved from a block of wood. There was some stirring, watching his hands at work, but vacations did that, didn't they, made you horny, made everything seem possible, a life completely different than the one you normally inhabited. She, Amanda, might be a mother temptress, sucking on a postadolescent's hot tongue in the parking lot of the Stop and Shop. Or she might just be another woman from the city spending too much money on too much food.

The boy, or maybe he was a man, put the bags into a cart and followed Amanda into the parking lot. He loaded them into the trunk, and she gave him a five-dollar bill.

She sat, the engine idling, to see if she had cell-phone service, and the endorphin rush of the arriving emails—Jocelyn, Jocelyn, Jocelyn, their agency director, one of the clients, two missives sent to the entire office by the head project manager—was almost as sexual as that flutter over the bag boy.

There was nothing important happening at work, but it was a relief to know that for certain rather than worry that there was. Amanda turned on the radio. She half recognized the song that was playing. She stopped at the gas station and bought Clay a pack of Parliaments. They were on vacation. That night, after hamburgers and hot dogs and grilled zucchini, after bowls of ice cream with cookies crumbled on top of them and maybe some sliced strawberries too, maybe they'd fuck—not make love, that was for home, fucking was for vacation, sweaty and humid and tantalizingly foreign in someone else's Pottery Barn sheets, then go outside, slip into that heated pool, and let the water wash them clean, and smoke one cigarette each and talk about what you talked about after you'd been married for as long as they'd been: finances, the children, fever dreams of real estate (How nice it would be to have a house like this all their own!). Or they'd talk about nothing, the other pleasure of a long marriage. They'd watch television. She drove back to the painted brick house.

4

CLAY BOUND THE TOWEL AROUND HIS WAIST. THE GESTURE of opening double doors was inherently grand. It was cold inside, and very hot outside. The trees had been pruned to keep the shade from the pool. All that sun made you lightheaded. His damp feet left marks on the wooden floors. They melted away in seconds. Clay cut through the kitchen and out via the side door. He retrieved his cigarettes from the glove box, wincing at the gravel. He sat on the front lawn in the shade of a tree and smoked. He should feel bad about this, but tobacco was the foundation of the nation. Smoking tethered you to history itself! It was a patriotic act, or once had been, anyway, like owning slaves or killing the Cherokee.

It was pleasant to sit outside, near naked, the sun and air on your skin reminding you that you're just another animal. He could have sat there nude. There were no other houses, there were no signs of human life, save an honor-system farm stand near a half mile back. There had been a time they'd been so naked together, Archie a wisp of bone and giggles sharing the tub with his parents, but you grew out of that unless you were a hippie.

He couldn't hear the children carrying on in the pool. The house between him and them was not so large, but the trees absorbed their noise as cotton might blood. Clay felt safe, cossetted, embraced, the rampart of hedge keeping the world at bay. As though he could see it, he pictured Amanda, adrift on an inflatable lounge, pretending dignity (hard to do: even the duck lacks that somehow, the water's undulations always ridiculous) and reading *Elle*. Clay unknotted the towel and lay back. The grass was itchy under his back. He stared at the sky. Without really thinking about it—but also kind of thinking about it—his right hand wandered down the front of his J.Crew suit, fumbled with his penis, gone cold and shy from the water. Vacations made you horny.

Clay felt light, unfettered, though he was not fettered by much. He was supposed to be reviewing a book for the *New York Times Book Review* and had brought his laptop. He only needed nine hundred words. In a couple of hours he'd put the family to bed, fill a tumbler with ice and vodka, sit shirtless on the deck, laptop illuminating the night, smoke cigarettes, and the thoughts would come and the nine hundred words would follow. Clay was diligent but also (he knew it) a little lazy. He wanted to be asked to write for the *New York Times Book Review* but didn't want to actually write anything.

Clay had tenure, and Amanda had the title of director, but they did not have level floors and central air-conditioning. The key to success was having parents who had succeeded. Still, they could pantomime ownership for a week. His penis jerked itself toward the sun, a yoga salutation, bouncing, then stiff at the house's allure. Marble countertops and a Miele washer and Clay had a full erection, his dick hovering over his belly like the searching needle in a compass.

Clay ground out his cigarette guiltily. He was never without breath mints or chewing gum. He tied the towel around his waist and went into the house. The garbage slid out on casters from beneath the countertops. Clay ran the butt under the faucet (imagine if he burned the house down?) then buried it in the refuse. There was lemon soap in a glass dispenser by the sink. From the window he could see his family. Rose was lost in a game of her own. Archie was doing pull-ups on the diving board, hoisting his skinny body heavenward, his bony shoulders the pink of undercooked meat.

Sometimes, looking at his family, he was flooded with this desire to *do* for them. I'll build you a house or knit you a sweater, whatever is required. Pursued by wolves? I'll make a bridge of my body so you can cross that ravine. They were all that mattered to him, but of course they didn't really understand that, because such was the parental contract. Clay found a baseball game on the radio, though he did not care about baseball. He thought the description comforting, the play-by-play like being read a bedtime story. Clay dumped two packages of the raw meat into a large bowl—Archie would eat three hamburgers—and diced a white onion, mixed that in, pinched in salt and ground in pepper, added Worcestershire sauce like daubing perfume onto a wrist. He molded the burgers and lined them up on a plate. Clay sliced cheddar cheese, halved the buns. The towel was slipping from his waist, so he washed the raw meat from his hands and tied it more tightly. He filled a glass bowl with potato chips and ferried the food outside. Every step felt familiar, like he'd been throwing together summertime meals in that kitchen all his life.

"Dinner in a bit," he called. No one acknowledged this. Clay switched on the propane, used the long lighter to make the flame catch. Half naked, he tended the raw meat, thinking he must resemble a caveman, some long-forgotten ancestor. Who was to say that one hadn't stood once on that very spot? Millennia earlier or even just centuries, some shirtless Iroquois in hide loincloth, stoking a fire that the flesh of his flesh might dine on flesh. The thought made him smile.

5

THEY ATE ON THE DECK, IN DISHABILLE, AN ASSEMBLAGE OF towels in garish colors and ketchup-stained paper napkins. Hamburgers the size of hockey pucks inside airy bread. Rose was particularly susceptible to the tart charms of vinegar potato chips. Crumbs and grease on her chin. Amanda loved that Rose could still reach girlishness. Her mind was one thing, her body another: it was the hormones in the milk or the food chain or the water supply or the air or who knew.

It was so hot that the parents didn't even bid the children shower, let them sprawl on the gingham-upholstered sofa in their fleshy bodies, Archie lank and Rose lush: visible ribs and a constellation of moles, dimpled elbows and a downy chin. Rose wanted to watch a cartoon, and Archie was secretly comforted by animation—wistful for his own youth! His skin prickled in the air-conditioned chill, the unfamiliar sofa was soft, and his mind and mouth felt thick and slow from the day's heat or exertion. He was too tired to get up for another hamburger, gone cold, doused in ketchup, which he'd eat standing up in the kitchen, the tile cold underfoot. In a minute, he thought, but his body was pleading with hunger from those hours in the pool or maybe just the hours cooped up in the car, his body always felt this way.

Amanda went to shower. The thing was fixed in the ceiling, the water falling onto you as rain might. She set it as hot as possible to banish the residue of the SPF lotion. That stuff always felt vaguely poisonous, an ounce of prevention, etc. She wore her hair neither short nor long, without bangs, which made her look youthful in a way that was not good in an office environment. Two different kinds of vanity at odds—a desire to look capable rather than girl-ish. Amanda knew that she looked like the sort of woman she was. You could read it on her from a great distance. Her poise and pos-ture, her clothes and grooming, all said who she was.

Her body still contained the secondhand warmth of the sun. The pool water had barely been a respite, the tepidity of bathwa-ter. Amanda's limbs felt thick and superb. She wanted to lie down and roll away into sleep. Her fingers strayed to the parts of herself where they felt best, in search not of some internal pleasure but something more cerebral: the confirmation that she, her shoulders, her nipples, her elbows, all of it, existed. What a marvel, to have a body, a thing that contained you. Vacation was for being returned to your body.

Amanda wrapped her hair into a white towel like a woman in a certain kind of film. She spread lotion across her skin, pulled on the loose cotton pants she favored in bed, summertime, and an old T-shirt with a logo that no longer meant anything to her. It was impossible to keep track of the provenance of all their earthly possessions. The shirt's cotton so worn that it shone. She felt alive and if not sexy, then sexual; the promise mattered more than the transaction. She still loved him, nothing like that, and he knew her body—it had been eighteen years, of course he knew it—but she was human, wouldn't have minded novelty.

She peeked out of the door to the living room. Her children looked dazed, fatted, odalisques on the couch. Her husband was bent over his phone.

"Bed in twenty minutes." Amanda gave Clay a suggestive look, then closed the door behind her. She stepped out of her pants and into the cool percale of the bed. She did not draw the curtains—let them watch, the deer, the owls, the stupid flightless turkeys—admire Clay's still impressive latissimus dorsi (he rowed at the New York Sports Club twice weekly), which she loved to sink her fingers into, catch the pleasant stink of his hairy armpits, applaud the practiced flick of his tongue against her.

The house was too far from the world to offer cellular service, but there was WiFi, a preposterously long password (018HGF234-WRH357XIO) to keep out whom—the deer, the owls, the stupid flightless turkeys? She tapped the glass, spelling it out, random as Ouija or the rosary, then the thing took and the emails arrived, piling the one atop the other. Forty-one! She felt so necessary, so missed, so *loved*.

In her personal account she learned that things were on sale, that the book club she'd been meaning to join was scheduling a fall get-together, that the *New Yorker* had written about a Bosnian filmmaker. In her work account, there were questions, there were concerns, and people were seeking Amanda's participation, her opinion, her guidance. Everyone had received her out-of-office reply, sunny and authoritative, but she broke the promise to be in touch upon her return. No, don't do X. Yes, email Y. Ask so-and-so about such-and-such. Just a reminder to follow up with that person about this matter.

Her arm grew tingly from the exertion of holding aloft the too-small phone. She flipped onto her stomach, the sheets warm from her body, so the transitive warmth against her vulva was that of her own body, and flopping around in the bed was an act of masturbation. She felt clean, ready to feel dirty, but she worked her way through the emails, distracting herself until at last Clay came to her, smelling of furtive cigarettes and the lemon wedges in his vodka.

The heat from the shower had softened her spine the way room temperature does a stick of butter. The occasional vinyasa class had made her more attentive to her bones. She let them give. She relaxed away from her usual resolve not to do the filthiest things they could conjure between the two of them. She let him knead his fingers into her hair and hold her head firmly but gently against the pillow, her throat a passage, a void to be filled. She let herself moan more loudly than she might have at home, because there was that long hall between them and the children's rooms. She bucked her hips back and up to meet his mouth, and later—it felt an eternity but was only twenty minutes—she took his wilting penis into her mouth, marveling at the taste of her own body.

"Christ." Clay was wheezing.

"You have to quit smoking." She worried about a cardiac event. They were not so young. Every mother had contemplated the loss of a child; Amanda had no emotions left around the theoretical death of her husband. She'd love again, she told herself. He was a good man.

"I do." Clay did not mean it. There was already so little pleasure in modern life.

Amanda stood, stretched, happily sticky, wanting a cigarette herself; the dizzying effect would put her at some remove from what they had just done, which you needed after sex, even with a familiar. That wasn't really me! She opened the door, and the night was shocking with noise. Crickets or whatever bug that was, various maybe sinister footfalls in the dried leaves of the woods beyond the lawn, the stealthy breeze moving everything, maybe the vegetal growth actually made a sound, even, the barest *scritch, scritch* of the advancing grass, the heartbeat throb of the oak leaves flowing with chlorophyll.

Amanda had a feeling like being watched, but there was no one out there watching her, was there? An involuntary shiver at the very idea, then a retreat into the adult illusion of safety.

The two of them crept, naked as Neanderthals, across the deck, the only light a slice of it falling through the glass door. Clay heaved the cover off the hot tub, and they sank into its froth, the steam obscuring his glasses, a satisfied sensual grin. Her eyes adjusted to the darkness. His pale flesh in stark relief. She could see him as he was, but she loved him.

6

NO ONE HAD BOUGHT CEREAL. ARCHIE WANTED A SPECIFIC taste less than the feel of processed grain gone soft enough in milk. He yawned.

"Sorry, champ. I'll make you an omelet." His dad had this stupid game of being the best at making breakfast. Though he was a good cook—he always put butter on the toast and then put it back into the toaster oven so it melted into the bread until the thing was sloppy like someone had already chewed it—there was something sad in the way he needed attention for it.

Amanda was spreading sunscreen on Rose's back. The television was on, but no one was actually watching it. She wiped her hands on her own bare legs and put the bottle into the tote bag. "Rose, you're bringing three books? For one afternoon at the beach?"

"We'll be gone all day. What if I run out of something to read?"

"The bag is already very heavy—"

Rose didn't want to whine, it just sort of happened.

"You can put them in this bag." Clay thought the girl's bookishness reflected well on them. "Archie, can you bring this bag?"

"I need to go to the bathroom." Archie lingered in there before the mirror. He was wearing his lacrosse shirt, the one he'd cut the sleeves off because he wanted people to see his muscles, and he studied them, happy with what he saw.

"Hurry up," Clay called to his son, the irritation that necessitated this relaxation.

"I've got lunch in there. And water. And the blanket and towels." Amanda was pointing at bags, sure they'd forget something even so, best-laid plans.

"I've got it, I've got it." A little *Christ* under the breath, which was more a reflex than he realized. Archie took the bag his father had left by the sofa. It weighed nothing! He was so strong.

The family trooped outside, loaded their things, and buckled their bodies. The GPS churned, unable to locate itself, or them, or the rest of the world. Without much thinking about it, Clay found the road to the highway and the satellite recovered its hold on them and they drove under its protective gaze. The highway turned into a bridge that seemed to lead to nothing, that led to the end of America itself. They wound into the empty parking lot (it was early) and paid five dollars to a khaki-uniformed teen who seemed himself made of sand—golden curls, freckles, browned skin, teeth like little shells.

There was a tunnel from the lot to the shore that carried them past a park, flagpoles towering as redwoods, flags of many nations cracking in the ocean air.

"What's this?" Archie, derisive even when he didn't mean to be.

They stood in flip-flopped feet in a little canyon of concrete, and Amanda read the inscription. "It's for the victims of Flight 800." TWA, bound for Paris. Everyone had perished. You heard that rendered as souls, sometimes, which made it sound more grand or old-fashioned or sanctified. Amanda remembered—conspiracy theorists said it had been an American missile, but logic said it was mechanical failure. We pretend otherwise, but these things happen.

"Let's go!" Rose tugged on the tote bag slung across her father's shoulder.

It was hot but the wind was relentless, bringing in a chill from the void of the ocean. There was something Arctic in it, and who was to say that wasn't literally the case. The world was vast but also small and governed by logic. Amanda struggled to spread the blanket, something she'd found on the internet, block-printed by illiterate Indian villagers. She placed a bag at each corner to weigh the thing down. The children shed their layers and bounded off like gazelles. Rose investigated the detritus washed up on the sand, shells and plastic cups and iridescent balloons that had celebrated proms and sweet sixteens miles away. Archie knelt in the sand some distance from their encampment, pretending not to stare at the lifeguards, hale girls, sun-lightened locks and red swimsuits.

Amanda had a novel she could barely follow, with a tiresome central metaphor involving birds. Clay had the kind of book he normally had, a slender and unclassifiable critique of the way we live now, the sort of thing it's impossible to read near naked in the sun but important to have read, for his work.

His glance kept straying to the lifeguards. So did Amanda's. How could they not? There was a metaphor less tiresome—what would stand between you and death at the hands of nature but beautiful youth, flat stomachs, nipples the size of quarters, swollen biceps, hairless legs, browned skin, dry hair, mouths perfected by orthodontia, unquestioning eyes behind cheap plastic sunglasses?

They ate turkey sandwiches and chips that kept breaking off in the pasty guacamole (a smaller portion without the acrid herb, for the doted-upon son), then watermelon, bracing and cold. Archie slept, and Rose read one of her graphic novels. Archie woke and goaded his father into the waves, which were terrifying. Amanda watched for sharks because she had heard there were sharks. What would one of those teenage lifeguards do if there were sharks?

It was pleasant, it was diverting, it was exhausting. The sun was not waning, but the wind was winning. "We should go." Amanda packed their empty plastic containers back into the insulated bag she'd found in the kitchen. It was in precisely the spot where you'd store an insulated bag in your kitchen (a cabinet beneath the microwave).

Rose shivered, and her father wrapped her up in a towel just as he had when she'd been a toddler fresh from the bath. The family trudged back to their car, strangely defeated, and drove back across the bridge.

"There's a Starbucks." Amanda pressed her hand onto her husband's right forearm, excited.

He pulled in to the lot, and Amanda went inside. Alee, away from that wind, the air was still hot. The shop was the same as all locations of a chain tend to be, but wasn't that comforting? The signature colors, those dependable brown napkins—always a stack in the car for blowing winter noses or mopping up spills—the green plastic straws, the heavyset devotees paying seven dollars for cream-topped milkshakes in cups the size of athletic trophies. She ordered black coffees, though it was after three and it would keep her up late, or maybe it wouldn't, because proximity to the ocean always made her so tired.

There was a desultory de-sanding of limbs, using the backyard hose. Archie sprayed the thing directly down the front of his suit, his balls shellacked with actual tiny shells, then figured that was good enough and dove into the pool. He rubbed his scalp and could feel sand being dislodged, drifting away into the water.

Amanda washed her feet and then went inside to shower. The house felt reassuringly familiar after fewer than twenty-four hours. She played a podcast on the computer—something to do with the mind, she barely paid attention to it—and shampooed her hair again, hating the effect of the salt water on it. She dressed and found Clay whistling as he rinsed the sandy Tupperware.

"I'll make pasta," Amanda said.

"The kids are in the pool. I'm going to run to the store and get some cereal for Archie." He meant he'd run to the store, smoke a cigarette in the parking lot, go inside, wash his hands, come back with a hundred dollars' worth of food. "They're saying it might rain tomorrow."

"You can almost feel it." A promise in the air, or maybe it was a threat. She had brought her computer into the kitchen with her so she could keep listening to the podcast. She set it on the counter. "Get something sweet? Like . . . a pie. Get a pie. And maybe some more ice cream?" The night before, postcoital and woozy from the hot tub, they'd eaten an entire pint between the two of them. "Maybe some tomatoes. Another watermelon. Some berries. I don't know, whatever looks good."

He kissed her, an unfamiliar thing to do when running out on a simple errand, but sweet.

The window meant that she could watch the children as she did something else. She zested the lemon, dumped that into the softening butter, minced garlic and added that. She used the kitchen shears to hack at the parsley, which had a sharp and astonishing smell. She folded this all together into a thick paste. The hot pasta would dull the taste of the garlic.

She used the pot filler over the stove, helped herself to the kosher salt in the pantry, poured a glass of red wine. It made her stomach churn, red wine over black coffee. The water boiled. Her attention had drifted. Beyond the pool, through the woods at the property's perimeter, Amanda saw a deer, then adjusted her eyes and saw two more, smaller. Mother and children! Wasn't that fitting. The animals were cautious, nosing through the brush in search of—what did deer eat? Her ignorance embarrassed her.

She strained the cooked pasta, dropped the herbed butter into the nest of noodles, replaced the lid, and opened the glass door. The air had grown cooler. It would rain, or something would happen, and they would have to spend the next day inside the house. There were board games, there was the television, maybe they'd watch a movie, there was a glass canister of dried corn in the pantry, maybe they'd pop some, lie about all day.

"It's time to come inside, guys."

Archie and Rose were in the hot tub, pink as cooking lobsters.

Amanda insisted the children bathe and banish that chlorine smell. She poured herself another glass of wine. Clay returned with a surprising number of paper bags.

"I went a little overboard." He looked sheepish. "I thought it might rain. I don't want to have to leave the house tomorrow."

Amanda frowned because she felt she was supposed to. It wouldn't ruin them to spend a little more than was usual on groceries. Or maybe it was the wine. "Fine, fine. Put those away and let's eat?" She wasn't sure she wasn't slurring a little bit.

She laid the table. The children, redolent of marzipan (Dr. Bronner's, in the green bottle), sat. They were the best kind of tired, docile, almost polite, no burping or name-calling. Archie even helped his father clear the table, and Amanda lay on the sofa beside Rose, her head in her child's warm lap. She didn't mean to sleep, but she did, full of wine and pasta and bored by the television's prattle. Amanda was perplexed when she was roused twenty minutes on by an especially shrill commercial and Rose's need for the bathroom. Her mouth was dry.

"Have a nice nap?" Clay was teasing, not amorous (he was still sated) but romantic—even better or rarer. They'd made a nice life for themselves, hadn't they?

Amanda did the *New York Times* crossword on her phone—she was afraid of dementia, and felt this was preventative—and the time passed strangely, as it did when measured in minutes before the television. If the night before she'd been eager to look at her work and fuck her husband, tonight it felt important to linger on the sofa with her children, Archie dopey in his too-big hooded sweatshirt, Rose infantile, wrapped in the itchy woolen throw left on the sofa's arm. Clay served bowls of ice cream, then collected the bowls, and the dishwasher ran with its reassuring gurgle, and Rose's eyes looked blank and Archie yawned loudly, suddenly, so like a man, and Amanda sent the children to bed, telling them to brush their teeth but not standing sentry to verify that they did.

She yawned, was tired enough to go to bed, but knew somehow that if she moved, she would not fall asleep. Clay changed the channel, pausing a moment on Rachel Maddow and then switching to a thriller that neither of them were able to follow, detectives and their prey.

"Television is idiotic." Clay turned it off. He'd rather play with his phone. He dropped some ice into a glass. "You want a drink?"

Amanda shook her head. "I'm done."

She didn't yet quite know which switch controlled which light. She flicked one, and the pool and the grounds beyond it were illuminated, pure white beams shot through the green branches overhead. She turned the light off, returning things to their black state, which seemed right, seemed natural.

"I need some water," she said or thought, and made her way into the kitchen. She was filling one of the IKEA glasses when she heard a scratch, a footfall, a voice, something that felt odd or wrong. "Did you hear that?"

Clay mumbled; he wasn't truly listening. He checked the little buttons on the side of his phone to make sure the sound was turned off. "It's not me."

"No." She sipped her water. "It was something else."

There it was again: shuffle, a voice, a quiet murmur, a *presence*. A disruption, a change. Something. This time Amanda was more certain. Her heart quickened. She felt sober, awake. She put her cup down on the marble counter, quietly—suddenly that seemed right, to move stealthily.

"I heard something." She was whispering.

Such moments, Clay was called upon. He had to be the man. He didn't mind it. Maybe he liked it. Maybe it made him feel necessary. From down the hall, he could almost hear Archie, snoring like a sleeping dog. "It's probably just a deer in the front garden."

"It's something." Amanda held up a hand to silence him. Her mouth was metallic with fear. "I know I heard something."

There it was, undeniable: noise. A cough, a voice, a step, a hesitation, that uncategorizable animal knowledge that there's another of the species nearby and the pause, pregnant, to see if they mean harm. There was a knock at the door. A knock at the door of this house, where no one knew they were, not even the global positioning system, this house near the ocean but also lost in farmland, this house of red bricks painted white, the very material the smartest little piggy chose because it would keep him safest. There was a knock at the door.

7

WHAT WERE THEY SUPPOSED TO DO?

Amanda stood, frozen, a prey's instinct. Gather your thoughts. "Get a bat." That old solution: violence.

"A bat?" Clay pictured the flying mammal. "A bat?" He understood, then, but where would he get a bat? When had he last held a bat? Did they even have a baseball bat at home, and if they did, had they brought it on vacation? No, but when had they decided to forsake that American diversion? In their foyer on Baltic Street they had a clutch of umbrellas of varying degrees of broken, an extra windshield scraper, Archie's lacrosse stick, some of those circulars, never asked for, a sheaf of coupons in rainproof plastic that would never biodegrade. Well, lacrosse was from the Indians, maybe that was more all-American. On a console table, beneath a framed photograph of Coney Island, there was a brass object, an artful little torque, the kind of made-in-China geegaw meant to add character to hotel rooms or model apartments. He picked it up but found it weighed nothing. Besides, what would he do, wrap his fingers around it, strike some stranger in the head? He was a professor.

"I don't know." Her whisper was built for the stage. Surely whoever was on the other side of the door could hear her. "Who could it be?"

This was ridiculous. "I don't know." Clay put the little objet d'art back in its place. Art could not protect them.

There was another knock at the door. This time, a man's voice. "I'm sorry. Hello?"

Clay could not imagine a killer could be so polite. "It's nothing. I'll get it."

"No!" Amanda had this terrible flash of feeling, a premonition if the worst came to pass and passing paranoia if it did not. She did not like this.

"Let's just calm down." Maybe he was unconsciously channeling behaviors seen in films. He looked at his wife until she seemed to calm, like what tamers did with their lions, dominance and eye contact. He didn't entirely believe in the act. "Get the phone. Just in case." That was decisive and smart; he was proud of himself for having thought of it.

Amanda went into the kitchen. There was a desk, a cordless telephone, a 516 number. In her lifetime the cordless telephone had been both innovation and obsolete. They still had one at home, but no one ever used it. She picked it up. Should she press the button, dial the nine and then the one and wait?

Clay unbolted the lock and pulled open the door. What was he expecting?

The interrogatory light of the porch revealed a man, black, handsome, well proportioned though maybe a little short, in his sixties, with a warm smile. It was funny, how quickly the eye could register: benign, or harmless, or instantly reassuring. He wore a rumpled blazer, a loosened knit tie, a striped shirt, those brown pants every man over thirty-five wears. He held up his hands in a gesture that was either conciliatory or said *Don't shoot*. By his age, black men were adept at this gesture.

"I'm so sorry to bother you." He sounded as people rarely did when saying those words: sincere. He knew how to put on an act.

"Hello?" Clay said it as if he was answering a telephone. Opening a door to an unexpected visitor was without precedent. Urban life contained only the guy who came to deliver an Amazon box, and he had to buzz first. "Hi?"

"I'm so sorry to bother you." The man's voice was gravelly with the gravitas of a news anchor. This quality, he knew, made him sound more sincere.

Beside but just behind the man was a woman, also black, also of an indeterminate age, in boxy linen skirt and jacket. "*We're* sorry," she corrected, an italicized *we*; it was so practiced that she had to be his wife. "We didn't mean to frighten you."

Clay laughed as though the idea were ridiculous. Frightened, he was not frightened. She looked like the kind of woman you'd see in a television ad for an osteoporosis medication.

Amanda lingered between the foyer and the kitchen, behind a column, as if this provided some tactical advantage. She was not persuaded. An emergency call might be in order. People in ties could be criminals. She had not gone to lock the children's bedroom doors; what kind of mother was she?

"Can I help you?" Was that what one said in such a circumstance? Clay was unclear.

The man cleared his throat. "We're sorry to bother you." A third time, an incantation. He went on. "I know it's late. A knock at the door, way out here." He had imagined how this would transpire. He had rehearsed his part.

Now the woman picked it up: "We couldn't decide if we should knock at the front door or the side door." She laughed to show how absurd this was. Her voice carried, implied long-ago elocution lessons. A trace of Hepburn that sounded like aristocracy. "I thought this might be less frightening—"

Clay protested too much. "Not frightening, just surprising."

"Of course, of course." The man had expected as much. "I said we should try the side door. It's glass, so you could have seen us and known that we're just—" He trailed off, a shrug to say *We mean you no harm.*

"I thought that might be stranger, though. Or frightening." The woman tried to catch Clay's eye.

Their near-unison seemed charming to the point of comedy, like Powell and Loy. Clay's adrenaline fermented into annoyance. "Can we . . . help you?" He hadn't even heard their car, if they had come by car, but how else would they have come?

Clay had said *we,* and so, telephone tight in her hand like a child's favored plush toy, Amanda stepped into the foyer. They were probably lost motorists, or had a flat tire. Occam's razor and all that. "Hi!" She forced in some cheer, as though she'd been waiting for them.

"Good evening." The man wanted to underscore that he was a gentleman. That was part of the plan.

"You startled us. We weren't expecting anyone." Amanda didn't mind admitting it. She calculated that it might establish her upper hand. She thought it might say *This is our house, now what do you want?*

There was wind, and it sounded like a chorus of voices. The trees swayed, their heads tossed with abandon. A storm was coming or out there somewhere.

The woman shivered. Her linen clothes could not keep her warm. She seemed pitiable, elderly, ill prepared. She was smart, and she'd been counting on this.

Clay could not help feeling bad, or rude. The woman was old enough to be his mother, though his own mother was long dead. Good manners were a tool that helped you deal with moments this strange. "You caught us by surprise. But what can we do for you?"

The black man looked at Amanda, and his smile warmed further. "Well, you must be Amanda. Right? Amanda. I'm sorry, but—" The breeze eddied around them, through their summer clothes. He said her name a third time because he knew it would be effective. "Amanda, do you think we could come inside?"

8

RECOGNIZING PEOPLE WAS ONE OF AMANDA'S SKILLS. SHE
bought cocktails for the apparatchiks from Minneapolis and Co-
lumbus and St. Louis who paid her. She remembered who was who
and asked after their families. This was a point of pride. She looked
at the man and saw only a black man she had never seen before.

"You know one another!" Clay was reassured. The breeze raised
the hair on his legs.

"We've not had the pleasure of meeting face-to-face." The man
had the practice of a salesman which was, ultimately, what he was.
"I'm G. H."

The letters meant nothing to her. Amanda couldn't figure whether
he was trying to spell something.

"George." The woman thought the name more gentle than the
initials, and this was a moment when they needed to seem human.
You never knew who had guns and was ready to stand their ground.
"He's George."

He thought of himself as George. He spoke of himself as G. H.
"—George, right, I'm George. This is our house."

Possession was some fraction of the law, and Amanda had de-
luded herself. She'd been pretending that this was their house! "I'm
sorry?"

"This is our house," he said again. "We emailed back and forth—about the house?" He tried to sound firm but also gentle.

Amanda remembered, then: GHW@washingtongroupfund.com—the formal opacity of those initials. The place was comfortable but sufficiently anonymous that she had not bothered to try to picture its owners, and now, seeing them, she knew that if she had bothered to picture them, her picture would have been incorrect. This didn't seem to her like the sort of house where black people lived. But what did she mean by that? "This is—your house?"

Clay was disappointed. They were paying for the illusion of ownership. They were on vacation. He closed the door, leaving the world out there, where it belonged.

"We're so sorry to bother you." Ruth still had her hand on George's shoulder. Well, they were inside; they'd accomplished something.

Why had Clay closed the door, invited these people in? It was so like him. He always wanted to handle the business of life but was not fully prepared to do so. Amanda wanted proof. She wanted to inspect the mortgage, a photo ID. These people and their disheveled clothes could be—well, they looked more like evangelists than criminals, hopeful pamphleteers come to witness Jehovah.

"You gave us a bit of a fright!" Clay didn't mind confessing his own cowardice, since it had passed. *A bit* barely counted, and it was, importantly, their fault. "Goodness, it's cold out all of a sudden."

"It is." G. H. was as good as anyone at predicting how other people would behave. But it took time. They were inside. That was what mattered. "Summer storm? Maybe it'll pass."

They were four adults standing about awkwardly as in those last anticipatory moments at an orgy.

Amanda was furious at everyone, Clay most of all. She twitched, certain one of these people would produce a gun, a knife, a demand. She wished she'd still been holding the telephone, though who could say how long it would take for the local precinct to get to their beautiful house in the deep of the woods. She didn't even say anything.

G. H. was ready. He had prepared, tried to guess how these people might react. "I understand how strange it must be for you, us turning up like this unannounced."

"Unannounced." Amanda inspected the word, and it didn't hold up to scrutiny.

"We'd have called, you see, but the phones—"

They'd have called? Did these people have her number?

"I'm Ruth." She extended a hand. Every couple apportioned labor by strength, even or especially at such moments. Her role was to shake hands and make nice and put these people at ease so they could get what they wanted.

"Clay." He shook her hand.

"And you're Amanda." Ruth smiled.

Amanda took the stranger's manicured hand. If calluses meant honest labor, did softness imply dishonesty? "Yes," she said.

"And I'm G. H., again. Clay, nice to meet you."

Clay applied more pressure than he normally might have, as he had a point to prove.

"And Amanda, it's nice to meet face-to-face."

Amanda crossed arms over her chest. "Yes. Though I have to admit that I wasn't expecting to meet you at all."

"No, of course not."

"Maybe we should—sit?" It was their house, what was Clay supposed to do?

"That would be lovely." Ruth had the smile of a politician's wife.

"Sit? Yes. Fine." Amanda tried to communicate something to her husband, but one look couldn't contain it. "Maybe in the kitchen. We'll have to be quiet, though, the children are sleeping."

"The children. Of course. I hope we didn't wake them." G. H. should have guessed there would be children, but maybe that helped the situation.

"Archie could sleep through a nuclear bomb. I'm sure they're fine." Clay was his usual joking self.

"I think I'll just go check on them." Amanda was icy, and tried to imply that it was her habit to peer in at her sleeping children every so often.

"They're fine." Clay couldn't understand what she was up to.

"I'm just going to go check on them. Why don't you—" She didn't know how to complete the thought, and so she did not bother.

"Let's sit." Clay gestured at the stools at the kitchen island.

"Clay, I should explain." G. H. took this on as a masculine burden, like arranging rental cars for trips out of town. He thought another husband might understand. "As I said, I would have called. We tried to, actually, but there's no service."

"We stayed not far from here a couple of summers ago." Clay wanted to establish that he had some hold on this geography. That he knew what it was like to have a house in the country. "Impossible to get a signal most of the time."

"That's true," G. H. said. He had sat, put elbows on marble, leaned forward. "But I'm not sure if that's what's happening at the moment."

"How's that?" Clay felt he should offer them something. Weren't they guests? Or was he the guest? "Can I get you some water?"

Down the dark hall, Amanda used her cell phone as a light. Having confirmed that Archie and Rose still existed, lost in the unworried sleep of children, she tarried just out of sight, straining to hear what was being discussed while trying to get her phone to engage. She gazed at it as if it were a mirror, but it did not recognize her—maybe the hallway was too dark—and did not come to life. Amanda pressed the home button, and it lit up, showing her a news alert, the barely legible *T* of the *New York Times* and only a few words: "Major blackout reported on the East Coast of the United States." She jabbed at it, but the application did not open, just the white screen of the thinking machine. This was a specific flavor of irritation. She couldn't be mad, but she was.

"Tonight we were at the symphony." G. H. was in the middle of his explanation. "In the Bronx."

"He's on the board of the Philharmonic—" Connubial pride, it couldn't be helped. She and George believed in giving back. "It's to encourage people to take an interest in classical music . . ." Ruth was overexplaining.

Amanda came into the room.

"The kids are okay?" Clay did not understand that this had been only pretense.

"They're fine." Amanda wanted to show her husband her phone. She didn't have any news beyond those eleven words, but it was something, and represented some advantage over these people.

"We were driving back to the city. Home. Then something happened." He wasn't trying to be vague. Even in the car he and Ruth hadn't spoken of it, because they were afraid.

"A blackout." Amanda produced this, triumphant.

"How did you know?" G. H. was surprised. He had expected to have to explain. They'd seen nothing but darkness all the way out, and then, through the trees, the glow of their own house. They couldn't believe it because it didn't make sense, but they didn't care to make sense. The relief of light and its safety.

"A blackout?" Clay was expecting something worse.

"I got a news alert." Amanda took her phone from her pocket and put it on the counter.

"What did it say?" Ruth wanted more information. She'd seen it with her own eyes but knew nothing. "Did it say why?"

"Just that. There was a blackout on the East Coast." She looked at the phone again, but the alert was gone, and she didn't know how to return to it.

"It is windy outside." Clay felt that the cause and effect was clear.

"It's hurricane season. Wasn't there news about a hurricane?" Amanda couldn't recall.

"A blackout." G. H. nodded. "So we thought. Well, we live on the fourteenth floor."

"The traffic lights would have all gone out. It would have been chaos." Ruth didn't want to bother explaining in more detail. The city was as unnatural as it was possible to be, accretion of steel and glass and capital, and light was fundamental to its existence. A city without power was like a flightless bird, an accident of evolution.

"A blackout?" Clay felt like he was simply offering the word to someone who had forgotten it. "There's been a blackout. That doesn't seem so bad."

Amanda didn't buy it. It didn't seem true. "The lights seem to be working here."

She was right, of course. Still, everyone looked at the pendants over the kitchen island, like four people seeking hypnosis. You couldn't explain electricity at all, neither its presence nor its absence. Were her words an act of hubris? There was the sound of the wind against the window over the sink. Immediately thereafter, the lights flickered. Not once nor twice; four times, like a message in Morse that they had to decipher, like a succession of flashbulbs, but it held steady, it held course, the light held the night at bay. The four of them had breathed in sharply; all four of them exhaled.

9

"JESUS CHRIST." THE LORD'S NAME IN VAIN MEANT BLAS-
phemy but also futility. Jesus cared nothing for Clay, but the power
didn't go out. Clay had already imagined Amanda and the other
woman (what was her name?) screaming. Maybe it was unkind to
equate femininity with fear. He'd have to reason with them—a
windy night, a far-off corner of Long Island. The world was so big
that much of it was remote. You could forget this if you lived too
long in a city. Electricity was a miracle. They should be grateful.

"It's fine." G. H. said it to himself, to his wife.

"So there was a blackout, and you drove all the way out here?"
Amanda couldn't make sense of this. Manhattan was so far away.
It didn't make any sense.

"These roads—they're familiar. I barely even thought about it.
We saw the lights go, and I looked at Ruth." G. H. didn't know
how he would explain what he didn't entirely understand.

"We thought we might stay," Ruth said. No sense dancing around
it. Ruth had always been direct.

"You thought you might stay—here?" Amanda knew these people
wanted something. "But we're staying here."

"We knew we couldn't drive into the city. We knew we couldn't walk up fourteen flights. So we drove out here and thought you might understand."

"Of course." Clay understood.

Amanda looked at her husband. "What he means is, of course we *understand*—" Did she, though? What if this was some con? Perfect strangers worming their way into the house, into their lives.

"I know it's a surprise. But maybe you can . . . This is our house. We wanted to be in our house. Safe. While we figured out what's going on out there." G. H. was being honest, but it still seemed like he was selling something.

"It's our good luck we had gas." Ruth nodded. "Honestly, I don't know how much farther we could go."

"Aren't there any hotels . . ." Amanda was trying not to be rude, but she knew this sounded rude. "We've rented the house."

Clay was thinking it over. He began to say something. He was persuaded.

"Of course! You've rented the house." G. H. knew they'd talk about money, because most conversations got there eventually. Money was his subject. It was no matter. "We could of course offer you something. We know it's an inconvenience."

"You know, we're on vacation." Amanda thought *inconvenience* too mild a word. It felt like a euphemism. That he'd been so quick to bring money into it seemed more dishonest.

G. H. had silvered hair, tortoiseshell glasses, a gold watch. He had presence. He sat higher in his seat. "Clay. Amanda." This was something he'd learned at business school (in Cambridge): when to deploy first names. "I could absolutely refund you your money."

"You want us to leave? In the middle of the night? My children are sleeping. And you just come in here and start talking about refunding our money? I should call the company, can you even do that?" Amanda walked to the living room to get her computer. "Maybe there's a phone number on the website—"

"I'm not saying you should leave!" G. H. laughed. "We can refund you say, fifty percent of what you paid? You know, there's an in-law suite. We'll stay downstairs."

"Fifty percent?" Clay liked the promise of a less expensive vacation.

"I really think we ought to look at the terms and conditions—" Amanda opened the laptop. "Of course it's not working now. Maybe the WiFi needs to be reset?"

"Let me try." Clay reached toward his wife's computer.

"I don't need your help, Clay." She did not like the implication of her inability. They both had a proximity to youth—college kids for him, for Amanda an assistant and junior staff. They'd both been subject to that humiliating inversion: watching, gleaning, imitating, like toddlers playing at dressing up. Once you were past a certain age, this was how you learned—you had to master technology or be mastered by it. "It's not connected."

"We heard the emergency broadcast system." Ruth thought this explained a great deal. "I thought to turn on the radio. 'This is the emergency broadcast system.'" Her tone was not mocking but faithful, sounding the right stresses and intonation. "Not 'a test.' Do you understand? Not 'This is only a test.' That's the only way I've ever heard it, so I didn't even notice at first, then I kept listening and I heard it again, again, again, 'This is the emergency broadcast system.'"

"Emergency?" Amanda was trying to be logical. "But of course, a blackout is a kind of emergency."

"Surely. That's one of the reasons we thought it best to just come home. It could be unsafe out there." G. H. rested his case.

"Well, we have a lease agreement." Amanda invoked the law. Fine, at the moment that document was filed away in cyberspace, a shelf they could not reach. Also the whole business felt off in some way she could not explain.

"May I?" G. H. pushed his stool back and walked to the desk. He took the car keys from his blazer pocket and unlocked a drawer.

He produced an envelope, the sort provided by a bank, and flipped through the currency inside it. "We could give you a thousand dollars now, for the night? That would cover almost half of what you're paying for the week, I think?"

Clay tried not to, but he always felt moved in a very particular way by the sight of lots of money. He wanted to count it. Had that envelope just been in a drawer in the kitchen all this time? He wanted a cigarette. "A thousand dollars?"

"There is an emergency outside." Ruth wanted to remind them of this. It seemed amoral to have to pay them, but she hadn't expected anything else.

"It's up to you." G. H. knew how to persuade someone. "Of course. We would be very grateful. We could show you how grateful we are. Then, tomorrow, we'll know a little more. We'll figure it out." He did not commit to leaving, which was important.

Clay continued to prod his wife's work-issued computer. "This doesn't seem to be responding." His intention had been pure. He wanted to be the one to show them that the world was chugging along, that people were still photographing their Aperol spritzes and tweeting invective about the mismanaged public transport system. In the minutes since that news alert had been issued, some intrepid reporter had likely figured the whole thing out. He could still hear the wind that he blamed. It was always some innocent thing. "Anyway. I think one night—"

"Perhaps we could discuss this privately." Amanda did not want to leave these people unattended.

"Right. Of course." G. H. nodded like this was the most sensible thing. He put the fat little envelope down on the counter.

"Yeah." Clay was flustered. He didn't know what there was to discuss besides that bundle of money. "Maybe we'll just go into the other room?"

"Say, you wouldn't mind if we have a drink?"

Clay shook his head.

G. H. used the keys once more, unlocking a tall cabinet by the sink. He rummaged around inside.

"We'll be right back. Make yourself—" Amanda didn't finish the sentence because it seemed silly to.

10

IT WAS COLDER IN THE MASTER BEDROOM, OR THE CHILL was something they carried with them.

"Why would you tell them they could stay?" She was angry.

Clay thought it was perfectly obvious. "There's been a blackout. They got scared. They're *old*." He whispered this, felt that it was disrespectful to point out.

"They're strangers." She said it like he was an idiot. Had no one ever warned Clay about strangers?

"Well, they introduced themselves."

"They just knocked on the door in the middle of the night." Amanda couldn't believe they were discussing this.

"Well, it's better than if they'd just burst in the door—" Wasn't that their right?

"They scared the shit out of me." Now that fear had passed, Amanda could admit to it. It was an insult. The temerity of these people—to scare her!

"They scared me too." Clay was downplaying it. It was in the past. "But they're just a little frightened themselves, I think. They didn't know what else to do."

Their onetime therapist had long ago urged Amanda not to be angry when Clay failed to act as she might have. People could not be blamed for being who they were! Still, she faulted him for it. Clay was too easily taken, too reluctant to stand up for himself. "Here's an idea. Go to a hotel."

"It is their house." These beautiful rooms seemed like theirs but weren't. You had to respect that, Clay thought.

"We rented it." Amanda was whispering still. "What are the kids going to say?"

Clay couldn't imagine what the children would say or whether they would say anything. The kids cared only for what directly affected them, and they let very little affect them. The presence of strangers might mean better behavior, but even that couldn't be counted upon. The children might bicker, swear, burp, sing, no matter who might overhear.

"What if they murder us?" Amanda felt her husband was not paying attention.

"Why would they murder us?"

This was harder to answer. "Why does anyone murder anyone? I don't know. Satanic ritual? Some weird fetish? Revenge? I don't know!"

Clay laughed. "They're not here to murder us."

"Don't you read the news?"

"This was in the news? Elderly black murderers are roaming Long Island, preying on unsuspecting vacationers?"

"We didn't ask for any *proof.* I didn't even hear their car, did you?"

"I didn't. But it's windy. We were watching television. Maybe we just didn't hear it?"

"And maybe they snuck up the road. To—I don't know. To cut our throats."

"I think we should just calm down—"

"It's a con."

"You think they sent a fraudulent news alert to your cell phone? They're more sophisticated criminals than I'd have guessed."

"It just feels a little improvised, is all. And suspicious. They want to stay here, with us? I don't like it. Rose is just down the hall. A strange man. What if he sneaks in there and— I don't want to think about it."

"You don't think he'd molest Archie, though. Amanda, listen to yourself."

"She's a girl, okay? I'm a mother, I'm supposed to be protective. And I just don't like the way the whole thing sounds. I don't even think this is their house."

"He had the keys."

"He did." She lowered her voice still more. "What if he's the handyman? What if she's the maid? What if this is just a scam, and the blackout or whatever is just a coincidence?" She was at least appropriately ashamed by her conjecture. But those people didn't look like the sort to own such a beautiful house. They might, though, clean it.

"He took that envelope out of that drawer."

"Sleight of hand. How do you know that drawer was locked? Maybe he just fiddled with his keys."

"I can't understand what they get out of giving us a thousand dollars."

Amanda picked up her phone to google the man. Washington groupfund.com seemed too opaque; probably fraudulent. The phone had nothing to offer her. Her daughter was asleep down the hall! "Also, he looks familiar to me. Like, really."

"Well, I've never seen him before."

"You're terrible with faces." Clay never recognized the children's teachers and often accidentally passed long-standing neighbors on the street without acknowledging them. She knew he liked to think this implied that he was lost in thought, when really he was merely inattentive. "I don't believe this bullshit about the emergency broadcast system. We were just watching TV!"

"That's easy enough." Clay walked down the short hall. He pointed the remote control at the screen mounted on the wall. He'd half hoped (more than half) to broadcast some pornography there. It added a certain twist to things, but the technology was hard for him to parse—you had to get the television and the computer to cooperate. The television lit up. The screen was that blank digital blue. "That's weird."

"Is it on the right channel?"

"I was watching this morning. I think it's out."

"But it's not the emergency broadcast system. The satellite is probably out. It's probably the wind." Amanda was not going to be persuaded, because she could sense those people trying to persuade them. There was dishonesty in it.

"Fine, it's a glitch. But they said they heard that on the radio. The one doesn't mean the other isn't true."

"Why are you working so hard to believe everyone but your own wife?"

"I'm only trying to calm you down. I'm not saying I don't believe you, but . . ." He hesitated. He didn't believe her.

"There's something happening." Wasn't this the plot of *Six Degrees of Separation*? They let those people in because they were black. It was a way of acknowledging that they didn't believe all black people were criminals. A canny black criminal could take advantage of that!

"Or they're scared old people who need a place to stay tonight. We'll send them away in the morning."

"I'll never be able to sleep with strangers in the house!"

"Come on." Clay did wonder. Maybe the thousand dollars was a ruse, or there was something worth more than that in the house. He couldn't think straight.

"I think I've seen him before, I'm telling you." Amanda felt that frustration of being unable to recall a specific word. What if this was a revenge killing? He was some man she'd slighted years ago.

Clay knew that he was not good with faces. And he knew that maybe, on some level, he was especially not good with black faces.

He wasn't going to say "They all look the same to me," but there was some evidence, actual biological, scientific evidence, that people were more adept at recognizing people of the same race. Like, it wasn't racist, was it, to admit that one billion Chinese probably looked more like one another to him than they did to one another. "I don't think we know him, and I don't think he's going to murder us." There was now some sliver, needle-sharp, of doubt. "I think we need to let them stay. It's the right thing to do."

"I want to see the proof." There was no way that she could make such a demand. "I mean, we have keys too! Maybe they rented it before us."

"This is their vacation house. It won't be on their license. I'll talk to them. If I get a bad feeling, we'll say, no, sorry, we're not comfortable with this arrangement. But if I don't, I think we let them stay. They're *old*."

"I wish I had your faith in other people." Amanda did not in fact envy Clay this trait.

"It's the right thing to do." Clay knew this would work; his wife felt it important, not to do the moral thing, necessarily, but to be the kind of person who would. Morality was vanity, in the end.

Amanda crossed her arms against her chest. She was right, in that she didn't know the whole story, nor did Clay, nor did the people in the kitchen, nor did the junior editor who, seeing the news cross the wire, issued the alert to the millions of people who had the *New York Times* app installed on their phones. The wind was so fierce, but even if it hadn't been, they likely would have been just too far from the flight path to hear the first planes dispatched to the coast, per protocol in that situation.

"We're going to be Good Samaritans." Clay turned the television off and stood, choosing in that moment not to mention the thousand dollars.

11

THAT DAY'S MORNING SEEMED DISTANT, LIKE A STORY ABOUT someone else Clay had once been told. He could almost see the beach towels, drying on the railing outside, and they were like the pinch you're supposed to administer when you think you're dreaming. Amanda followed just behind him, and they came into the kitchen and found these strangers there, moving around like they owned the place, which, perhaps, they did.

"I made drinks. Felt like it was in order." G. H. gestured at the glass in his hand. "Our private reserve. I'm happy to get you one."

The man had left a cabinet ajar, and Clay could see inside of it bottles of Oban, wine, that expensive tequila in the porcelain vessel. He had done an inventory of the kitchen. Had he missed this, or had it been locked? "You know, I might have a drink."

G. H. poured one. "Ice? No ice?"

Clay shook his head and took the glass being offered. He sat at the island. "That's lovely, thank you."

"It's the least we can do!" The man gave a mirthless laugh.

There was a temporary silence, as though they'd planned it to memorialize someone now gone.

"I might need to excuse myself," Ruth said.

"Of course." Clay didn't know what was required of him. She wasn't asking his permission, and it wasn't his to grant.

Amanda watched the woman leave the room. She poured herself a glass of the wine she'd opened earlier because she wasn't sure what else to do. Her wine, the wine she'd paid for. She sat beside her husband. "It is a beautiful house." What a thing, to make small talk now.

G. H. nodded. "We love it. I'm happy to hear you do too."

"Have you been here long?" Amanda was trying to interrogate, hoping to catch him.

"Bought it five years ago now. We spent quite a while on the renovations, almost two years. But at this point it's home. Or home away from home."

"Whereabouts do you live in the city?" Clay knew how to make small talk too.

"We're on Park, between Eighty-First and Eighty-Second. What about you?"

Clay was cowed. The Upper East Side was uncool, but still holy. Or maybe so uncool that it was in fact cool. They'd held on to their place so long he could no longer comprehend real estate, the local sport. Still, he'd been in apartments on Park, upper Fifth, Madison. It always felt unreal, like a Woody Allen film. "We live in Brooklyn. Carroll Gardens."

"It's really Cobble Hill," Amanda said. She thought that more respectable. A better riposte to his uptown address.

"That's where everyone wants to live now, I guess. Younger people. I imagine you have more space than we do."

"Well, you have all this space here, in the country," Amanda said, reminding him of what she thought was his cover story.

"A big part of the reason we bought out here. Weekends, holidays. Get out of the city and into the fresh air. It's so different out here, the air."

"I like what you all did." Amanda stroked the countertop like it was a pet.

"We had a great contractor. So many of the little things were his idea."

Returning from the bathroom, Ruth paused in the living room to switch on the television. The screen was that vintage shade of blue from some simpler technological era, white letters important: emergency broadcast system. There was a beep, then a quiet hiss, the sound of something that was not much of a sound, then another beep. They kept coming, the beeps. There was nothing but the beeps, steady but not reassuring. The three others walked into the living room to see it for themselves.

"So, no news there," Ruth said, mostly to herself.

"It's probably just a test of the emergency broadcast system." Amanda was skeptical.

"It would say so if it was," Ruth said. It was common sense. "You see this."

They all saw it.

"Change the channel." Clay had faith. "We were just watching a show!"

Ruth scrolled through every available channel: 101, 102, 103, 104. Then more quickly: 114, 116, 122, 145, 201. All blues, those meaningless words. "This is some emergency broadcast system we've got."

"I'm sure it's nothing." Clay looked at the built-in shelves with remaindered art books and old board games. "It would tell us more if there were more to tell." Ipso facto.

"The satellite television is so unreliable. But it's impossible to get them to run the cable out this far, so it's the only option." Ruth had wanted the house to be far from everything. She'd been the one who wrote that Airbnb listing, and she meant it. That the house was a place apart from the rest of the world was the best thing about it.

"The wind is enough to knock it out." G. H. sat in one of the armchairs. "Rain. It's not very reassuring, that rain can affect a satellite. But it's true."

Clay shrugged his shoulders. "So there's an emergency. The emergency is that New York City is without power. But we still have it, even if we don't have TV or the internet. So that's got to make you feel better, I'd imagine? You were right to get out of the city—it must be a mess."

Amanda didn't believe this, but she also wondered. Should they fill the bathtub with water? Should they find batteries, candles, supplies?

"I think you should stay here tonight." Clay had seen enough evidence. "Tomorrow we'll sort out what's happening."

Amanda had nothing to say about the emergency broadcast system.

"A blackout could be something. It could be a symptom of something bigger." Ruth had ninety minutes to work it out and wanted to say it. "It could be fallout. It could be terrorism. It could be a bomb."

"Let's not let our imaginations run away." Clay's mouth was sugary from the drink.

"A bomb?" Amanda was incredulous.

G. H. didn't like to ask, but he had to. "You know, I'm sorry to trouble you, but we didn't have dinner. Some cheese and crackers before the concert."

The party—was it a party now?—retreated to the kitchen. Clay took the leftover pasta, still in its pot, out of the refrigerator. He was suddenly aware how messy the room was, how thoroughly they'd made themselves sloppily at home. "Let's eat something." He said it like it was his idea. Professors learned that, taking the occasional insightful classroom comment and transforming it into fact.

Ruth noticed that the sink was full of dirty dishes. She pretended not to be disgusted. "A dirty bomb in Times Square? Or some coordinated effort at the power plants?" She had never thought of herself as imaginative, but now she was discovering a flair for it. It only sounded like paranoia if you were wrong. Think of what had been done and forgotten in their lifetimes—in the past decade alone.

"We shouldn't speculate." G. H. was reasonable.

Someone had left the tongs inside the pot. The metal was cold to the touch. Clay filled four bowls, microwaved them in turn. "Where are the power plants in New York City?" There was so much you never knew in life, even someone smart like he was. Clay found this marvelous or meaningful. "They must be in Queens, I guess. Or by the river?"

"Some guy blows up a suitcase in Times Square. His pals do the same thing at the power plants. Synchronized chaos. The ambulances couldn't even get through the streets, if all the lights were out. Do the hospitals even have generators?" Ruth accepted a bowl of pasta. She didn't know what else to do, so she ate. Also, she was hungry. The pasta was too warm, but good, and she was unsure why this was something she begrudged. "This is very kind of you."

Amanda slurped accidentally. She was suddenly ravenous. Sensual pleasures reminded you that you were alive. Also, drinking too much made her hungry. "It's nothing."

G. H. could feel the food working on his chemistry. "It is delicious, thank you."

"It's the salted butter." Amanda felt the need to explain because it was unclear whether she was guest or host. She liked clarity about the role she was meant to discharge. "That European kind, shaped like a cylinder. It's a very simple recipe." She thought chat might salve the discomfort. She was embarrassed to have served this to strangers. The meal was just an improvisation that had ended up part of her repertoire. She liked to imagine some future summer, at some other rental house, the children back from Harvard and Yale, requesting this special dish that reminded them of their sun-filled childhood. "On vacation, I like to keep it simple. Burgers. Pancakes. That kind of thing."

"I'll do the washing." Ruth thought restoring her kitchen to order might soothe. Also it was only polite.

"We're here now. We're grateful to you both. I feel so much better, having eaten. I think I might have another drink." G. H. refilled. It was a whisky old enough to vote. It was for special occasions, but surely this counted.

"I'll join you." Clay slid his glass toward the man. "You see, there's nothing to worry about here." *Tumbler* was somehow fitting; the glass was heavy and expensive and it kept him from tumbling to the floor.

These strangers didn't know him, so they didn't know that G. H. was not given to hyperbole. In the hour and a half drive his fear had doubled like resting dough. "Well, it was disturbing." He had what he wanted, but now he wanted this man and this woman to understand him. He could sense their suspicion.

Ruth was calmed by the suds, the yellow sponge, the lemon scent, the squeak of a clean, hot plate. The preceding ninety minutes she'd been both suspended and speeding—modern life had an uncanny tempo, one man was never meant for. Cars and planes made time travelers of all of us. She'd looked out at the black night and shivered. She'd put a hand on G. H.'s knee. She'd thought about this place, this house, solidly made and tastefully furnished, beautifully situated and absolutely safe but for the complication of these people in her kitchen. "That's an understatement."

"A blackout. Like Hurricane Sandy." Clay recalled unfounded reports of an explosion, Superfund sludge from the Gowanus spilling into the water supply, every sip a carcinogen. They were without power a day and a half. It had been a kind of charming emergency; hunker down with playing cards and books. When the lights came back on, he had baked an apple pie.

"Or in 2003," Amanda said. "The electrical grid, remember that?"

"I walked across the Manhattan Bridge. Couldn't reach her on the phone." Clay put a hand on his wife's, nostalgic and possessive. "I was so worried. Of course, we were all remembering 9/11, but it was so much better than that day." That parochial one-upmanship New Yorkers think their own, special remit, but everyone is possessive of the places they inhabit. You recount the disasters to demonstrate your fidelity. You've seen the old girl at her worst.

"I thought of 9/11, of course." Ruth washed the food scraps down the drain and switched on the disposal. "What if people are dying right now? Remember a few years ago, that guy drove his truck on the bike path on the West Side? Just rented a truck in New Jersey and killed all those people? It's not even *difficult*. Like how much planning could that have possibly taken?"

"The lights. All the lights—" G. H. knew that no one was interested in hearing about the dream you had last night. This had been real, but maybe some things you had to see for yourself.

Clay believed if you said it, it would be true. "I think in the morning—"

"It *is* morning, now." Ruth met Clay's eyes in the reflection of the window, a neat little trick.

"I guess what I mean is that things always look different in the light of day. I guess self-help clichés are rooted in truth." Clay sounded apologetic, but he believed it. The world was not as fearful as people thought.

"I don't know how to explain it." Ruth dried her hands on a towel and hung it back where it belonged. A building lit up was alive, a beacon; dark, it vanished, like David Copperfield had made the Statue of Liberty do that one time. Ruth associated the sudden absence of light with something being extinguished, with a switch being flipped, with a change, and this invited the question: What had been extinguished, what switch flipped, what had changed?

"You've had a scare." Clay understood.

Ruth had learned only one thing from the current reality, and it was that everything held together by tacit agreement that it would. All it took to unravel something was one party deciding to do just that. There was no real structure to prevent chaos, there was only a collective faith in order. "I was scared. I am." This last part she didn't quite whisper. She wasn't ashamed, but she was embarrassed. Was this it, then; was she a fearful old woman now?

"We'll find out more tomorrow." Clay believed this.

"What if it's the North Koreans? That fat one who fed his own uncle to the dogs." Ruth could not stop herself. "What if it's a bomb. A missile." A year ago, was it, there was that false alarm in Hawaii where, for some terrible stretch, vacationers and honeymooners and dropouts and housewives and surf instructors and museum curators thought that was it, a missile was on its way from the Korean peninsula to obliterate them. How would you spend the last thirty-two minutes: looking for a basement or texting your friends or reading a story to your children or in bed with your spouse? People would probably monitor their own destruction by CNN play-by-play. Or the local stations wouldn't cut away, and you could go out watching *The Price Is Right*.

"The North Koreans?" Amanda said it like she'd never heard of the place. What if it was the Outer Mongolians? The Liechtensteiners? The Burkinabé? Did they even have the bomb in Africa? She'd watched Lorin Maazel conducting in Pyongyang. Some cable correspondent had promised détente, some previous president had promised them all peace. Amanda didn't have time to think about the North Koreans, and had no idea, even, what Ruth was talking about, feeding people to dogs; she thought the rap on the Koreans was that they were the ones who ate dogs.

"It's not the North Koreans." G. H. shook his head, but this was as remonstrative as he was willing to get. You didn't scold Ruth. She was a Barnard girl: she had ready answers. He fiddled with the heavy watch on his wrist, a nervous tic he knew was a tic. He had his money on Iran, maybe Putin. Not literally so; that was against the law. But he was no fool.

"How do you know?" Now that they were safe—but there was a question mark there—Ruth could cede to the panic that had been in her throat as they drove. She could say what she'd been unable to in the car, afraid of jinxing them with an empty tank or a punctured tire. She kept her silence and pictured the faces of her daughter and grandsons, the atheist's prayer. Muslim fundamentalists! Chechen true believers! Rebels in Colombia, Spain, Ireland, every country had its madmen.

"Wouldn't there have been a boom?" This was a familiar feeling for Clay, whenever he had to assemble furniture or the car made funny noises: how little he *knew*. Perhaps that was why, in his estimation, true intelligence was accepting how limited one's intelligence always is. This philosophy let him off the hook. "You would have . . . *heard* something. Like if it had been a bomb."

"I was having breakfast at Balthazar on 9/11." G. H. remembered the silky omelet, the salty French fries. "Can't be more than twenty blocks from the towers, right? I didn't hear a goddamn thing."

"Can we please not talk about 9/11?" Amanda was uncomfortable.

"I heard the sirens, and then people in the restaurant started talking, so—"

Ruth idly rapped her fingers against the countertop. There was no way to explain that the thing about dark is that it's rare. There's always some ambient light. There's always that contrast that helps you understand: *This is dark.* The pricks of stars, the leak beneath the door, the glow of an appliance, something. Wasn't its ability to assert itself, and at breakneck speed at that, light's most remarkable quality?

Without thinking, Clay gave his phone his fingerprint. The phone showed him a photograph of the children, Archie, then eleven, Rose, only eight, rounded, small, innocent. It was startling to look at this evidence of the selves now gone, though he often didn't truly see this picture, obscured by little squares of information, the seductive glow of the phone itself. He felt phantom tingles when the phone was not at his side. Clay recalled that in January, in the spirit of resolution, he'd tried leaving his phone in another room while he slept. But that was how he did most of his newspaper reading, and staying informed was as worthy a resolution. "Still nothing," he said, answering a question they all wanted to ask, even if none of them had bothered to. They decided to go to bed.

12

THEY HAD FINISHED THE BASEMENT FOR RUTH'S MOTHER, A
dignified, withered creature, silk scarves and color-coordinated suits.
She'd come to live with them when she turned ninety—much complaining, but the winters in Chicago were terrible, and there was no
one left there to keep a close watch on her. Ruth had handled the
sale of the house, sent disbursements to her sister and their brother,
then moved Mama into the guest room. She liked to walk to the
Met, look at the Impressionist paintings, then sit at the diner with
a cup of tea and a Manhattan clam chowder. Had she not died,
she'd be stranded in the dark three-bedroom on the fourteenth
floor. Small mercy.

G. H. led the way downstairs, where they almost never went—
that city dweller's fantasy: rooms you barely need—switching on
the lights as he went. He had not realized how much light con-
noted safety, and how much dark its opposite. Even as a boy he'd
not feared the dark, so this was a surprise. "Just watch your step,"
he said, some tenderness for his wife.

"This is my house." Ruth was holding tight to the railing. She
felt it important to underscore this fact.

"Well, they paid for it." G. H. had driven fast, but there were
some things that couldn't be outrun. His reticence was because of

a very particular burden: he knew that something was wrong, truly wrong. "I can't exactly throw them out." G. H. didn't want to say that he had known something was coming. His business was clairvoyance. You looked at the yield curve arching and slumping like an inchworm making its inefficient progress, and it told you everything you needed to know. He had known not to trust that particular parabola. It was more than portent, it was a promise. Something was upon them. It had been decreed.

"You saw how dirty they had the kitchen." Ruth didn't need to say *What would Mom think of that?* because Mom hovered around. The basement had been intended for her—an exterior ramp around the back of the house, easier than the stairs—but she died before she got to visit. Ruth knew she was evolving into a pale imitation of the woman. Another way of saying she was old. It just happened. You found yourself holding your grandbabies—twins!—and not saying anything about the fact that they had two moms. Clara was a professor of classics at Mount Holyoke. Maya was the headmaster of a Montessori school. They had a big, cold clapboard house with a turret. Mom would have got a kick out of her mocha-colored greatgrandsons, made of the genetic issue of Clara's brother, James, who did something in Silicon Valley. The boys looked just like both of their mothers, something you'd not have thought possible, but there it was, in black and white, ha ha ha.

G. H. flicked on lights, forgetting to pause in gratitude that they still worked. There was a big closet: a cache of Duracells, a flat of Volvic, some bags of Rancho Gordo beans, boxes of Clif Bars and Barilla fusilli stored in a heavy-duty plastic bin because there were mice in the country. Cans of tuna, a gasoline canister's worth of olive oil, a case of a cheap Malbec that was not half bad, bed linens in those vacuum bags that sucked out all the air. The two of them could be comfortably housebound for a month, if not longer. G. H. practically dared a snowstorm to arrive, but thus far none had. They said that was global warming. "Everything in order."

She murmured something to show she heard him. They'd spent too much remodeling. Improvement was an addiction. G. H.'s business was money's preservation. Actual spending was so abstract to him that he did as the contractor said. Danny was one of those men other men didn't want to seem a fool in front of. He had a power over men that was almost sexual, in the way that sex always ends up being about power. You'd do what he said, and maybe in your worst moments you'd worry that Danny was laughing at you. Their checks had certainly paid for Danny's daughter's year at private school. That's why they rented: to recoup.

"It smells down here." Ruth made a face, but it didn't really smell. Rosa cleaned the place, her husband tended the lawn, and their kids came out and assisted. It was a family affair. They were from Honduras. Rosa would not have left a smell. The carpet's nap said that she vacuumed even the unused basement. There was a bedroom, with a sofa and a table and a wall-mounted television, the bed made up and expectant. She sat and slipped off her shoes.

"It doesn't." G. H. sat on the edge of the bed, more heavily than he meant to. He couldn't stop himself sighing when he did things like that. He tried to imagine the morning's relief. The funny news on the radio—a band of raccoons broke into a substation in Delaware and knocked out power all over the East Coast, or some subcontractor's most junior employee had a terrible first day. What were we worried about, what were we afraid of? Market confidence would be restored; there would be a windfall for certain stoic bettors.

Ruth was at a loss. Their normal routine was to first unlock all the cabinets filled with their special and necessary things: swimsuits and flip-flops, Shiseido sunscreen, a wool Hermès picnic blanket, and in the pantry, a tin of Maldon salt, a bottle of olive oil from Eataly, the horrifyingly sharp Wusthof knives, four jars of Luxardo cherries, Clase Azul, Oban, Hendrick's, the wines guests had brought as hostess gifts, dry vermouth, bitters. They'd reunite with those possessions: rub them on their skin, scatter them around the rooms, and feel truly at home. They'd pull off their clothes—what was the point having a home in the country if you couldn't walk around mostly naked?—and make Manhattans and slip into the pool or the hot tub or just into the bed. They still went to bed with each other, aided by those most effective blue tablets. "I'm scared."

"We're here." He paused because it was important to remember. "It's safe here." He thought of his canned tomatoes. There was enough to last them for months.

There were unopened toothbrushes in the bathroom drawer. There were fresh towels, rolled jauntily and stacked in a little pyramid. Ruth showered. Feeling clean made such a difference to her. In the bedroom dresser there was an old T-shirt from a charity run she couldn't remember, a pair of shorts she could not identify. She put these on, felt immediately ridiculous. She didn't want the people upstairs to see her in these cheap clothes.

G. H. tried the bedroom television, because he was curious. It showed nothing, just a blue screen, channel after channel. He undid his tie. When she'd been alive, G. H. had felt Mom's presence as an indictment. G. H. was so accustomed to being who he was and had come to believe that was success. When Mom had come out to inspect Maya, she'd rebuked him for his fourteen-hour days, for living so high up (unnatural!), for the delusion of their New York lives. It had shaken him. They changed their lives. They bought the place on Park, sent Maya to Dalton, and lived prudently. Sometimes he did miss the ground underfoot. The wisdom of the elders.

Ruth returned in a billow of steam.

"I tried the television. Same thing." He had to share this with her, though he had not expected otherwise.

She shifted and adjusted under the clean bedding. The wind was noisy. "So, what do you think it is?" She didn't want to be humored.

G. H. knew her. It had been decades! "I think it's something we're going to laugh about when we hear what it was. That's what I think." He didn't think this. But it was right to lie sometimes. He looked at himself in the mirror and thought about their apartment, their home, the suits in his walk-in closet, the coffee maker he'd settled on after spending weeks researching. He thought about the planes over Manhattan and how it must have looked to their passengers as the place went dark. He thought about the satellites over the planes over Manhattan and the pictures they were taking and what they would show. He thought about the space station over the satellites over the planes and wondered what the multiracial, multinational crew of scientists would have made of the whole thing from their unique vantage. Sometimes distance showed a thing most clearly.

G. H. understood electricity as a commodity. This wasn't some vicissitude in the market. You couldn't pull the plug on the nation's financial capital. Insurance companies would be in litigation for decades. If the lights went out in New York City, that was act-of-God stuff. Act of God. The kind of thing his mother-in-law might have said.

13

———

YOUR KID'S VOICE COULD WAKE YOU UP, YOUR KID'S PRES-
ence could wake you up. Amanda felt Rose's fat little body rock
into the gulf between her and Clay even before she felt the girl's wet
breath too near her ear.

"Mom, Mom." A soft hand on her arm, gentle but also insistent.

She sat up. "Rosie." The previous year the girl had declared she
was done with the *ie*. "Rose."

"Mom." Rose was wide awake. Rose restored by the night. Rose,
abloom. It had been this way her whole life. Mornings, she was
dying to *do*. She opened her eyes and jumped to the floor. (Mrs.
Weston, the neighbor downstairs, had raised two daughters in the
same eleven hundred square feet, so she never complained.) Rose
didn't understand how her brother could stay asleep until eleven,
twelve, one. Mornings, everything seemed thrilling to her—wash
face, choose clothes, read a book. Rose was enthusiastic. Everything was possible. When you're the younger child, you learn to
fend for yourself. "There's something wrong with the TV."

"Honey, this is not an emergency." Then she remembered: *This
is the emergency broadcast system.* Amanda slapped the too-slack pillows into obeisance.

"It's all messed up." The first few channels were black and white, dancing light. After that, all white, just nothing.

They'd forgotten to draw the blinds. Outside it was light, but indirect. Not clouds but the early hour. The storm they'd thought was coming wasn't after all. As she looked at it, the squat clock bedside ticked from 7:48 to 7:49. So: electricity. Some blackout. "Honey. I don't know."

"Can't you fix it?" Rose was just young enough to believe her parents could do anything. "It's not fair, it's a vacation, and you said on vacation we can watch as much television or have as much screen time as we want."

"Daddy's sleeping. Go wait in the living room, I'm coming."

Rose stomped away—that was how she walked—and Amanda picked up her phone. The screen woke up, happy to see her, and she was happy, too: not one news alert but four. But just as before, she couldn't see more than the dispatch. She pressed on the alert and the screen tried and failed to connect. The same headline—"Major Blackout Reported on the East Coast of the United States"—then "Hurricane Farrah Makes Landfall in North Carolina"—then "Breaking: East Coast of the United States Reports Power Failure"—then a final "Breaking" followed by nonsensical letters. She hoped the television would work. But they'd stopped listening to NPR when four-year-old Rosie had intoned "I'm David Greene," and seven-year-old Archie asked about Pussy Riot. They'd protected the kids from so much.

Amanda smoothed the sheet under her hand, bumped Clay's ass. "Clay." He mumbled, and she shook him by the shoulder. "Get up. Look."

His mouth was sour, eyes unfocused. Amanda had her phone in his face. He made an unintelligible sound.

"Look." She shook the phone again.

"I can't see." In those moments of waking, it was impossible to see anything. You had to force your eyes to focus. But really he meant the phone had gone dark.

She jabbed at it. "Oh, here."

"What?" He remembered last night, but could not push himself from sleep into wakefulness so quickly. "It looks like no one murdered us."

She ignored this. "The news."

The screen before him said nothing. "Amanda, it doesn't say anything." Just the date, just the same photograph, a snapshot of the kids they'd used as their Christmas card two years before.

"It was just there." She needed Clay to share the burden of this information.

He yawned; it went on for a long moment. "Are you sure? What did it say?"

"Of course I'm sure." Was she? Amanda studied the phone. "How do you see the alerts? It's not opening the app. But there were four. That same one about the blackout, then another one about the blackout, and something about that hurricane, and one that just said 'breaking,' and it was—"

"Breaking what?"

"It just said a bunch of gibberish."

"They abuse that 'breaking.' Breaking, polls show the Liberal Democrats take the lead in the Austrian congressional races. Breaking, Adam Sandler says his new movie is his best work yet. Breaking, Doris Who Gives a Fuck, inventor of the automatic ice cream maker, dead at age ninety-nine."

"No, like it was. Not even words. Just letters. It must have been a mistake."

"Maybe that's the network. The cell network? Maybe there's something wrong with that? Would a blackout affect that?" Clay didn't know how the world fit together. Who truly did, though?

"You think there's something wrong with the cell phones? Or is it just where we are? Because my phone's been spotty since we got here. It worked in town, when I went to the grocery."

"We are sort of far away. This happened last year, too, remember? And that place we rented wasn't nearly as remote."

Or, she didn't say, something so bad happened that even the *New York Times* was affected. Amanda stood and drank from the bottle on the bedside. It was room temperature, and what she most wanted was cold water. "Four news alerts. I didn't even get that many on election night." She went to the bathroom, studied the phone as she peed. It did not tell her any more.

Clay pulled on the boxer shorts he'd lost in the night and looked out at the backyard. Despite the portent of storm, it seemed like any other summer morning. Even the wind seemed to have abated. Indeed, had he looked—closer than it was possible for him to look— he'd have understood the stillness as a response to that wind. He'd have noticed that the insects had gone quiet; he'd have noticed that the birds were not calling. Had he noticed, he'd have noted that it was like those strange moments when the moon passed before the sun, that temporary shadow the animals did not understand.

She left the bathroom and passed her husband waiting for his turn. "I'll make some coffee." The phone felt heavy in her thin cotton pocket.

Rose was at the kitchen island with a bowl of cereal. Amanda remembered (it was not so long ago) when the girl had needed adult intercession to fetch the bowl, fill it, slice the banana, pour the milk. She had tried not to resent it at the time; she had tried to remember how fleeting those days were. And now they were gone. There was a last time that she had sung the children to sleep, a last time she had wiped the feces from the recesses of their bodies, a last time she had seen her son nude and perfect as he was the day she met him. You never know when a time is the last time, because if you did you could never go on with life. "Hi, baby." She scooped dry coffee into the paper filter. Another normal, beautiful day, right?

"Can I watch a movie on your computer?"

"The internet is out, honey, otherwise I'd let you watch Netflix. Listen. I have to tell you—"

"This vacation sucks." Rose had a point to make. Injustice.

"—last night, these people—the Washingtons—the people who own this house, they had to come by, there's been—" What noun did she need? "There was a problem. With their car. And they were not far from here, so they came here, even though they rented the house to us for the week." You had to be willing to lie, to be a mother or maybe just a person. Sometimes you had to lie.

"What are you talking about?" Rose already didn't care. She wanted to text Hazel and see what she was doing. Hazel was probably watching television right that very minute.

"There was a problem with the car and they weren't far away and they knew we were here, but they thought maybe they could just come and explain and—" It was not even hard to dissemble. The children couldn't hold complex things—even simple things, really—in their heads, and also they didn't care, beautiful narcissists.

Clay in his boxer shorts and sleepy eyes. "I'll take some of that coffee."

Amanda filled a mug. "I was just telling Rose about the Washingtons."

"Dad, the TV isn't working." Rose tugged on his arm. He was the one who would care. He was the one who would help her.

The hot liquid splashed onto his right foot. "Easy, baby."

"Did you forget to put your bowl in the sink?" Amanda had read a book on how to talk so kids will listen. "Clay, you should put clothes on. Those people are here." She heard the rudeness in this. "The Washingtons. They're just downstairs."

"Dad, can you fix it?"

"Let's just slow it down." Maybe they'd been too permissive about screen time, parceled out like the narcotic that it was. Clay was unable to resist her entreaties. As a toddler, she'd called for Daddy in a way that was very specific. A girl needed her father. He put his coffee down and fiddled with the remote control. Snow, a bit of poetry for what you saw when the signal was broken. "Yeah. This doesn't look like it's working."

"Can't you, like—reset it or something? Or go up onto the roof or whatever?"

"No one is going on the roof," Amanda said.

"I'm not going on the roof." He scratched at his belly, stippled with hair, swollen from midnight pasta. "Besides, I'm not even sure if the problem is here, on the roof, or—somewhere else." His gesture indicated everything around them. Who could answer for the world at large? Was it even . . . still there? "Why don't you go sit outside. I'll come join you—I just need to talk to Mom for a second."

Rose would have preferred television, but also she just needed a task. She would accept her father's attention. "You're coming."

"Just give me two minutes." He looked past her at the morning, pale yellow and reluctant.

She said "Fine" the way adolescents learn to pronounce it, with all the fervor of any four-letter word. The morning was quiet. It was pretty, but not as interesting as a television show.

Rose slammed the door behind her without entirely meaning to. It was definitely nicer wherever Hazel was. Her television would never not work. Her parents let her have an unlocked Instagram account. Rose sat on one of the white metal chairs and looked at the woods.

Where the yard shrugged away from the house, the grass grew patchy and was then just dust and leaves and weeds at the hem of the woods or wilderness or whatever it was. In the space beyond that, Rose saw a deer, with abbreviated velvet antlers and a cautious yet somehow also bored mien, considering her through dark, strangely human eyes.

She wanted to say "A deer," but there was no one there to hear her. She looked over her shoulder into the house and saw her parents talking. She wasn't supposed to go in the pool, but she wasn't going to go in the pool. She walked down the steps onto the damp grass and the deer just watched her, barely curious. She hadn't even seen that there was another beside it—no more. There were five deer, there were seven; every time Rose adjusted her eyes to try to understand what she was seeing, she was seeing something new. There were dozens of deer. Had she been up higher, she'd have understood that there were hundreds, more than a thousand, more than that, even. She wanted to run inside and tell her parents, but she also wanted to just stand there and see it.

14

RUTH WOKE WITH LUCID EYES AND SUDDEN MEMORY. THAT familiar sensation of jerking awake when you're falling asleep, something you take for private idiosyncrasy then learn is part of the human condition. The quotidian sounds of morning: water in pipes, someone else's footsteps, a conversation from another room. She was desperate for Maya. She was in bed but also still in the car, thinking of the girl: baby at her breast, toddler on her lap, ten with thick limbs and box braids, terse teen in flannel shirt and too many earrings, college girl, blushing wife, radiant mother. Every version of Maya overlapped in Ruth's mind. The green light on the cable box showed her that the power still flowed. Her cell phone still did not seem to reach the world, but she hadn't expected it to. She let George sleep, crept upstairs.

In the kitchen, Ruth picked up the telephone Danny had suggested installing. The contractor had some kind of hold over George. Men of G. H.'s generation didn't think of affection for other men. That had made it the more charming and then annoying to watch G. H. fall under Danny's spell. The man was a manual laborer; G. H. had gone to Harvard Business School. But Danny was muscled and capable in his chambray shirts, sleeves rolled over firm forearms, sunglasses perched on the back of his head. She pressed the receiver against her ear. Not the steady basso of a phone ready to be dialed; the dirge that told you the thing was already dead. For a terrible moment Ruth couldn't quite imagine the sound of her daughter's voice. What did Maya, today's Maya, the real person, sound like?

As an adult, she was the same as she'd been as a child, mostly bemused by her parents. She favored long, strange dresses in a riot of colors and patterns. Her children were called Beckett and Otto and toddled around on the back lawn naked. Ruth didn't understand their names or the fact that they had foreskins, but she kept this to herself. She put the phone down, too forceful, maybe.

The couple were in the living room. The man was barely dressed, the woman in her comfortable clothes.

Amanda tried not to show that she was startled. "Good morning."

Ruth returned this pleasantry, as was normal. It was insincere or inaccurate, or perhaps both. "The telephone is still out."

"We were just— Amanda had alerts on her phone this morning."

"What did they say?" Ruth wondered why her phone had told her nothing. She never could quite master the damn thing.

"The same thing, a blackout. Then something about that hurricane. Then an update, then something that was just gibberish." This was the third time she'd explained it; the information felt even more meaningless now.

"Let me get you some coffee," Clay said. He felt embarrassed, undressed.

"A hurricane. That's something." Ruth tried to make it mean something.

"Is it?" Clay handed her a mug (her mug).

"Well, yes, maybe it's related. To the power outage. That could be. There was Hurricane Sandy, of course. I don't remember hearing that this one was bound for New York, but I wasn't paying close attention, I have to admit." They'd all heard, she knew, that those storms of the century were going to be storms of the decade. That there might have to be a new category introduced to accurately describe the kinds of storms, now that humankind had so altered the ocean.

"I'm not sure what to tell the kids." Amanda looked at the stranger as though she might have some advice, then turned toward the French doors, and they all did, all looked at Rose, standing down in the yard.

"How old is she?" Years ago, Ruth was asked to help out in the school office. Dalton wanted to increase *diversity*. Now Ruth was immune to kids' germs and mostly impervious to their charms.

"Just thirteen. Last month." Amanda was protective. "But still kind of a baby at heart. So I would love to keep . . . things between the adults."

"There's no need to worry them." At school, Ruth treated kids as the selves they'd inevitably be. The boys who would turn out handsome and therefore catered to, the girls who would turn out pretty and therefore cruel, the rich ones who would become Republicans, the rich ones who would become drug addicts, the rich ones who would exceed their parents' expectations of them, the poor ones who would prosper and the poor ones who would skulk from Princeton back to East New York. She knew that childhood was a temporary condition. But being a grandmother had made her soft.

"I don't want the kids to panic over nothing." Amanda tried not to imply that this was what Ruth and her husband had done.

Ruth's mother would have invoked God. Life was about making sure your children do better than you did, and Ruth's atheism was a definite improvement. You can't get through life dismissing the incomprehensible as divine. "I don't want to scare anyone." But she was afraid. "Thank you for the coffee."

"We have—there are eggs, cereal, you know." Clay held a banana, not knowing how like a primate he looked in that moment. "I'm going to go get dressed," he said, quite forgetting his promise to his daughter. He had a plan.

Ruth sat. She felt safe in small talk. "So. What is it you do?"

This Amanda understood. "I'm in advertising. On the client side. Manage relationships." She sat, too, crossed one leg over the other.

Ruth took her turn. "I'm retired now. I was in admissions. At the Dalton school."

Amanda couldn't help sit up a little straighter. Perhaps there was an angle. Her children, not exceptional (still wonderful in her estimation!), could do with an advantage. She knew the tuition was a suggestion. Families like theirs relied on the largesse of luckier people. "That's so interesting."

From her old office Ruth sometimes saw Woody Allen, poking around in the house directly opposite. That was one of three or four interesting things about it. She was happy to be free. "And your husband?"

"Clay? He's a professor. English, but also media studies."

"I'm not sure I know what that means." She said it like a little joke on herself.

Amanda was never entirely clear on it either. "Films. Literacy. The internet. The truth, that kind of thing."

"At Columbia?"

"City College." It seemed like a disappointment, since the woman's first guess had been the Ivy but Amanda was proud.

"I was at Barnard. Then Teachers College." Ruth was doing this routine because she wanted to understand these people a little better. It was a give-and-take.

"A true New Yorker. I went to Penn. Philadelphia seemed so urban to me. So exotic." She remembered driving onto campus, her parents' Corolla bursting with jersey sheets, desk lamp, shower caddy, Tori Amos poster. The place had looked flat. She heard "city" and had been picturing buildings reaching for the sky. Still, it was better than Rockville. REM was right: nobody says hello, don't talk to anybody they don't know. "I wish I'd gone to college in New York."

"Well, I'm from Chicago." Ruth said it like it was the best place to be from. "But I suppose I'm a true New Yorker now. More years there than not."

G. H. had dressed—skipping the dirty underwear and sweat-in socks, not bothering with the tie—and made up the bed. Not making up the bed was no kind of life. He had tried to prepare himself, the usual ablutions, but was vague about what he was preparing himself for. "Good morning."

Amanda stood to greet him, some formality she did not know was her nature.

"Any news?" He listened to Amanda's report of what they barely knew and wished he could see the news, but he also wished he could see the market. He wanted information but also vindication. "The storm, I'm sure. A downed limb."

"The landlines *don't* go. That's the whole reason Danny said to put one in." Ruth didn't mind being mollified, but she did not want to be lied to.

"The power is still on." G. H. did not want this overlooked. "Maybe today we should drive over to Danny's." If you were going to be under some kind of terrorist siege, you'd want to be with Danny.

"Who's Danny? Are there neighbors nearby? We passed that farm stand, just before the turn onto the lane. There must be someone there. Maybe they know something." Amanda did not know that the itch she felt was so like the one that afflicted her husband when he was too long without nicotine. She wanted away.

"What if. Collective hysteria. Groups of people get some malady that turns out to just be a shared delusion. Hundreds of people with tremors and fever, imagining a rash. They can even make their skin turn pink." G. H. was only offering a theory.

Ruth brought her husband a coffee. "You're going to call me hysterical—the word people, *men*, use for women." Cassandra had, of course, been right about Troy.

"We saw the same thing. Something happened, sure, I think

we can agree." But this was a technicality, it was the nature of the world, things happening.

"You drove." She meant he ran. "You were as afraid as me."

"Well, the elevator." Their floor was termed the fourteenth, but it was not. The building lacked a thirteenth floor because that was terrible luck. Simply pretending it wasn't there was better.

Amanda felt embarrassed. She didn't know these people and couldn't watch them bicker. "Where does Danny live?"

"Not far. You can't do anything in life without the right information. I'll drive over there." G. H. looked out at the day. The morning looked odd to him, but he could not articulate why, could not be certain it was not context instead of fact.

"I don't want you going anywhere." Ruth scoffed at the idea of seeking refuge at Danny's, like he was their son instead of someone they paid. She was working through all the possible scenarios. Some Muslim with nothing to live for strapped into explosives. Another plane crash—why didn't those happen more? It was brilliant to turn a plane into a weapon.

The little house felt safe. Amanda understood.

"I need my clothes. I need clean clothes." Ruth looked toward Amanda.

"Oh. Of course."

"I just need to go into my closet." They rented the house, but they'd never actually seen strangers inside it. They always had Rosa in before they came out. They always found the house spotless and chilled and ready to receive them.

"Clay's just getting dressed, I'll ask him to hurry."

Ruth didn't need to say anything about the look on their faces when they'd opened the door to them. Guess who's coming to dinner? "Thank you."

Ruth was sixty-three years old. She hadn't been raised to *do*—though that had been expected—but to convince. This was, her mother understood, how women made their way in the world: convincing men to do the things they wanted. "I'm scared." She was confessing. "Maya and the boys. She's probably trying to call us."

"Our daughter," G. H. explained. He put a hand on his wife's shoulder. "Don't worry about that now."

She mostly could bear not thinking about the ice caps or the president. She could hold fear at bay by focusing on the small matter of her own life. "You remember that year we went to Italy?"

Dry heat, a luxury hotel, Maya in her pigtails. They'd sipped glasses of sweet juice, they'd eaten pizza topped with rosemary and potatoes, they'd rented a car, they'd stayed in a villa in the country. It was a flat, near treeless place with the mercy of a swimming pool. Maya, taking in the rubble that was the Forum, asked why they'd come there to see a place so wholly wrecked. History meant nothing to her. Time was unimaginable at nine. Maybe it was at sixty-three too. There was only that moment, the current moment, this life. "What made you think of that?"

"I don't know what else to think about," Ruth said.

15

ROSE TURNED THE SECRET OF THE DEER OVER AND OVER, AS you would a hard candy on your tongue. She was not yet old enough that her words would be believed. They would say she'd made it up. They would say she'd exaggerated. They would say she was a child. But Rose felt the change in the day, even if no one else did. For starters, it was hot, impossibly so, given the sun had not fully come up. The air felt artificial, like inside a greenhouse or some botanical garden exhibition. The morning was too quiet. It was telling her something. She tried to hear what.

In the kitchen, her father was talking to an old man she'd never seen. Rose did not bother reminding her father that he'd been supposed to come see her outside. It was better that he had forgotten. He made introductions.

"Nice to meet you." Rose was well brought up.

"A pleasure." G. H. couldn't help think of his own daughter. He remembered he'd used her name for the combination to the lockbox.

"Did you brush your teeth?" Clay wanted to get rid of the girl.

"It's super hot outside. Can I swim?"

"Fine with me. Just find your mother first. Tell her I said it was okay. I need to talk to Mr. Washington."

In the night, somehow, each man had forgotten the other, would have been unable to describe him to a police sketch artist. They said eyewitnesses were unreliable anyway; most people cared only for themselves. That was true of both these men, rudderless without precedent for etiquette, in a house to which they each laid claim.

Seeing the man again, in the day's light, was like seeing a stranger with whom you'd had sex. "G. H., would you mind if we stepped outside?" This sounded so masculine and decisive if you didn't know that Clay wanted a cigarette.

"Let's do that." G. H. chuckled a little. It was hard not to assume the role of genial sitcom neighbor. Television created the context, and black people had to play along. But this was his house. He was the protagonist of his story.

They left through the side door. G. H. was proprietary about even the grounds. Thicket was right—the lawn petered out at a wall of trees. It was different than having a home at the sea. The ocean loomed. The trees were protective. "Hot out." He looked at the sky and noted how pale it was.

Clay produced cigarettes from his pocket. "A little vice—I'm sorry."

G. H. understood: man to man. Men didn't say such things anymore, they just implied them. Once it had been one of the secretary's responsibilities to empty the desktop ashtrays. Now you didn't even say "secretary" but "assistant." "I understand."

They walked past the hedgerow. The gravel crunched pleasantly underfoot. Clay went farther than necessary—the hedge obscured them, the children would not see—because he felt this was respectful. "I wouldn't smoke in the house, you know."

"There's a reason we ask for the security deposit." They'd had fine luck with renters. A broken wineglass, a loose doorknob, a missing soap dish that Ruth had replaced with a large seashell.

"Amanda told you what she saw? The news alerts." These didn't worry him, only the one that was gibberish. He worried about the technology more than the nation.

G. H. nodded. "Do you know what I do for a living? I manage money. And do you know what you need to do that job? Information. That's it. Well, money. But information. You can't make choices, you can't assess risks, unless you know something."

But Clay wanted to be the one. Clay wanted to put everyone at ease. Clay was just selfish enough. "I'm going to drive into town. It's the only way."

"I suspect it's terrorism. But that's not what scares me. Terrorists are dumb hicks. That's how you convince them to incinerate themselves for God. They're patsies. But what comes next?" G. H. once had faith in the institutions of American life, but he had less now. "Let's say something happens in New York City. Do you think this president will do the right thing about it?" This kind of thing used to sound like paranoia, but now it was just pragmatism.

"Well, I'm going to get to the bottom of it." Clay was proud of himself. His chest swelled in some primate's instinct.

"My contractor lives just a few miles down the road. He's a good man. I trust him. We could head over there." G. H. was mostly thinking out loud.

Clay was relieved by the nicotine. "We're safe out here, I think."

G. H. was less certain. "It seems so. At the moment."

"I don't think we need to bother your friend. I'm going to go into town. Buy a newspaper. Find someone who knows more than we do."

"I'd say I'd join you, but I'm not sure if Ruth would approve." He was a dealmaker by trade. He didn't want to go.

"You stay here." Clay was thinking, on some level, of his father. "You see those rentals where the homeowner is on the premises. Hosts. It's really not so odd." He worried about them driving more. He thought this was decent of him. He wanted to be seen to be good.

G. H. looked again at the sky. "It looks like it might be a nice day. Very hot out already." When you got older you could say that kind of thing, as though you were somehow in tune with nature's secret rhythms, as though G. H. had spent his life on a fishing trawler instead of in a Midtown skyscraper. Maybe he'd have a swim.

Clay looked up too. The yellow was setting into blue. He'd thought it seemed like rain, but now it felt like summer. How wrong they'd been!

16

HE PRESSED THE BUTTON TWICE TO LOWER ALL FOUR WIN-
dows simultaneously. Clay appreciated this feature, the brainstorm
of one particularly insightful engineer who understood that on a hot
day the first thing you wanted was air. There was, though, a kind of
pleasure in the close dry heat inside the car, flecks of dust, the way
you could almost smell the sunlight. The wheels made a particular
noise on the gravel, then cleared that and moved smoothly over
the asphalt. He drove slowly, nonchalant, to make himself feel the
more brave. Also, he figured, the longer those people stayed, the
more right he had to their thousand dollars.

There was a field of something being cultivated, but Clay had
no idea what it was. Were soybeans the same thing as edamame,
or were they something else, and what could they be used for? He
drove slowly past the little shack selling eggs. The road was an in-
termediate thing, still narrow, not quite real; he waited for the GPS
to register, but hadn't he found the way to the shore only yesterday
morning? Clay knew what he was doing.

Someone had once told him that people found smoking calming
because it was essentially deep breathing. There was no shoulder, so
he simply stopped in the road, turned the machine off, depressed
the button to bring the windows back up in beautiful unison. He

stood ten feet away because he didn't want the smell of smoke to permeate the car.

There was that familiar, pure rush of satiety. There was an almost swoon. He had nothing to lean on, so he simply drew himself up taller and looked around at the world, which was quiet. He had a fleeting desire for the clarity of a cold Coke, to shake off the vague hangover. That's what he would do. He'd drive down this road, turn onto the main road, wind around the curves and end up at that four-way intersection and instead of bearing right, toward the sea, he'd go left, toward the town. There was a gas station, there was a public library, there was a junk shop and an ice cream parlor and a motel, and farther down the road one of those depressing low-lying complexes with a grocery, drugstore, dry cleaner, and chain sandwich shop tidily arrayed before a parking lot so large it would never fill up. That's where he'd go in search of knowledge, not to the library but to the place where things were sold. You could get a Coke almost anywhere.

Clay looked at his phone. Habit was powerful. It showed him nothing. He dropped the cigarette and stepped on it, then got back into the car. The brain was a marvel. You could drive without wholly thinking about driving. Sure, familiar routes, the everyday commute—start the car, find the highway, maneuver through lanes, take the usual exit, glide to stops at red lights, move forward at green ones—while not exactly hearing the top stories being reiterated on NPR, or thinking about some slight at the office, or remembering a production of *The Pirates of Penzance* you saw the summer between sixth and seventh grades. Driving was rote. It was something you just did.

He wasn't actually thinking about the production of *The Pirates of Penzance* he'd seen the summer between sixth and seventh grades, though he remembered that as the golden, temporary season in which he'd still been his mother's favorite child, but he must have been thinking about something because Clay turned, at some point, and drove for some distance—he found estimating distance and measures of volume impossible—and realized that though he was definitely on a road, a more serious, two-lane road, the sort of road the GPS would know and name, he could not be certain, not really, that it was the road he'd wanted. There were directions written down in Amanda's notebook, of course, but Amanda's notebook was back at the house, in Amanda's Vuitton bag. Anyway, the ability to take written directions to one destination and simply invert them to move in reverse was an obsolete art. It was like winding the car windows down with a crank. Human progress. Clay was lost.

Everything was very green. There was nothing to hold on to. There were some trees. There was a field. A glimpse of a roof and the promise of a building, but he couldn't say whether it was a barn or a house. The road curved, and then he emerged somewhere else where there was another field and some more trees and another slice of roof of barn or house and Clay thought of those old cartoons that recycled their backgrounds to create the illusion of movement. It was impossible to say what was more sensible—to stop the car and backtrack or to forge ahead as though he knew where he was going. He didn't even know how long he'd been driving, or whether he'd know the turn back onto the road that led to the gravel driveway up to the house where his family waited. He didn't know whether that road was marked by a sign or what the sign would say. Maybe he ought to have paid closer attention; maybe he ought to have taken this errand more seriously.

The sound of the wind and the sensation of it on his face was distracting. Clay slowed the car a little and sent the windows back up, then jabbed at the center panel until the air-conditioning came to life. He continued straight, but that wasn't exactly correct, since the road undulated and twisted and maybe he'd gone in a complete circuit and that was why the trees and occasional buildings looked so familiar: because they were. He found a piece of gum and put it in his mouth. Fine.

There were no other cars, and he didn't know if that seemed odd or not. Anyway, it was not the kind of road for stop signs. The local planners trusted the local people. He pulled onto the dusty shoulder and turned the car around and drove in the direction from which he'd come. Now nothing looked familiar, though he'd just driven through it. It was all inverted, and he noticed things on the left side of the road that he'd missed when they had been on his right: an amateurish painted sign reading "McKinnon Farms," a lone horse standing in a field, the remains of a building that had burned down. He drove and then slowed, because he felt he must be close to the turn back to the house. But he wouldn't take that, he would drive on in the other direction, where he knew the town waited.

There was a road on his right, and he turned to look up it as he passed, but it was not the road that led to the house, because that road had that little painted shack where you could get a dozen eggs for five dollars. He sped up and drove on. There was another turnoff, but again, no painted shack. Then he wondered whether he'd turned twice to get to the road where he now found himself, and was looking for a landmark that did not exist. Clay took out his phone, though he knew you weren't supposed to look at your phone as you drove, and was surprised that it did not seem to be working. Then he remembered that of course it had not been working, that was the real purpose of this errand, not an ice-cold Coke. He had driven out to show everyone that he was a man, in control, and now he was lost and felt ridiculous.

He tossed the phone into the seat beside him. Of course there were no other cars. These were rural roads, for the convenience of a handful of people. The day only seemed strange because the night had been strange. He was a little turned around, but he would find his way; he hadn't gone so far that he'd need rescue. He thought of how the government sent helicopters for the antisocial weirdos who insisted on living atop wildfire-prone mountains. People thought fire a disaster, failing to understand it was an important part of the life cycle of the forest. The old burned. The new grew. Clay kept driving. What else was he supposed to do?

17

───────

THE SUN CREPT ACROSS THE SKY AS EVER IT HAD. THEY WEL-
comed it; they worshipped it. The prickle on the skin felt like punishment. The sweat felt like virtue. Cups collected on the table. Towels
were used and abandoned. There were sighs and feints toward conversation. There was the plash of water and the sound of the door
opening and closing. It was the kind of heat you could almost hear,
and in that kind of heat what could you do but swim?

Amanda worried fresh sunscreen into her chest and could feel
the stuff of herself, ropy and fibrous, beneath her skin. It was an
improvisation. Someone in the audience's shadows had shouted out
this scenario. It made no sense, and she was tasked with performing
as though it did. Clay driving into town. She was doing this. She
thought of that movie where the man pretended for his son that
life under the Nazis was normal, beautiful even. Something about
that seemed prescient now that she thought about it. You could fake
your way to a lot.

Ruth told the children there were more pool floats in the garage.
They returned with sagging plastic mini Oldenburgs. Archie put
the little nub between his lips (it was meant to look like a doughnut,
sprinkled, with a bite taken out of it), the effort of exhalation expos-
ing the filigree of his ribs.

It was so unfair, how much more capable Archie was. Three years of advantage. Rose couldn't get a single breath into her float, which was just a round raft, but looked comfortable. It was annoying. Archie was basically a grown-up, and she was stuck being just herself.

"I'll do it, honey." Amanda took the limp thing between her legs and, perched on the edge of the wooden chaise, coaxed it into shape.

"I like the doughnut one better." Nothing went her way and she couldn't stop herself from noting it.

"Too slow, stupid." Archie tossed the ring onto the surface of the pool. He bounced from the diving board, landing only half on the thing as though he'd meant to. He was unbothered by his sister's protests, had long learned how to ignore most of the things his sister had to say.

"The raft is more comfortable." Rose was the sort of plain, chubby girl Ruth couldn't help feel sorry for. Ruth thought Archie so like every boy she'd seen troop through the halls of her school, convinced of his own charms. Maybe this was something mothers did to sons. She worried about her grandsons, mothered/smothered twice over.

Rose was old enough to know how to feign manners. Still, she whined. "But the doughnut is funny." Rose spoke in that particular mode kids deploy when appealing to adults who are not their parents.

"Funny is no good in the long run." At the umbrellaed table, Ruth crossed her legs. She wore her clean things. She'd stalked into the master bedroom, wincing at the unmade bed, the spent washcloths on the bathroom floor, the scattered dirty laundry. She felt better. Almost relaxed.

"This is harder than it looks." Amanda thought of Clay's cigarettes, stealing her breath. She knew it wasn't fair, not to have a vice. The modern world was so joyless. When had they turned into parents to each other?

Rose was impatient as any thirteen-year-old. "Mom, hurry."

She pulled the translucent nipple, shining with saliva, from her mouth. "Here you go." That was good enough.

Rose stood on the steps, tepid water to her shins. She and Archie vanished into their game, the private conspiracy of childhood. Children sided with one another, the future against the past.

Amanda often thought that siblings were like long-married couples, all those shorthand arguments. This endured only in childhood. She had little to do with her brothers beyond the occasional too-long email from her older brother, Brian, the rare misspelled text messages from her younger brother, Jason. "How long has he been gone?" Amanda checked her phone. At least the clock was working.

"Twenty minutes?" G. H. looked at his own watch. It was that long into town, more if you drove slowly, as a man who didn't know the place might. "He'll be back soon."

"Should I make lunch?" Amanda was less hungry than bored.

"I can help." Ruth was already on her feet. Hard to discern even to her whether she wanted to or felt she had to. She did like cooking, but was that because convention forced her into the kitchen until she'd learned to enjoy time spent there?

"The more the merrier." Amanda didn't want the woman's company, but maybe it would distract her from thinking about her husband.

It was cooler inside, though Ruth had adjusted the thermostat so that it wasn't too cold. She felt this was wasteful. "You shouldn't worry, you know."

This was a kindness, Amanda understood. Clay had bought brie and chocolate. There were sandwiches, a particular favorite of Rose's, a recipe he used to make on New Year's Day for some reason; traditions just begin, somehow, then they end. "I'll warn you, this recipe sounds odd, but it's so good." She laid out ingredients.

Ruth was the one who submerged the Thanksgiving bird in salty water. She was the one who stretched bacon on the rack and let it crisp in the oven. She was the one who used a knife to sunder the flesh from the grapefruit's membranes. This was her room. "Chocolate?"

Amanda looked at the things arrayed on the counter, each individual chocolate chip somehow lovely, the soft wedge of cheese remarkable. "Salty and sweet, some kind of magic there."

"Opposites attract, I guess." Was Ruth flirting? Maybe she was. Were she and Amanda actually opposites? Random circumstance had brought them together, but wasn't everything random circumstance in the end? She chopped basil.

Ruth filled a bucket with ice. She produced cloth napkins, folded them into precise squares, and laid these out on a tray.

Amanda sniffed the fragrant tips of her fingers. "You're the gardener?"

"You won't catch George doing any of that old-people stuff." Ruth thought her more grandmotherly inclinations—the crossword, gardening, fat paperback histories of the Tudors—didn't seem evidence of anything. She was just a woman who liked what she liked. She wasn't old.

Amanda tried to guess. "He's in law? No, finance. No, law." She thought the expensive watch and neatly groomed salt-and-pepper hair and fine spectacles and luxurious shoes explained just what type of man G. H. was.

"Private equity. Should I slice this cheese?" Ruth had explained this before many times. It still meant very little to her. So what? G. H. didn't understand the particulars of what she had done at Dalton. Maybe no one, however much in love, cares about the minutiae of someone else's life. "So, finance, you could say. But not for a big bank. A small firm, a boutique operation." This was her way of explaining it to people who were as confused as she was.

"Just slice it thin, for a grilled sandwich." They had enough for four but not precisely enough for six. She'd make one and leave it aside for Clay. For no reason but thinking of him, tears welled in her eyes. She wanted the news he would bring, but also she just wanted him back.

"At least the children are enjoying themselves." Ruth didn't want these people here, but she couldn't help but feel some human connection to them. Ruth worried about the world, but to care for other people felt something close to resistance. Maybe this was all they had.

Amanda melted butter in the black skillet. "There's that." Archie was almost a man. A century ago, he'd have been sent to the trenches of Europe. Should she tell him what was happening, and what would she tell him if she did?

"I found this onion dip. Maybe as a snack?" Ruth took out a bowl and a big spoon, and they worked in silence.

Amanda could not bear it, and so she broke it. "What do you think is happening out there?"

"Your husband will be back soon. He'll find out something." Ruth tasted the dip with her pinkie, an elegant gesture. She didn't want to play guessing games. She suspected Amanda didn't believe them. Ruth didn't want to be embarrassed.

Amanda removed a finished sandwich. "My kids rely on their phones to tell them how the weather is. To tell them what time it is, everything about the world around them, they can't even see the world anymore but through that prism." But even Amanda did this. She'd mocked the television commercial in which Zooey Deschanel seemed not to know whether it was raining, but she'd done the very same thing. "Without our phones, it turns out we're basically marooned out here." That's what it was. The feeling was withdrawal. On planes, she turned off airplane mode and started trying to check her email once you heard that ding that meant you were fewer than ten thousand feet aloft. The flight attendants were buckled in and couldn't scold. She'd pull and pull and pull at the screen, waiting for the connection to be established, waiting to see what she had missed.

"You'll believe it when you can see it on your phone." Ruth didn't even blame her for this. All these years debating the objectivity of fact had done something to everyone's brains.

"We just don't know anything. I'll feel better once we do. Do you think it's taking Clay a long time?"

Ruth put the dirty spoon in the sink. "There's an old idea, you're trapped on a desert island. You're far from society and people and maybe you have to choose the ten books or records you can take with you. Sort of makes the thing seem like paradise instead of a trap." A desert island sounded nice to her, though the seas were rising; maybe all such islands would vanish.

"But I don't have ten books. If we had the internet, I could get into my account and download all the books I've bought for my Kindle. But we don't have that." What she didn't say: We have the pool, these brie and chocolate sandwiches, and though we're strangers to one another, sure, we have one another too.

18

AMANDA BROUGHT OUT WINE. IT WAS A VACATION. ALSO:
the hair of the dog. When the children complained it was too
early to eat, Amanda let them vanish into their game, relieved.
She poured pale pink wine into acrylic glasses and handed them
around, ceremonial, almost religious. Someone attentive and patient had pressed the cloth napkins. She wondered if it had been
Ruth.

"Your children are so polite." G. H. considered this the highest
of praise.

"Thank you." Amanda was not sure this was not flattery, or just
something to say, but she was pleased. "You've got a daughter?"

"Maya. She teaches Montessori in Massachusetts." G. H. still
wasn't entirely certain what this entailed, but he adored her.

"She runs the school. She doesn't just teach. She's in charge of
the whole operation." Ruth bit into a baby carrot. She felt light.
Maybe some part of her remembered reading once that people with
fatal diagnoses entered a period of remission, calm, almost good
health, once that's been established. A honeymoon. An interlude
of joy.

"That's wonderful. We used to send Archie to a Montessori when
he was small. It was amazing. Changing into their inside shoes.

Washing hands. Saying good morning like colleagues at the office." She'd loved how he'd referred to play as "work." Those bumbling toddlers practicing for adulthood by lifting glass beads with a teaspoon, sponging up lunchtime spills.

"They say it's important for development. Maya is very passionate about it. The boys will start there, goodness, in only a couple of weeks, I suppose it'll be." Ruth was defensive.

"It can't be already!" G. H. knew that every cliché turned out to be true, that they do, in fact, grow up so fast.

"September." Ruth said it with hope. Her mother would have brought God into it—*God willing*, a reflex like drawing breath. They hadn't scorned it, but they hadn't learned that woman's devotion. Maybe she was onto something. Maybe it was a folly to assume anything happened without someone—God, sure, why not him—willing it.

Why did Amanda think of the Earth, Wind and Fire song, or why did the thought seem racist? No, some of their best friends were not black. Their friend Peter was married to a woman named Martika, whose mother had been a famous black model in the 1970s. Their neighbor on the ground floor was black, but also transgender, or nonbinary, or—Amanda always referred to this person by name just to be safe: *Jordan, so good to see you*; *Jordan, how is your summer going?*; *Jordan, it's been so hot out lately*. "It does fly by. Older parents always said that to me when Archie was a baby, and I would think, Well, I can't wait for this to go by. Because I was exhausted. But now I realize they were right." She was babbling.

"I was about to say as much to you. You beat me to it. I remember Maya at this age." G. H. was wistful, but also he was worried. They'd had fine lives, long lives, happy lives. Maya and her family were the only thing that it amounted to, of course, and that was something. A father should protect, and as he'd driven the night before, he'd worked through what he might do for her from the distance of Long Island and realized there wasn't much. But Maya wasn't the one who needed help; they were. Maya and the boys were fine.

Ruth wondered what version of the girl was in her husband's mind. She didn't want to ask. It was too private in front of this stranger. It was odd enough that they were all sitting there in their swimsuits.

"It must be fun to be grandparents. You get to do all the spoiling and don't have to get up all night or scold them for bad report cards or whatever." Amanda's own parents discharged that office with indifference. They didn't dislike Archie and Rose, but they didn't dote upon them. They were two of seven cousins, and her parents had retired to Santa Fe, where her father painted terrible landscapes and her mother volunteered at a dog shelter. They were determined to enjoy the liberty of their old age in that strange place where it took longer for water to boil.

"These sandwiches are good." Ruth had doubted they would be. Also she wanted a change of subject. The truth was, Maya guarded Beckett and Otto. She thought her parents feeble, or conservative, unable to comprehend the philosophy of it, what she and Clara had agreed upon. Ruth would come bearing bags from Books of Wonder, and Maya would pore over them like a rabbi, searching out their sins. It was well intentioned. Her distrust was not of her parents but of the world that they had made, and maybe she was right. Ruth could not resist buying them adorable things—little gingham shirts, like you'd put onto a teddy bear—and Maya would try to conceal her disdain. No matter, Ruth just wanted to be humored, and hold the boys' clean-smelling bodies close against her own. It was remarkable, how that made her feel. Invincible.

"They are good," G. H. agreed.

"Well, we do some spoiling," she allowed. "When we get the chance." That's what she wanted, the chance to see her family.

Amanda no longer thought they were con men, but was this the precursor to dementia, the first warning sign, like keys left in the refrigerator or socks worn into the shower or thinking Reagan was still president? Wasn't that how it worked: first fiction, then paranoia, then Alzheimer's? She felt the same way about her parents— their volition seemed suspect. They'd moved to Santa Fe after skiing in New Mexico once or twice a decade earlier; it made no sense to her, and their contentment seemed a bit like delusion. "It's the whole point of being a grandparent."

"George is worse than I am—"

"Wait." She was more rude than she'd meant to be, and gave the people a sheepish look. "I just realized. Your name is *George Washington?*"

There was no particular shame in it. He'd been explaining it for sixty-plus years. "My name is George Herman Washington."

"I'm sorry. That was rude of me." It was the wine, maybe? "It's just that it seems somehow fitting." She couldn't explain it, but maybe it was self-evident; someday there would be an anecdote, the time she sat poolside with a black man named George Washington while her husband went forth to figure out what had gone wrong in the world. They'd traded their disaster stories the night before, and this would just be one more of those.

"No apologies necessary. Part of the reason I settled on using my initials early in my career."

"It's a fine name." Ruth was not insulted, just marveled at the familiarity with which this woman talked to them. She knew it made her sound even more like an old woman, but she missed a sense of propriety about things.

"It is that! A fine name. And wonderful initials, I think. G. H. sounds like a captain of industry, a master of his business. I would trust a G. H. with my money." Amanda was overcompensating now, but also a little tipsy, the wine, the heat, the strangeness. "Clay should be back soon, don't you think?" She looked at her wrist but was not wearing her watch.

19

THE CHILDREN WERE BORED BY THEIR LEISURE. OUTNUM-
bered, Archie and Rose rediscovered some connection, were again
a five-year-old and two-year-old cooperating toward some unstated
goal. They'd left the pool, left the grown-ups, were into the grass,
the shade the relief the pool had not been.

"Let's go in the woods, Archie." She thought about what she'd
seen. It didn't make sense, even to her. "I saw something this morning. Deer."

"They're everywhere, dumbass. They're like squirrels or pigeons.
Who cares." She wasn't terrible, his sister, and she was still a little
kid, so she couldn't help being a dumbass. Had he been that stupid
at thirteen?

"No. I mean like. Come on." Rose looked over her shoulder at the
adults eating lunch. She couldn't say "Please" because begging would
turn him off. She had to make it sound appealing. She wanted to
pretend they were exploring, but they actually would be exploring,
so it wasn't even a game. "Let's see what's out there."

"There's nothing out there." Still, he kind of wondered what was
out there. Indian arrowheads? Money? Strangers? He'd found, in
various woods he'd visited in his life, some weird shit. Three pages
torn from a dirty magazine: a lady with old-fashioned hair, tan skin,

immense boobs, pouting and bending her body this way and that. A dollar bill. A jar filled with not-quite-clear liquid he was sure was piss but didn't know how to prove that because he didn't want to open a jar that might contain someone else's piss. There were mysteries in the world, was all Rosie was saying, and he knew it but didn't want to hear it from her.

"What if there is? Maybe there's a house back there." She was imagining something as yet unclear even to her.

"There's no other houses anywhere near here." Archie said it like he couldn't believe it, or like he regretted it. He understood. He was bored too.

"There's that farm. We saw them selling the eggs, remember?" Maybe those farmers had kids, maybe they had a daughter, maybe her name was Kayla or Chelsea or Madison and maybe she had her own phone, and maybe she had money, or an idea for something that would be fun to do. Maybe she'd invite them inside, and it would be air-conditioned, and they would play video games, and eat Fritos, and drink Diet Coke with ice cubes in it.

Rose was hot and itchy. She wanted to go into the woods with her brother, to go where the adults couldn't see them, bother them. She imagined evidence out there. Footprints. Tracks. Proof.

Archie retrieved a stick from the ground, heaved it into the trees like a javelin. Kids loved sticks the way dogs did. Take a kid to the park, and they pick up a stick. Some kind of animal response.

"There's a swing. Cool." It hung from a tall tree. There was a small shed that could have been a playhouse or full of tools. Beyond, the grass ebbed until there was nothing but dirt and trees. Rose trotted toward it and sat.

Archie swore and felt like a man, complaining about the knots and rocks under his feet. "Shit."

"What's in that thing?" Something about the shed made Rose cautious. Anything could be inside it. Rose had started pretending, or she never stopped pretending.

"Let's open it and see." Archie sounded confident but privately shared his sister's awe at the thing. It could have been the playhouse of some kid who was dead now. There could be a person inside it, waiting for them to open the door. It was something from a movie, or the kind of story they didn't want their life stories to be.

The adults were behind the fence; it was like they had ceased to be. Rose hopped from the swing and stepped toward the little structure. She broke a spiderweb, invisible until it was not, felt that terrible shiver you do in that moment. The body knew what it was doing. It was scaring you away in case the spider was poisonous. She told herself not to scream—her brother had no patience for girlie things like that. A sound emerged all the same, a kind of strangled disgust.

"What?" Archie looked at his sister, some concern mixed with his disdain. That, too, was an animal response, the big brother's.

"Spiderweb." She thought of *Charlotte's Web*. She knew spiders did not have human personalities and voices, but worried about the spider she might have displaced, could not but imagine it a kindly female spider. She did not know that she limned generosity with femininity, part of the moral of that particular story. She did not know that her mother objected to that, when rereading it aloud a few years ago, when they were small enough to be read to at night.

The boy and the girl moved together through the thick grass, their bodies near naked and pinked from the sun, prickled from the cooler air beneath the boughs, goose fleshed from the spider's silk and the fear that was the best part of exploration. Seen from far away, they looked as the fawns did when you saw them early in the morning, young, hesitant, ungainly, but graceful for being only what they were.

Archie thought, but did not say, *Pussy*. It was a reflexive response to the perception of weakness, but she was his little sister. "Open it."

Rose hesitated and then did not. She had to be brave, that was the game. There was the kind of notch you depress with your thumb, over a handle she gripped but lightly. The metal was weathered, and the touch felt charged. Rose pulled open the door, which made a loud creak. Inside: nothing, a scattering of dried leaves in the corner that looked almost deliberate. Rose's heart was thudding so that she could hear it. "Oh." She was a little disappointed, though she couldn't say what she had expected to find in there.

Archie ducked his head into the building, but did not enter it. "This stupid fucking place is so boring."

"Yeah." Rose dug into the ground with a toenail that had been painted pale blue weeks before.

Now Archie understood it was an improvisatory game. "Maybe this is just where he sleeps, though. Where he hides at night."

Immediately afraid. "Who?"

He shrugged his shoulders. "Whoever made that impression." Archie pointed at the leaves, which had once been wet but had dried into a thick, contoured surface. "I mean, if you were in these woods with nowhere to go and no place to sleep—what would you do?"

She didn't want to think about it. "What do you mean?"

"You couldn't like—climb a tree, and sleep up there. But anywhere on the ground would be like—unsafe. Snakes and shit like that. Rabid animals. Four walls! And a roof. It's basically luxurious. And there's this window—" Archie gestured at the dirty pane cut into the side of the shed, which they had not noticed until they opened it.

"Yeah, I guess." She definitely wouldn't want to sleep outside. She couldn't imagine sleeping in the branches of a tree. She didn't think she could even climb a tree. They'd done rock climbing at Park Slope Day Camp a couple of years ago. She'd been tethered at her waist, had worn a helmet and kneepads, but still refused to go on halfway up the wall, hanging there shrieking until her counselor Darnell worked the rope to get her back down.

Archie paused meaningfully. ". . . So he can see."

"See what?"

Archie bent back into the shed, looked through the window. "Into the house, of course. See for yourself. There's a perfect view."

Rose stepped forward, recoiling a little at the bare dirt under her feet. She did not have to bend, she was not as tall as her brother, but she did, her hand on his forearm to steady her. She could, in fact, see the house from that vantage.

He went on. "Isn't that . . . the room you're sleeping in? Wow. Correct me if I'm wrong. But I'm pretty sure it is. Just imagine, when it's dark out here but the house is all lit up. Your little bedside lamp is glowing, and you're reading, nice and cozy under the covers. He could just follow that light right up to you. I bet you could see right in the windows without even having to stand on tiptoe."

She pulled her body back, knocking her head against the threshold. "Shut up, Archie."

He stifled a laugh.

"Just shut up." She folded her arms against her chest. "Listen. This morning I saw deer. Not a deer. A lot of deer. A hundred. Maybe more. Right here. It was so weird. Do they go around in big groups like that?"

Archie walked toward the tree in whose shade the little playhouse was nestled. He reached up and leaped just slightly, took hold of the lowest limb, lifted his knees to his chest, and swung, animal and mischievous. He dropped to the ground with a thud. He spat into the dust. "I don't fucking know anything about fucking deer."

Peach-colored, fuzzed, sticky, their bodies dissolved into the foliage; they couldn't be seen, heard, spied, as they investigated.

They wanted something to happen, but something was happening. They did not know it, and it did not involve them, not really. It would, of course; the world belonged to the young. They were babes in the woods, and if the tale were to be believed, they would die, the birds would see to their bodies, maybe escort their souls to heaven. It depended on which version of the story you knew. The dark that had settled on Manhattan, that tangible thing, could be explained. But beyond the dark was everything else, and that was more vague, hard to hold on to as spider's silk, there but not there, all around them. They walked farther into the woods.

20

IT HAD BEEN FOURTEEN MINUTES SINCE HE'D LEFT THE house. He remembered checking the display as he started the car. Maybe it was sixteen. Maybe he was misremembering. Maybe it was fewer! Then he'd stopped to smoke that cigarette, which he usually said took seven minutes but actually took closer to four. So Clay had been driving for ten minutes, which was not really so long, and meant he couldn't truly be lost. He told himself to calm down, then pulled the car into the McKinnon Farms driveway to smoke a cigarette. He could, of course, continue down the drive, to the farmhouse or some other building where people would be, but that would mean he was truly panicked, which he was not. So he smoked and tried to find the relaxation inherent in the act, then stubbed the thing out before it was truly done, impatient. He couldn't remember, when they'd driven to the house that first day, if theirs had been the only car. That first day seemed weeks in the past.

He closed the door harder than he meant to, though it was not exactly a slam. It was loud enough to underscore the general quiet. He told himself that this was normal, and it was. It would have seemed peaceful had he been prepared to find peace. It seemed irritating at best and menacing at worst. Symbols don't mean anything;

you invest them with meaning, depending on what you most need. Clay chewed a piece of gum and started the car. He turned left out of the farm's access road and drove slowly, noting every possible turn on the right. There was one, then another, then, finally, another, but none looked familiar, and none were adjacent to a stand selling eggs. There was a sign that read only "Corn," but this didn't seem to indicate anything at all, and must have been old.

He thought of the mental and actual preparation they'd put in to prepare Archie to ride the subway alone. The way they'd insisted the boy memorize their phone numbers, in case his telephone was lost or broken, the plan they'd agreed upon should he find himself on a rerouted train bound for some part of the city where he'd never been. Now he rode the subway all the time. Clay rarely thought about it. That was how it worked, maybe. You prepared your child to sleep through the night or wield a fork or piss in the toilet or say please or eat broccoli or be respectful to adults, and then the child was prepared. That was the end of it. He didn't know why he was thinking about Archie, and he shook his head as though to clear it. He would have to turn around and take one of the three, four, five turnoffs he'd passed, determine where they led, see if they were the right way. One of them had to be. He needed only to be methodical. He'd trace the route back to the house, then begin again, more cautious, more attentive, and work his way to town, where he had intended all along to end up. He really wanted that Coke now. His head hurt from lack of caffeine.

Their vacation was ruined. The spell had been broken. Truly, what he should do was drive back to the house and have the kids pack their things. They'd be back in the city before dinner. They could splurge at that French place on Atlantic, order the fried anchovy, the steak, a martini. Clay was only decisive after the fact. And now he was—well, he would say turned around, not lost. He felt a strangely powerful desire to see his children.

He took the first left, and drove only a few yards before understanding that this was not the route; it pitched uphill, and he knew the road had been level. He turned the car around and turned back onto the main road, barely slowing, knowing there was no traffic coming in either direction. He took the second left, and this seemed like it might be the way. He drove on, then turned right, because he could. Perhaps that was it, and the painted egg shack was just up that road. Everything looked familiar because trees and grass only ever looked precisely as you'd expect them to.

He turned the car around again, went back to the road onto which he'd turned from the main road, and there, across that main road, he saw a woman. She was wearing a white polo shirt and khaki pants. On some women it would have looked like leisure wear, but on this woman, her face a broad, indigenous shape (ancient blood, timeless dignity), it looked like a uniform. The woman saw him, raised a hand, waved at him, gestured at him, beckoned him. Clay pulled into the road, more slowly now, and glided to a stop. He lowered the passenger window and smiled out at the woman, the way you're taught to smile at dogs so you don't betray your fear of them.

"Hello, there!" He wasn't sure what he'd say. Would he admit to being lost?

"Hello." She looked at him and then began speaking, very quickly, in Spanish.

"I'm sorry." He shrugged. It sounded, he hated to admit even in his private thoughts, like gibberish. He didn't speak any other languages. Clay didn't even like to attempt it. It made him feel like a fool, or a child.

The woman continued. The words poured out of her. She barely took a breath. She had something urgent to say, and had maybe forgotten what English she possessed—*hello* and *thank you* and *it's ok* and *Windex* and *telephone* and *text* and *Venmo* and the days of the week. She talked. She kept talking.

"I'm sorry." He shrugged again. He did not understand, of course.

But maybe he comprehended. Oh, that was a word: *comprende.* They said it in movies. You couldn't live in this country and not know some Spanish. If he'd had time to think about it, if he'd forced himself to calm down, he could have communicated with this woman. But she was panicked, and she was panicking him. He was lost and wanted his family. He wanted a steak at that restaurant on Atlantic Avenue. "No Spanish."

She said more. Something something. He heard *beer* but she said *deer*; they sound alike in both tongues. She said more. She said *telephone*, but he didn't understand. She said *electric*, but he didn't hear. Tears welled at the corners of her small eyes. She was short, freckled, broad. She could have been fourteen or forty. Her nose was running. She was weeping. She spoke louder, hurried, was imprecise, maybe lapsing out of Spanish altogether into some dialect, something still more ancient, the argot of civilizations long dead, piles of rubble in jungles. Her people discovered corn, tobacco, chocolate. Her people invented astronomy, language, trade. Then they'd ceased to be. Now their descendants shucked the corn they'd been the first to know about, and vacuumed rugs and watered decorative beds of lavender planted poolside at mansions in the Hamptons that sat unused most of the year. She forgot herself, even, put her hands on his car, which they both knew was a violation. She held on to the two-inch lip of window that was sticking up out of the door. Her hands were small and brown. She was still talking through the tears; she was asking him a question, a question he could not understand and anyway would not have been able to answer.

"I'm sorry." He shook his head. If his phone had worked, he might have tried Google Translate. He could have urged her to get into the car, but how would he have made her understand that he was lost, not driving in circles because he meant to kill her or lull her to sleep, as suburban parents did with their infants? A different man would respond differently, but Clay was the man he was, one

unable to provide what this woman needed, one afraid of her ur-
gency, her fear, which did not need translation. She was afraid. He
should be afraid. He was afraid. "I'm sorry." He said it to himself,
more than to her. She released the window as he started to roll it
up. He drove farther down the road, quickly, though he'd intended
to investigate all those driveways. He needed to be away from her
more even than he needed to be with his family.

21

IN THE WOODS YOU HAD THIS SENSE OF SOMETHING YOU couldn't see no matter how you tried. There were bugs, dun-colored toads holding still, mushrooms in fantastical shapes that seemed accidental, the sweet smell of rot, inexplicable damp. You felt small, like one of many things, and the least important too.

Maybe, maybe, something had happened to them. Maybe something was happening to them. For centuries there was no language to describe the fact that tumors blossomed inside lungs, beautiful volunteers like flowering plants that take root in unlikely places. Not knowing what to call it did not change it, death by drowning as your chest filled with sacs of liquid.

Rose felt eyes on her, but then she pretended, often, that she was being watched. She saw herself at the remove of a cell-phone camera. She was young and didn't understand that was how everyone saw themselves, as the main character of a story, rather than one of literal billions, our lungs slowly filling with salt water.

In the woods, the light was different. The trees interfered with it. The trees were alive and felt like Tolkien's majestic creatures. The trees were watching, and not impartially. The trees knew what was up. The trees talked amongst themselves. They were sensitive to the seismic reverberations of bombs far distant. Trees miles away—where the ocean had begun to breach the land—were dying, though it would take years for them to be reduced to albino logs. The trees had all the time the rest of us do not. The mangroves could outsmart it, pull up their roots like a Victorian lady's skirts, sip the salt from the ground, so maybe they'd be fine, with the alligators and the rats and the roaches and the snakes. Maybe they'd be better off without us. Sometimes, sometimes, suicide is a relief. That was the right noun for what was happening. The sickness in the ground and in the air and in the water was all a clever design. There was a menace in the woods and Rose could feel it, and another child would have called it God. Did it matter if a storm had metastasized into something for which no noun yet existed? Did it matter if the electrical grid broke apart like something built of Lego? Did it matter if Lego would never biodegrade, would outlast Notre Dame, the pyramids at Giza, the pigment daubed on the walls at Lascaux? Did it matter if some nation claimed responsibility for the outage, did it matter that it was condemned as an act of war, did it matter if this was pretext for a retaliation long hoped for, did it matter that proving who had done what via wires and networks was actually impossible? Did it matter if an asthmatic woman named Deborah died after six hours trapped on an F train stalled beneath the Hudson River, and that the other people on the subway walked past her body and felt nothing in particular? Did it matter that machines meant for supporting life ceased doing that hard work after the failure of backup generators in Miami, in Atlanta, in Charlotte, in Annapolis? Did it matter if the morbidly obese grandson of the Eternal President actually did send a bomb, or did it matter simply that he could, if he wanted to?

The children couldn't know that some of this had happened. That in an old-age home in a coastal town called Port Victory a Vietnam vet named Peter Miller was floating facedown in two feet of water. That Delta had lost a plane traveling between Dallas and Minneapolis during the disruption of the air traffic control system. That a pipeline was spilling crude onto the ground in an unpopulated part of Wyoming. That a major television star had been struck by a car at the intersection of Seventy-Ninth and Amsterdam and died because the ambulances couldn't get anywhere. They couldn't know that the silence that seemed so relaxing in the country seemed so menacing in the city, which was hot, still, and quiet in a way that made no sense. Nothing matters to children but themselves, or perhaps that is the human condition.

Barefoot, bareheaded, bare-breasted, the children moved gingerly, feet arching, toes recoiling. Branches grazed their skin, and you could not see the marks they made. The illness of the planet had never been a secret, the nature of it all had never been in doubt, and if something had changed (it had), the fact that they didn't yet know it had no bearing on the matter at all. It was inside them now, whatever it was. The world operated according to logic, but the logic had been evolving for some time, and now they had to reckon with that. Whatever they thought they'd understood was not wrong but irrelevant.

"Archie, look." It came out as a whisper. She'd lowered her voice, assuming respect, as you might inside a holy place. She pointed. A roof. A clearing that became a lawn. A brick house, like the one where they were staying, a pool, a sturdy wood swing set.

"A house." He wasn't even derisive, just declarative. Archie hadn't been expecting to find anything. Ruth had told them there was nothing out here, but they had gone farther than Ruth ever had, were curious about the world in a way Ruth was not. This was a satisfying discovery. Other people. Archie had left his phone charging in his bedroom. He wished he'd brought it, tried to borrow these people's WiFi.

"Should we go up there?" She was thinking of the swing set and that maybe the kids had outgrown it. She was thinking that not talking to strangers was a matter for the city only.

"Nah. Let's go." Archie turned toward what he believed was

the direction from which they'd come. He didn't feel the tick burrowing into his ankle any more than he could Earth's deliberate daily rotation. He didn't feel anything in the air because it felt unchanged.

They walked, not slowly, but not in a hurry. Time passed differently in the woods. They didn't know how long they'd been gone. They didn't know what they'd intended to do. They didn't know why it felt satisfying, just strolling through the shade of the trees, air and sun and bugs and sweat on skin. They didn't know that their father was even then driving past, less than a half a mile away, less than a quarter mile, near enough they could run to him, save him. From where they stood they couldn't hear the road, and they weren't thinking about their father, their mother, anyone.

As they walked, Archie and Rose barely spoke, mucking through the leaves, shivering a little. Their bodies knew what their minds did not. Children and the very old have this in common. Born, you understand something about the world. That's why toddlers report conversing with ghosts and unnerve their parents. The very old begin to remember it, but can rarely articulate it, and no one listens to the very old anyway.

They were not afraid, the children, not really. They were at peace. A change was upon them; a change was upon it all. What you called it didn't matter. Overhead, the leaves shifted and sighed, and there was the sound of Archie and Rose saying something to each other, something impossible to make out, something that existed only between them, the private language of youth. And save that there was only the gentle rustle of the trees adjusting their limbs and the susurrus of unseen insects. Those would settle, soon, the way that things grow quiet before the sudden summer rainstorm, because the bugs knew, and would hold their bodies tight to the stippled bark of the trees and wait for whatever was coming.

22

SO HE'D BEEN GONE FOR FORTY-FIVE MINUTES. IT MEANT he'd stopped to smoke. It meant he'd stopped for groceries. Amanda: What, me worry?

Ruth put a bowl of cherries, more black than red, onto the table. It had the air of ceremony.

"Thank you." Amanda didn't know why she was thanking the woman. Hadn't she spent eleven dollars on these cherries?

A cloud, one of those soft, cottony ones, all curves like a child's drawing, seeped across the sky. The change was severe enough that G. H. shivered. "I could almost use a minute in the hot tub."

Amanda took this for an invitation. She left the table, sank into the froth beside the strange man. The water made you buoyant, and so it made it hard to sit. Amanda leaned forward to look toward the trees. She could not see the children any longer.

"They're fine, I expect." George understood. You had a child and were forever vigilant. "There's nothing back there but more trees."

Ruth looked at the two of them. Wine with lunch had made her drowsy. "I might make some coffee then."

"That would be nice, love, thank you."

Amanda smiled. "Can I do anything?"

"You relax." Ruth went back into the house.

"The pool. The hot tub. They cost a fortune in electric bills. We're going to have solar panels put up. I didn't want to do it during the season, when we use the house. I'm waiting until September, October. My contractor told me he generates enough that he sells power back to the grid. More people should do that." G. H. was almost beginning to enjoy this woman's company. He liked an audience.

"Clean energy. Should save the planet. Should be a law." Sometimes at the movie theater or on the sidewalk Amanda would see wind energy proselytizers with pamphlets and free buttons, but it always seemed like a scam. "How did you get into your line of work?" More small talk.

"I had a mentor, in college. It was him who made me—I mean, I didn't know what people did for a living. My mother ran a hair salon." His tone conveyed his respect for his mother's work. She died of cancer—liver, stomach, pancreas—probably from handling the chemicals women like her used to make their hair respectable. "Stephen Johnson. Gone now, but what a life."

"I guess it's like having a green thumb. Or being good at doing the Rubik's cube. Some people can make money, some people can't." She knew who she and Clay were.

This was one of G. H.'s hobbyhorses. "That's the conventional wisdom. You have to ask yourself why that is. Who wants you to believe that it's not possible to get, if not rich, at least comfortable? It's a skill. You can be taught. It's just about information. You have to read the paper. You have to listen to what is happening in the world." Of course, he thought you had to be *smart*, but he considered that a given.

"I read the paper." She was a woman of the world, she believed. She wanted to say something about her work, but there was little to say.

"You only have to understand the patterns that govern the world. Did you ever hear about that guy who beat the game show *Press Your Luck*?" G. H. looked down at her over the rims of his Ray-Bans. He wanted a newspaper now. He thought of the numbers. He wondered what had moved.

"Whammy? No Whammy?"

"All he did was pay attention and learn that the Whammy wasn't random at all. It always appeared in a certain sequence. That information was just there, but no one had ever bothered to look for it." Rich people didn't have a moral authority. They just knew where the Whammy was.

"That's interesting," she said, indicating that she did not find it so at all. Where were the kids? "I'm glad to be away from my work, for the moment. Don't get me wrong—it's interesting, to me, anyway, helping people tell the stories of their companies, helping them find consumers, make that connection. But it's a lot of diplomacy. It gets tiring."

George went on. "My mentor was one of the first black men at a Wall Street firm. We had lunch one afternoon—lunch! I was twenty-one." How to communicate that he'd never previously considered eating lunch at a restaurant, never mind one like that, carpeted, mirrored, brass ashtrays and solicitous uniformed girls in ponytails? He'd showed up without a tie, and Stephen Johnson took him to Bloomingdale's, bought him four from Ralph Lauren. G. H. hadn't known how to put them on; the ones he'd worn at Christmas were clip-on.

"I've always thought that women need to stick together in the workforce. Or maybe everywhere. I'd be nowhere without my mentors." This was not entirely true. Amanda had worked for women, but secretly preferred working with men. Their motivations were so simple.

"He said to me, 'We're all machines.' That's it. You get to choose the nature of the machine you are. We're all machines, but some of us are smart enough that we get to determine our programming." What he'd said: Fools believe rebellion is possible. Capital determines everything. You can either calibrate yourself to that or think you've rejected it. But the latter, Stephen Johnson said, was a delusion. You were either going to get rich or not. You only had to choose. Stephen Johnson and he were the same kind of person. He was who he was—patriarch, intellect, husband, collector of fine watches, first-class traveler—because he'd chosen to be.

Amanda was lost. They were talking around each other, not to each other. "You must love what you do."

Did he care about it, or had he come to care about it, as the spouses in an arranged marriage find, over time, a transaction settled into something like affection? "I'm a lucky man."

The heat was clarifying in the way of orgasm, akin to blowing your nose. The hot sun, the hot water, but still this energy: she could have run around the block, or taken a nap, or done pull-ups. She was waiting for Clay to drive up the road. It had been an hour, right? She listened for the sound of the car.

They should leave. If they timed it right, they'd be home for dinner. They could treat themselves to one of the neighborhood restaurants that was just slightly too expensive to be a regular haunt. She didn't know, of course, that Clay had the same thought. She didn't know this bespoke how well suited to each other they were.

The yard was quiet but for the steamy undulation of the tub. She looked at the woods, and she thought she saw something moving but couldn't pick out their bodies. She thought a mother should be able to do that, once upon a time, but then she'd actually taken the toddlers to the playground and lost them immediately, a sea of small humanity that had nothing to do with her. She was happy the children had each other, were still children enough to get lost in their games, tromping through the woods like she imagined country kids did.

She was sitting there, not doing anything more, when it happened, when there was something. A noise, but that didn't cover it. Noise was an insufficient noun, or maybe noise was always impossible to describe in words. What was music but noise; could words get at Beethoven? This was a noise, yes, but one so loud that it was almost a physical presence, so sudden because of course there was no precedent. There was nothing (real life!), and then there was a noise. Of course they'd never heard a noise like that before. You didn't hear such a noise; you experienced it, endured it, survived it, witnessed it. You could fairly say that their lives could be divided into two: the period before they'd heard that noise and the period after. It was a noise, but it was a transformation. It was a noise, but it was a confirmation. Something had happened, something was happening, it was ongoing, the noise was confirmation even as the noise was mystery.

Understanding came after the fact. That was how life worked: I'm being hit by a car, I'm having a heart attack, that purple-gray thing emerging from between my legs is the head of our child. Epiphanies. They were the end of a chain of events invisible until that epiphany had been reached. You had to walk backward and try to make sense. That's what people did, that's how people learned. Yes. So. The thing was a noise.

Not a bang, not a clap. More than thunder, more than an explosion; none of them had never heard an explosion. Explosions seemed common because films so often depicted them, but explosions were rare, or they'd all been lucky to be spared proximity to explosions. All that could be said, in the moment, was that it was noise, big enough to alter forever their working definitions of noise. You'd cry if you weren't so scared, surprised, or affected in some way impossible to understand. You might cry even so.

The noise was quick, maybe, but the air buzzed with it for what seemed like a long time. What was the noise, and what was the noise's aftereffect? One of those unanswerable questions. Amanda stood up. Behind them, the glass pane of the door between the bedroom and the deck cracked, a fine but long crack, beautiful and mathematical and something no one would notice for a while yet. The noise was loud enough to make a man fall to his knees. That's what Archie did, distant, in the woods: fell to his bare knees. A noise that could make a person fall to their knees was only nominally a noise. It was something else for which there was no noun necessary, because how often would one use such a word?

"What the fuck?" This was, maybe, the only proper response. Amanda was not talking to George. She was not talking to anyone. "What the fuck?" She said it a third time, a fourth time, a fifth time, it didn't matter. She kept saying it, and it was unanswered, as a prayer.

Amanda was trembling. Not shaken but shaking, vibrating. She went quiet. A noise so big, how could you meet it but with silence? She thought what she was doing was screaming. The feeling of a scream, the emotion of a scream, but in fact she gasped, like a fish flipped out of its pond, the noise deaf-mutes make in moments of passion, the shadow, the silhouette, of speech. Amanda was angry.

"What—" She didn't feel any particular need to finish her sentence because she was talking to herself. "What. What. What."

George had leaped from the tub, didn't even cover his body with a towel. Everything in the world was quiet, except, maybe, that sense of afterglow, the void where the noise had only just been. Perhaps her ears were damaged, and it was an illusion. Perhaps her brain was damaged. There had been that story, about consular employees in Havana who developed neurological symptoms believed to be linked to noise. It had never occurred to Amanda that a weapon could be sonic, had never occurred to her that a noise might be something to fear. You told kids and pets not to worry during thunderstorms.

Amanda was shaking. There was a sharp taste, like she had a Kennedy half dollar sitting on top of her tongue. If she moved, the noise might recur. If it did, she was not sure she would be able to bear it. She never wanted to hear it again. "What was that?" This was more to herself than anything. Was it localized—inside the house, within the perimeter—or was it something related to the weather or interstellar or the parting of the heavens to herald the arrival of God himself? As she asked, she knew that the noise would never be satisfactorily explained. It was past logic, or explanation, at least.

It was very slow at first. She walked and then leaped down the steps. She had just been looking out at the trees. She tried to find their bodies in all that green and brown. She should call for them, and it seemed like she did, but she did not. Her voice did not work, or couldn't catch up to her body. She just moved. Slow, then fast, jog then run, Amanda went down past the pool, shoving open the gate, and into the grass. Her children, their perfect faces, their flawless bodies, were there, somewhere. She could see only the single mass of the landscape. It looked to her as it might had she been nearsighted and without her glasses, indistinct, bright, impossible.

She ran farther. The yard was not so big, there was not so much to run into. Still she did not call, only ran. There was a little shed in the shadows. She pulled open the door and it was empty. All in one movement—she didn't truly stop running—she continued to the edge of the yard, soft dirt and dry leaves. The noise was over, but there was still a noise, her blood in her veins, her heart resilient enough. She needed her children's bodies against her own.

Amanda leaped over a stick, small enough that she could have stepped over it, and her feet were in the carpet of humus, here catching a pebble, pointed bark, a thorn, something wet and unpleasant. She should call out to them but didn't want to drown out their voices should they be calling to her, urgent *Mom*s, as convicts were said to utter upon their executions.

The kids, where were her kids? The trees barely seemed to move. They just stood, indifferent to her. Amanda sank to the ground. The touch of leaves, bark, dirt, was almost a comfort. The mud on her pink knees was almost a balm. The clean soles of her feet were blackened and pocked but not painful. At last she found herself. She intended to call out for the children, to call out the names they'd chosen so lovingly, but instead of "Archie" and "Rosie" (for the diminutive would surely have emerged, love and longing), Amanda only screamed, a terrible, animal scream, the second most shocking noise she had ever heard.

23

THEY SPOKE MORE QUIETLY THAN NORMAL. THEY WERE DEF-
erential, of course, to the noise. They were waiting for it to come
back. They didn't want to be caught unawares, but how could you
anticipate that, even having heard it before? All the same: there was
disagreement.

G. H. did not wholly believe what he was saying. "It could have
been thunder, I suppose." Sometimes you could will yourself to
believe what you said.

"There are no clouds!" Amanda's fury was blunted, a bit, by relief. She had found her children, wide-eyed and filthy as mendi-
cants, and would not let them go. She had Rose's right hand in hers
as she used to, years ago, when the girl was misbehaving. On the
girl's left hand the palm was etched red, a perfect, unbroken line.
Abraded skin on her left knee, smudges on her chin and shoulder
and the soft midriff—she'd campaigned for months for a two-piece
swimsuit—and greasy hair and red eyes, but otherwise the girl was
fine. The children looked fine. They seemed fine.

Amanda had plunged headlong into the woods and found them
by some instinct she'd forgotten she possessed, or perhaps it was
dumb luck. The noise sent the three of them running, and their

paths happened to intersect. The noise saw Clay stop the car beside the maddeningly empty road, open the door, and consider the heavens. The noise startled Ruth, filling the coffeepot, dropping a spoon to the ground. The noise bade those deer, more than a thousand in number, already heedless of the property lines drawn by men, to stampede through gardens without even stopping for a nibble. Homeowners were too distracted—by the shattered windows, by the screaming children, by the infant eardrums, irreparably affected—to gawk at all those animals.

Amanda and the children emerged from the woods, and though they were strangers there was real joy at their reunion. Ruth had put an arm around the boy's bare shoulders. G. H. had squeezed Amanda's forearm in paternal relief. The aftermath of the noise—a hum, a sense of vibration—seemed to linger. It was like a swarm of persistent insects, the biting flies you sometimes encountered at the beach. There and not there. Dogged. Amanda suggested they go inside, articulating what everyone was feeling. The sky was quite blue and very pretty, but the out-of-doors seemed somehow untrustworthy. The noise seemed to belong to nature, but as Ruth knew, the bricks had not been enough to keep the sound away. "Was that a bomb?" Visions of mushroom clouds.

"Where's Dad?" Regressing as you did after a trauma, Archie's voice broke, high and awkward, on *Dad*. Where was Dad?

"He ran an errand." Amanda was terse.

"I'm sure he'll be back any moment." Ruth filled glasses with water. The children were filthy and sweaty. She wasn't sure how to help, and that was what she wanted to do. She couldn't hold her grandchildren close. She could get this stranger's children a glass of water.

"Thank you." Archie remembered his manners. That was a good sign.

"Why don't you go wash? I can stay with Archie." Ruth bent to pick up the dropped teaspoon with which she'd been measuring the coffee grounds. She wanted to help, but mostly she wanted a distraction.

Amanda took Rose to the bathroom, cleaned her wounds. They were minor. The ritual was a comfort to both of them: damp toilet paper and Neosporin, her child's face close enough that she could smell her hot breath. After the genocide, beauty parlors helped Rwandans cope. Touching another human being was a curative. She swabbed the child's face with a damp washcloth, dressed her in a sweatshirt and shorts. Rose, who no longer wanted to be seen naked, did not even protest that. The noise had terrified her.

Ruth had to do *something*. "Drink your water, sweetie." The blandishment did not come naturally. At school, they called every child "friend." Even in trouble they were not subjected to "ma'am" and "sir" but "friend." Friend, we need to talk about your behavior. Friends, please lower your voices. It was holy in a noncommittal way.

Archie's hairless back was coated with a paste of sweat and dust. You could have inscribed a word in the filth on his skin, the way pranksters wrote "Wash me" on untended cars. Dutiful, he took a sip. "My ears feel weird."

"It's probably normal." Ruth's ears didn't feel weird, but her everything else did. "That was—loud." It might have damaged their eardrums.

Amanda returned, the clean little girl holding her hand, made a child again. "Oh Archie. You're a mess." She stroked his grimy back, reassured and reassuring.

G. H. peered out the window, suspicious of everything he could see, the pool, the rustling trees. That was all that was out there, that was all he could see, but he wasn't expecting to see—what? A bomb? A missile? Were those the same thing?

"Was it a plane?" Amanda was trying to reconstruct it, but a noise was like pain: your body couldn't remember its specifics. It might have been mechanical, and planes seemed the highest form of machine.

"A plane crashing?" Ruth didn't know if that was what she meant and couldn't guess what sort of sound it would make, a plane exploding like that one over Lockerbie or felled like the one that was destined for the US Capitol. Again she only had Hollywood films.

"Or breaking the sound barrier. A sonic boom. Was that a sonic boom?" They had flown on the Concorde once, a lark, their fifteenth anniversary. François Mitterand had been on their flight. "I think you can't break the sound barrier when you're over land. But it gets lost over the ocean. I think that's right."

"Planes don't usually break the sound barrier." Archie had done a report on it in sixth grade. "The Concorde doesn't fly anymore."

He was right in that the Concorde had only ever terrified the whales in the North Atlantic. But these were extraordinary times. He didn't know that the planes dispatched from Rome, New York, usually flew north, the most direct route to the open sea. But they were off to intercept something that approached the nation's eastern flank. The circumference of the noise they created was about fifty miles—a rend in heaven right over their little house.

Ruth had thought of it over their repast of strange sandwiches. "I noticed today—did you? There was no air traffic. Not one plane, not one helicopter."

G. H. knew, as his wife said it, that this was true. "You're right. I mean, usually we hear so many. Planes, helicopters."

"What do you mean?" Amanda asked. "There must have been—"

"Hobbyists taking lessons. Impatient people flying out from Manhattan. It's a big issue in the local op-eds." Ruth herself had become inured enough to the noise pollution that she noticed, instead, its absence. She didn't know what this meant, but thought it might mean something.

Amanda wanted to send the children out of the room, but there was no television to distract them. "Archie, why don't you go put on your clothes." Her hand on his gritty back. He was hot to the touch. "Drink more water. Maybe you should take a shower?"

Ruth understood; maybe any parent would. "Rose, maybe you should go lie down."

The girl didn't know if this strange woman was meant to be obeyed. She looked up at her mother to see what to do.

"That's a good idea, honey." Amanda was grateful. "Go curl up in Mommy's bed. Read your book."

"I'm going to go take a shower." Archie was suddenly conscious of being undressed. He couldn't confess this, but he'd pissed in his swimsuit when he heard that noise, like a baby. There was a point, when he was younger, where he'd dreamed of understanding grown-up conversation. Now he could, and realized he'd overestimated it. "Come on, Rose." A big brother's kindness.

Amanda waited until the children were gone. "What was that?"

Ruth looked past her husband to the window, the flat blue sky. "It's not the weather—" Ideal day for swimming, and anyway there had never been thunder so loud, that lasted so long. If they lived in Hawaii, she might have said it was a volcano.

G. H. was impatient. He was done with this. "We can agree that we don't know what it is," he said.

"Where is Clay?" Amanda looked at Ruth as though the woman were responsible. As the noise changed the girl from teen to child, it left Amanda soft, helpless.

Ruth had lost track of the time. "It wasn't so long ago. It just feels that way."

"He'll be back soon." G. H. was making promises.

"This settles it, though. Something is . . . happening." The lack of a cellular signal was an assault. The absence of television was a tactic. "We have to do something!"

"What should we do, sweetie?" Ruth didn't disagree, but she was at a loss.

"We're being attacked. This is an attack. What are you supposed to do in the event of an attack?"

"We're not being attacked." G. H. was not entirely certain, though, and it showed. "Nothing has changed."

"Nothing has changed?" Amanda was louder. "We're just sitting here, like, I don't know what. Is that what sitting ducks are? Ducks just sitting and waiting to be shot?" What a stupid expression. Why would a duck sit?

"I mean, we still don't know what's happening. We should just wait for Clay to come back, and we'll see what he's learned."

"Should I drive into town and look for Clay?" She didn't want to leave the house, but she would. Something had to be *done*. "Should we fill the bathtubs? Do we have batteries and Tylenol? Should we find the neighbors? Is there enough food? Is this an emergency?"

G. H. put his brown hands on the Vermont stone countertops. "This is an emergency. We're prepared. And we are safe here." Those were the facts: his energy bars, his case of wine.

"Is there a generator? Is there a bomb shelter? Is there— I don't know. A hand-crank radio? One of those straws that makes it safe to drink dirty water?"

"He'll be back soon, I'm sure." G. H. was trying to convince himself as well. "We'll stay here. We're safe here. All of us. We'll stay here."

"It's fifteen minutes to town. Then fifteen minutes back. That's half an hour. At least." Ruth fidgeted. What were they doing? "Maybe it's longer if you don't know the way. Maybe it's twenty minutes. Forty, there and back."

Amanda was mad at all of them. "What if he's not coming back? What if the car died, or that noise did something to him, or—" What did she envision? Clay, gone forever.

"George is right. We're safe. Let's just sit tight."

"How can you say we're safe when you don't know what's happening to us?" Amanda hoped the children could not hear her. She wept, now.

"We heard that noise." Ruth was logical. "We should just wait. To see what we're going to have to do next."

Amanda was furious. "We don't have the internet, we don't have our phones, we don't know what anything is." She blamed it on these people. They'd knocked on the door and ruined everything.

"Maybe it was like—what was that? Ten Mile Island?" Ruth wanted a drink, but couldn't decide if this was a good idea. "There are power plants out here, aren't there?"

"Three Mile Island." G. H. always knew that sort of thing.

Amanda knew it from history books. "A nuclear accident?" The abiding fear of her youth: presidential red telephones, flashes of light, fallout. She'd forgotten all that at some point. "Oh my god. Should we tape the windows shut? Are we going to get sick?"

"I don't know that that would account for the noise." G. H. tried to remember: the steam was produced by the sea water used to cool the material that produced the reaction that created the energy. An earthquake in Japan had shown the fallacy; the sea water could flow back, poison could travel across the ocean. They'd found debris in Oregon. Would a nuclear incident make such a noise? Did the nuclear plants out here supply the city, and would their damage account for the blackout?

"A missile?" Amanda was thinking out loud. "North Korea. Ruth, you brought up North Korea."

"Iran." G. H. said it without meaning to.

"Iran?" Amanda said it like she'd never heard of the place.

"We shouldn't speculate." G. H. regretted it.

"Maybe this was. You know. The blackout then—the source of that noise, a bomb or whatever." Terrorists were planners. The action itself felt like impulse, because televisions couldn't show what preceded it: meetings, strategy, sketches, money. Those nineteen had practiced in flight simulators! Where would you even find a flight simulator?

"We're just getting worked up—" G. H. felt it was important to stick to what they could see.

Ruth would have a drink. She found the wine key. She went to the cabinet and took out a cabernet. "But . . . Clay. What if—what if he found something?" What was worse: he was not coming back, or he was, and had found something out in the world truly unbearable, worse than they were able to even guess at, and had to come back with news of it and force these people to bear it with him?

Amanda wept, more now. "But we won't know what is happening until we do. We're just . . ." She looked at the pendant lamps, new but made to look like something from a turn-of-the-century schoolhouse, at the clever cabinetry that concealed the stainless steel dishwasher, at the milk-glass bowl full of lemons. The house had seemed so alluring. It didn't feel as safe anymore, it didn't feel the same, nothing did.

"Maybe the television will come back on." Ruth tried to sound optimistic.

"Or our cell phones will work again." Amanda said it like a prayer. She looked down at the countertop, noticing, maybe for the first time, the beautiful abstraction of stone. It didn't seem strong or solid, but it did seem newly beautiful. That was something.

24

MASCULINE RESPONSIBILITY, CLAY REALIZED, WAS UTTER bullshit. The vanity in wanting to save them! That noise made him want to be at home. He didn't want to protect; he wanted to be protected. The noise brought tears, frustrated, irritated tears. He was turned around and felt utterly lost. He didn't even want to smoke, but he was slowing the car to a stop when it happened, when the skies opened up and this intangible thing fell all around them. He didn't notice if it startled the birds and squirrels and chipmunks and moths and frogs and flies and ticks. He was paying attention only to himself.

Clay idled there, because there was no traffic to block. He waited eight minutes, sure the noise would come back. It did, but over Queens; distant enough that he couldn't hear it. Solitude made the noise unbearable for Clay, but so did its opposite. In Queens, crowds formed and panic metastasized. People ran. People wept. The police barely bothered to pretend to do anything.

Then: Clay found the way. It was like the previous forty-four minutes had never happened. He turned right and saw the sign promising eggs. It was too ridiculous to think about. Clay had no information, no cold Coke. Minutes before, he had decided that when he got back to the house, he'd bundle his family into the car and leave this place. He'd never wanted to see the house again.

Now the painted brick greeted him as an old friend. He cried from relief instead of fear. He turned off the car. He looked at the sky. He looked at the car. He looked toward the trees. As he ran toward the house, he began to recount what he knew.

The seas were said to be rising. People had been talking about Greenland a lot. Hurricane season was particularly bad. The forty-fifth president of the United States seemed to have dementia. Angela Merkel seemed to have Parkinson's disease. Ebola was back. There was something happening with interest rates. It was the second week of August. Classes would begin soon enough that you could measure the distance in days. His editor at the *New York Times Book Review* had probably emailed back with her comments on his review.

If the noise returned, say tonight, once the sun had set—once the profound dark of the farmland all around them asserted itself—he wouldn't survive it. You couldn't. That was the nature of the noise; it was horror, in some distilled way, in a single, very brief moment. He was rough with gooseflesh just revisiting it, trying to remember what it had sounded like as a means of deducing what it had been. He feared even going to sleep. How was he supposed to drive away?

Clay thought of his father. It seemed all too possible that his father, at home watching television in Minneapolis, knew nothing of a cryptic noise over Long Island. Something had to be truly big to affect life. When he was a teenager, his mother had suffered from what she assumed was the flu, a sleepiness she couldn't shake. She was dead of leukemia a few months after. Fifteen-year-old Clay had learned to cook Hamburger Helper and separate the white laundry from the colored laundry. People dropped dead, but you still needed to eat dinner. Maybe a war had begun, maybe there'd been some kind of industrial accident, maybe thousands of New

Yorkers were trapped belowground in subway cars, maybe a missile had been fired, maybe some thing they'd never conceived of being possible was unfolding—all this was more or less true, as it happened—but Clay still felt like smoking a cigarette, or worried about the children's manners, and thought about what they would eat for dinner. Business as usual, the business of being alive.

Amanda, G. H., and Ruth were inside. They looked at him like people in a play, like they'd rehearsed this moment—you stand here, you stand here, you stand here, you come in. He felt like he should wait for applause, then wait for that to die down before he spoke. What was his line, anyway?

"Jesus Christ." Amanda did not race to hug him, did not shout it, it only fell out of her, a thud of relief.

"I'm back." Clay shrugged his shoulders. "Is everyone okay?"

G. H. looked vindicated. He looked pleased.

Amanda embraced him. She didn't say anything. She pulled away and looked up at him, then embraced him once more.

He didn't know what else to say. He'd heard the noise and winced and then the noise had abated and he could hear the blood thrumming through his body. "I'm okay. I'm here. Are you okay? Where are the kids?"

"We're okay," G. H. asserted. "Everyone is here. Everyone is okay."

"Maybe you'd like to join us." Ruth pushed the wine bottle in his direction like a bartender in a movie. She was more relieved than she had thought she would be. She realized it with shame, and then a sense of horror: she hadn't actually expected Clay to come back.

Clay scraped the chair's feet on the wood floor and sat. "Did you hear that?"

"Did you go into town? What happened?" Amanda held her husband's hand.

Clay couldn't reckon with that noise; he had to reckon with his own shame. He didn't know if he could admit it. "I didn't." He just said it, flat, no intonation.

"You didn't?" Amanda was confused, but they were all confused. "Where have you been?" She was angry.

Clay grew red. "I didn't get very far. And then I heard that noise—"

"But what were you doing?" Amanda was confused. "We've been waiting for you, I was going crazy—"

"I don't know. I had a cigarette. I was just gathering my thoughts. I had another. I started to drive, and then I heard that noise, and I came right back." He was lying because he was ashamed.

Amanda laughed. It came out cruel. "I thought you were dead out there!"

"So you didn't see anyone. Or anything that might help us figure out what's happening." G. H. wanted to keep them focused.

"You're here. Let's go. Let's get out of here. Let's go home!" Amanda wasn't sure if she meant it, or if she wanted to be persuaded otherwise, or what.

Clay shook his head. It was a lie. He had seen that woman. She'd been weeping. Had she found someone to help her? He couldn't bear admitting what sort of man he was when tested. It was easy enough to tell himself that that woman didn't matter. He could barely remember what she looked like. He wondered what she'd done when she heard the noise. "I didn't see anything or anyone. No cars, nothing."

"That's what it's like out here." G. H. tried to be rational. "That's why we like it out here. You often see no one."

They were all quiet.

Ruth was looking out the window, toward the pool. "It's dark out. It was just so clear." She stood. "Storm. Maybe that was thunder."

"That was not thunder." The sky was now, it was true, fat with clouds, gray fading to black. But Clay knew that much.

Ruth turned to look at them. "Years ago, G. H. took me to the ballet. *Swan Lake.*"

The kind of thing Clay claimed was the reason to live in New York to begin with. But it was a logistical nightmare. Tickets for a mutually agreeable night, a place to have dinner at 6:30, eighteen dollars an hour for the sitter. They were too *busy*, committed to the notion of their own overcommitment. Could they not spare a few hours for transcendence?

"I remember thinking at first, oh, this is so odd. People in span-gled costumes. They'd dance for a few minutes, then scurry off the stage, and then they'd do it again. I thought it was a story, but a ballet is just a bunch of short things loosely organized around a theme that doesn't make much sense to begin with."

Like life, Clay didn't say.

She went on. "Birds in white and birds in black, big sweeping music. I got interested. I think it was the most beautiful music I've ever heard in my life. There was this one dance I'd never heard before, and I don't know why they don't use it in movies and commercials, it's so beautiful. I bought the CDs. *Swan Lake*, conducted by André Previn. I remember the name of the piece. 'Pas d'Action,' 'Odette and the Prince.' " You never heard anything more—sweeping and romantic and then so sweet and alive."

"Probably." Amanda had no idea about ballet. She was happy the woman was talking, filling the silence.

"Tchaikovsky was thirty-five when he composed *Swan Lake*, did you know that? It was considered a failure, but you know—it's the very idea of ballet: a dancer dressed as a bird." She hesitated. "I remember thinking—well, it's a maudlin thought, but I suppose we all have thoughts like this from time to time—if I had to die, and we all do, if I could hear music, as I was dying, or have a piece of music that I knew would be the last thing I heard before I died, or that came to my mind as I was dying, even just the memory of it, I would want it to be that. Tchaikovsky, this dance from *Swan Lake*. That's what I'm sitting here thinking about. Though perhaps you won't like to hear it, but I was thinking, goddamn, I have those CDs in my apartment."

"You're not going to die out here, Ruth." Here? In this charming little house? Impossible. "We're safe here," Clay said. It was like that childhood game of telephone. They were talking amongst themselves and had lost track of things.

"How do you know?" She was calm. "The fact, the unfortunate fact, is that you don't know that. We don't know what is going to happen. I may never hear 'Pas d'Action,' 'Odette and the Prince,' ever again. I think I have it." She tapped a temple. "I think I can hear it. The harp. The strings. But I might be wrong. What I have in here is beautiful, though."

"We're not on Mars. There are people just a few miles away. We'll hear something. We heard something. Maybe we'll hear it again." This was G. H., trying to be reassuring and rational at the same time. "We'll drive out to the neighbors. Or someone will come by. It's just a matter of time."

"I never want to hear that thing again." Clay wished he could have denied hearing the noise altogether. He wished he could imagine doing what G. H. described, but he couldn't. He was scared. He didn't want to leave, not because it wasn't prudent but because he was too afraid.

Amanda pulled away from her husband, who still had his arms on her, dazed relief, and looked at G. H. "You know, you look a little like Denzel Washington."

G. H. wasn't sure how to respond, and also it was not the first time he'd heard this.

"Has anyone ever told you that? And your last name is Washington! Any relation?" Amanda looked at her husband. "His name is *George Washington*. I don't know—I'm sorry, I know it's rude." She laughed, and none of them said anything.

25

FROM THE OTHER ROOMS, THE CHILDREN COULD NOT HEAR their mother's laughter. From the other rooms, the children had not heard their father's return. The little house was so well made (walls so solid!) and so seductive too that it made you forget other people altogether.

Archie ran the shower very hot. His balls were tight against his body, bumpy like he'd just got out of the pool. The muscles in his back softened as he watched the water twist down the drain, dirty and then clear. He dried his body on white towels. He put on boxer shorts and took to bed, where, unable to watch *The Office*, he diverted himself with that important repository, the hidden album on his phone. The pictures were mostly beautiful. The stuff Archie liked best was not so terrible. He was weirded out by the internet's complex configurations: three women, five women, seven women, massive dicks (his dick would never get so big, he worried), two men, three men, pretended incest, racial violence, spit, ropes, athletic equipment, public spectacle, stage lights, mussed makeup, swimming pools, toys and tools he didn't know the name of, the supposed beauty of punishment. He just liked women. Dark hair and tan skin. He preferred them to be completely naked, rather than posed with clothes to emphasize the parts of their body there for you to see: wooly sweater raised over heavy breasts with satin nipples, plaid skirt up over pale hips to show off what he called pussy because he was sure he didn't know the exact word for it, denim shorts slashed or torn, lips protruding. He liked her to look pretty and happy. Archie wanted to please and be pleased.

Rose pulled the down comforter of her parents' bed up to her chin, then over it, up to her nose, drawing in the smell of detergent and bath soap and her own skin and the lingering traces of her parents' chemical signature. This was comforting, almost canine. Her book was not an escape (adolescence's trials, the body's betrayals, the heart's new desires) but preparation, the Fodor's to a country she planned on visiting soon. But it couldn't hold her attention. She thought about the quiet of the woods, punctured by that bang overhead. She could barely picture her little bedroom in Brooklyn. She shook her head to clear it, but that didn't do anything.

She didn't want to hide in bed. Rose didn't want to hide at all. She stood up and stretched as you might after a restorative night's sleep. She stretched her arms and legs, and they both felt powerful and alive. Rose walked to the window and tried to see into the trees. She wasn't sure what she was looking for, but she would know it when it appeared, and knew, too, that it would appear. Earlier, she'd wanted to prove that she'd seen those deer, but the ground had showed no sign of them. The beasts trod lightly on this earth.

She was standing before the glass back door, looking out at the flat sky, clouds close enough to touch. She saw that there was a crack in the pane and understood this had not been there before. It made sense. The rain was as it always was: hesitant at first, then confident. The trees were so thick with leaves, they'd sop up most of the water before it touched the ground. The overflow from the gutter over the door made a kind of waterfall. What did the deer do when it rained? Did animals care about getting wet? Rose wished she could go for another swim, or just sit in the hot tub. She wished for a little more vacation, even just an hour.

The phone in one hand and himself in the other, Archie's body did not respond as it usually did. He could come in the morning's shower and in his nighttime bedroom lit by the laptop, volume turned low. Sometimes afternoons too: huddled in the drafty pee-smelling cubicle, spit on palm. First ropes of cum, then an abbreviated sneeze of the stuff, finally a dry shudder, his dick red and tired and maybe a little sore. He'd always swear it off but—it finds a way. It was life!

There was a storm forming outside, and the light was strange, but even if not for that, Archie would have had no idea how to guess what time it was. He knew it was odd that the people who owned the house had shown up, but he didn't care, or they seemed nice. Mr. Washington had asked him the kinds of questions that grown-ups always asked, and had seemed nice. Archie abandoned his phone. He slipped into the beautiful void. If he dreamed of anything (the noise?), it was with some part of his mind so distant he barely controlled it.

Did he feel warm? Well, he'd just taken a shower. When he tucked his wrist under his cheek, that told him nothing; touching your own skin is not diagnostic. The body was a splendid and complicated machine, almost always humming along happily. When something went wrong, the body was smart enough to make accommodations. The light was muddled and soupy, the room filled with the music of rain on the roof overhead and the unassuming sound of objects in space—the presence of Archie's body, his bed, his pillows, his glass of water, his paperback of *Nine Stories*, the wet towel curled on the floor like a napping pet. It was like the white-noise machine his parents had used to trick the infant him to sleep.

Washing her hands, Ruth could not hear the rain. Then she left the guest bath and saw the tumble of water and understood. The wine had done nothing to her. She was not sleepy, or pacified, or distracted. She gathered their dirty clothes into a little pile. How were there so many already? There was something comforting about the yellow of the bedside lamps and the gray outside the windows. She could have got into that bed and read a book. She might even have dozed in that indolent way you do when you're in a vacation home—not for need of rest but because you can.

Instead, she went to the walk-in closet down the hallway, found a laundry basket on the shelf beside all of George's provisions, those bottles of wine, those helpful tins, those sturdy plastic containers of thousands and thousands of calories. She allowed herself to think—*good*. They were prepared for whatever this was. She'd have thought this might comfort her, but she didn't want cans of tomatoes or sticky Kind bars. It was fruitless to dwell on what it was she wanted, which perhaps explained her resolve to simply *do* something. Ruth filled the basket with their dirty laundry. She righted the throw pillows on the bed. She put the useless television remote control back onto the dresser. She turned off the reading lamps that no one was using. She retrieved the damp towels from the bathroom.

It was too intimate, but she knew she should invite Amanda to put in her dirty clothes. It would be a more efficient use of power and water. It would be neighborly, though that word didn't describe their relationship—maybe no word could. Ruth knew a conversation was warranted, and knew that it would demand that she pretend to be a better person than she felt like being. She thought of the satisfying weight of her grandsons on her body.

Rose put her hand on the window. It was cold, as glass tended to be. There was something satisfying about the surface of the swimming pool, roiled and rippled by the steady rain. There was no thunder, and anyway, Rose understood that the noise before had not been thunder. She saw the temptation in believing that, but she knew in her own teenage way that belief and fact had nothing to do with each other.

The question was not what that had been; the question was what they would do next. Rose knew that her parents did not take her seriously, did not think her grown. But Rose knew that their troubles were not a matter of some sound overhead. She'd seen what the problem was, and she'd try to solve it. Then she remembered that her mother had promised her that when it rained, they would bake a cake, so Rose forgot her book and went to do just that.

26

TELEVISION WOULD HAVE BEEN PALLIATIVE. TELEVISION would have stunned them, entertained them, informed them or helped them forget. Instead: the three of them sitting around a television that showed them nothing, the pleasant orchestra of the rain against skylight, roof, deck, canvas umbrella, treetop, and the clatter of Rose—"I can do it by myself!"—in the kitchen, and then the chemical scent of her cake from a box, puffing up in the gas oven.

"We need to fill the bathtubs." Amanda wasn't sure what was required. She was guessing.

"Fill the bathtubs?" Clay took it for a figure of speech.

She lowered her voice. "In case—the water."

"Does the water not run if the power goes out?" Clay had no idea.

It did not. The next day, or the day after that, certainly the day following that one, some residents of the uppermost apartments in Manhattan would fall into the delirium that presaged their eventual dehydration. "I think that's right. An electric pump fills the reservoir. So if the power goes, the water does too." G. H. marveled that their power still held on. He credited the well-made little house, even though he knew that had nothing to do with it.

"Do you think the power is going to go out?" Clay thought

the day—the smell of yellow sponge, the percussion of the rain—seemed almost unnervingly normal.

"It goes out in storms, doesn't it? Like, downed branches? And if there's something wrong in the city. And then that noise, whatever that was? I think we're lucky that it's still on, but maybe we shouldn't push our luck." Amanda looked at her husband. "Go!"

Clay got up and went to do as entreated, without mentioning the fact that they weren't his tubs and it wasn't his water.

Amanda leaned forward in her seat, toward G. H. across from her. "There's no thunder. No lightning, even. Just rain."

"I didn't really think it was thunder anyway."

"So what was it?" She was whispering because she did not want Rose to hear. She did not think the girl stupid, she just thought she might protect her.

"I wish I knew."

"What are we doing?"

"I'm waiting for the cake your daughter is baking."

"Should we leave?" She looked at the older man like he was the father she had never had, the one she could trust for sound advice. "Wouldn't we be better—safer—at home, in the city, around other people?"

"I don't know."

"I would feel better if I just knew what was happening." Amanda looked toward the hall, could hear the plash of water in the bathtub. These words were not true, but she did not know that.

Clay returned, wiping hands on shorts. "That's done."

"There's a tub downstairs. I'll do the same." G. H. nodded his thanks.

"So there's that." Amanda was trying to convince herself. "We have some water. And we don't even need it. Maybe we won't at all."

"Better to be prepared," Clay agreed.

"Do you think we should go home?" Amanda looked at her husband.

"Or we can just go back to town tomorrow? Or go for the first time," G. H. corrected himself.

"I'm sorry." Clay put his hands on his knees. The gesture was sheepish.

"What?" Amanda asked.

"I should have— I heard the noise and I came back, I was worried. But! I didn't see any cars." Clay did not tell them about the woman. He wondered if she was out in the rain.

"I thought you were— I didn't know what had happened to you."

G. H. was understanding. "You see no cars a lot of the time. It depends on the time of year, I guess. But it's quiet. That's why we moved here in the first place."

"I think we should just sit tight." Clay didn't want to go back onto those confounding roads.

"How can you say that?" Amanda asked. Parenthood required pretending bravado, derring-do, courage, conviction. It was just instinct, it was just love.

"It's pouring. Maybe it's not the best idea to trek out in a storm."

"Fine. But tomorrow." Amanda was prompting him.

"We'll go to town," Clay said. "Then we can—decide. If the power is out in the city maybe we should wait things out."

"Here?" They did have the lease. That didn't seem to matter as much. Amanda would prepare to demonstrate her faith. She'd pack up their things, be ready to leave. It was a statement of purpose.

"Tomorrow. Clay, you and me, we'll go in the morning. I know the way." G. H. didn't believe Clay's story, and he was right not to. "Then we'll see where we are after that. If there's power, if there's a problem, what that noise was. We'll know more, and once we know more, we can decide the best thing to do." He looked up at the girl approaching the adults. G. H. felt the same urge Amanda had. "It smells delicious in here." He said it jauntily but meant it sincerely.

"It just needs to cool before I frost it."

"It's done already?" Amanda tried to determine the time. "We should save it for after dinner."

"I made layers, so it bakes faster. Two little cakes instead of one big one. I wish I had things to decorate it. Sprinkles and stuff."

"You might want to look in the pantry. Go ask Mrs. Washington to show you where she keeps all the baking things. I wouldn't be surprised if we had some supplies on hand." The girl was nothing like his daughter, but naturally that was who he thought of.

"I should get something together for dinner." Clay thought it atonement for his earlier failure. He'd filled the tubs, he'd feed them dinner, he'd prove his value. "Rose, before you get into the cake decorating, let's tidy up the kitchen."

"Where's Archie?" Amanda wanted the children out of sight but could not get them out of mind.

Clay shrugged. "Maybe he's napping."

"I should get him up." There was that danger, she knew, in napping too late—the grogginess nothing would dispel. As a toddler, he'd wake with his face creased from the bedding, red from the exertion of rest, grumpy and unable to do more than pout for at least ten minutes. She offered G. H. an "Excuse me," then went to the boy's door. Amanda knocked, because teenagers needed the respect of that first (she'd seen some things), then pushed the door open, saying his name.

The boy did not stir, did not seem to register her presence.

"Archie?" She could see his shape, twisted in the blankets. "Honey, are you sleeping?"

He said nothing, if he heard her, so Amanda pulled the covers from his face, revealing his hair, in glorious disarray, tendrils this way and that like the roots of an old tree. She smoothed his locks, a palm on his forehead by reflex. Was he warm from fever or warm from slumber? "Archie?"

He opened his eyes, not blinking; asleep and then not. He looked at his mother, but she did not come into focus.

"Archie? Are you feeling okay?"

He exhaled slowly, a long and tremulous breath. He did not know where he was, he did not understand what was happening. He sat up, this movement abrupt too. He opened his mouth, not to speak, but to move his jaw, which hurt, or of which he was aware, in some way that seemed new or different or wrong. "I don't know."

"What do you mean, you don't know?" She pulled the duvet back, revealing his thin frame, releasing the radiant heat of his body, so powerful she could feel it without laying hands on him. "Archie?"

He made a sound, like a hum. He leaned forward and vomited onto his own lap.

27

PARENTHOOD HARDENED YOU. YOUR TASK WAS UPKEEP OF the body, and you understood what that entailed. The sight of vomit once made her retch, but her children's—Amanda faced it. Crisis made her rational. She called to Clay. She washed her son's body just as she had when he'd been a boy.

When they were babies, Clay and Amanda played man-on-man defense. That first wretched winter, Clay would take Archie to the New York City Transit Museum, an indoor attraction but always very cold, since it was built in an old subway station. Amanda would pace the apartment with Rosie, desperate for the tit, listening to the album Björk had made about how great it was to have sex with Matthew Barney. If she thought about it, Amanda could still hear the creak of floorboard underfoot in that one spot near the kitchen. If he thought about it, Clay could still picture the trains from a more innocent era—rattan seats, ceiling fans—parked on the museum's obsolete tracks. Amanda stripped the soiled bedding. Clay took the boy to the living room.

"We have a thermometer." Ruth, prudent, had stocked the bathroom. Analgesics for adults and children, bandages, iodine, saline, petroleum jelly.

"That would be great." Clay helped the boy into his too-big sweat-shirt; he smoothed his mussed hair. He sat beside him on the sofa, and they looked toward the back of the house, at the drama of the rain filling the swimming pool.

Maternal muscle memory was strong. Ruth returned with sup-plies. "Let's take his temperature."

So, too, was paternal instinct. G. H. helped Rose find the hidden stores: icing sugar, tubes of decorative gels, birthday candles, sprin-kles rattling in plastic jars. Rose was not a fool, but happy enough to be diverted. They coaxed the cake onto a plate, and she spun it expertly beneath the spatula, stationary, thick with frosting.

"Thank you," Clay said.

Ruth held the boy's chin, placed the point of the glass tube be-neath his tongue. "You do feel warm. But let's just see how warm."

"How do you feel now, bud?" Clay relied on these masculine af-fections when he was most worried. He'd already asked. Archie had already answered. He wanted to put an arm around him, wanted to fold him into his body, but the boy wouldn't like that because the boy was nearly a man.

"I'm fine." Archie mumbled through the thermometer, unable to achieve his characteristic adolescent disdain.

Ruth studied the inscrutable instrument. "One hundred and two. Not so bad. Not so good."

"Drink your water, pal." Clay pressed the glass into the boy's hand.

"Take these." Ruth shook out two Tylenol just as G. H. and Rose were peppering the cake with sugar confetti, a nice little duet.

Archie did as he was bid. He held a sip of the liquid in his mouth, then put the pills into that. He swallowed and tried to tell if his throat was tender. He wanted to watch television, or go back to his house, or lose himself in his phone, but none of these were possible, so he just sat there, saying nothing.

"I'm going to go help Amanda." Ruth was pleased to have a

problem to solve, or a problem that she might solve. "You just rest here."

Finding the bathtub full of the water that was meant to save their lives, Amanda took the soiled sheets to the master bathroom, rinsed the (mercifully watery) vomit in the tiled shower. She squeezed them as dry as she could, twisting the cotton until she feared it would rend. She was angry, and this was something to do with that feeling. She dried her hands and went into the bedroom. How quickly they spread out: a tangle of dirty underwear, used paper napkin, magazine, glass of water, all these little signs that they existed and endured. Trees marked their lives in rings that can't be seen; people, in the garbage they left everywhere, a way of insisting on their own importance. Amanda began righting the room.

"Knock knock." Ruth said it like a character in a television show as she strode down the hall and into the room, laundry basket at her hip. "I don't mean to interrupt. I thought I might do the wash anyway, though."

Amanda performed a kind of curtsy for some reason. Well, it was the woman's room. "I'm sorry. I can do Archie's sheets."

"Don't be sorry. Just throw them in here. He seems fine. A temperature. One hundred and two."

"One hundred and two?"

"It sounds high, but you know they are high when they're kids. Those showroom-new immune systems working overtime. I gave him some Tylenol."

"Thank you."

"You can put your clothes in too. I just—while the power is still on."

It was too intimate, but Ruth had foresight. It would save them the trek to the Laundromat when they got home. Amanda did not know that the Laundromat was closed. She did not know that the Chinese man who ran it was inside the elevator that carried passengers between the turnstiles and the platform at the R train station in Brooklyn Heights, and he'd been there for hours, and he'd die there, though that was many hours in the future yet. "That's smart. Thank you."

They considered each other like they were meant to duel. Maybe that was inevitable. Ruth pitied the woman. She knew what was required of her, and hated it. She had to pretend her way to being a good person. But what about Maya and the boys? "You know, you could stay. If you wanted."

The little house as life raft. Ignorance as a kind of knowing. This did not seduce Amanda. An eternity (as though that were granted) with these people. Part of her still wondered whether this wasn't a con or a delusion. It was torture, a home invasion without rape or guns. Still, this woman was the nearest an ally Amanda had. She shook her head. "Archie needs a doctor."

"What if we all do? What if it's inside us? What if something is beginning, or everything is ending?" This subtext was inescapable. People kept calling the Amazon the planet's lungs. Waist-deep water was lapping against Venetian marble, and tourists were smiling and taking snapshots. It was like some tacit agreement; everyone had ceded to things just falling apart. That it was common knowledge that things were bad surely meant they were actually worse. Ruth wasn't this kind of person, but she could feel disease blooming inside her body. It was everywhere, inescapable.

"I can't think about what we don't know. I need to focus on this. Archie needs a doctor, I'll take him to a doctor tomorrow morning."

"But you're afraid. I'm afraid."

"That's not getting us anywhere. I can't stay here. I can't hide. I'm his mother. What else can we do?"

Ruth sat on the bed's edge. She couldn't go to town or beyond, to Northampton. She wanted to just lie in her bed. "I guess you're right."

"Say something to make me feel better." Amanda was searching for friendship or humanity or reassurance or relief.

Ruth crossed her legs and looked up at her. "I can't do that. Comforting."

Amanda was immediately disappointed.

"Maybe I need it. Comforting." She was eager to wash the clothes. The neutral smell of the soap, the thunder of the water. "So I can't provide it. But stay. I think you should. I think it makes sense. Even if I can't make you feel better. I can't say something wise and churchy for you."

"I know—I know you can't."

"At least you have your children here with you. I don't know what's happening to my daughter. I don't know what's happening to my grandsons. We don't know anything about the world. That is what it is."

Amanda knew this was the way it had always been. She couldn't help but wish it were otherwise. Her clothes smelled of her son's vomit, and the air smelled of her daughter's cake. "Let's eat something. I'm going to take a shower, and then we should eat something. I think that will help." No, that wasn't quite it. "I can't think of anything else to do."

28

THERE WAS ALMOST SOMETHING FESTIVE ABOUT IT. A DRINK before the war. Seen one way, it was placid, it was inviting, it was a vacation. Enterprising Ruth had produced a can of chicken soup, which Archie reluctantly spooned. Amanda tucked him into his remade bed. Enterprising Rose remembered: she had downloaded a movie to her mother's laptop a year earlier. She wasn't that interested in it, but it was better than nothing. Amanda sent her to bed with a slice of cake and the almost-obsolete computer, and the four adults had an adult evening, or the candor they couldn't enjoy when little ears were listening. G. H. paged through an old *Economist*. Ruth filled porcelain bowls with baby carrots and hummus. Amanda nursed a glass of wine. Clay stood at the island, improvising a sausage pasta.

The rain had abated, the deck dry beneath the eaves. But they'd dine inside, not for fear of the mosquitoes in their end-of-season death throes. The woods menaced them. The moon was waxing, pale yellow, proud through the broken clouds. There was no aftershock to the noise, or there was, and it was all in their heads. Maybe what they'd heard was the sky itself cracking, like Henny Penny foretold. It seemed likely as anything. No one knew what was happening to them, and maybe because of that the rite was strangely joyous, or maybe it was collective hysteria, or maybe it was the chardonnay, cold and the color of apple juice.

It felt practiced or familiar as Thanksgiving, the passing of food on plates, the filling of glasses, the chitchat. Did anyone want to hear George's stories? A client bilked out of a fortune when a Basquiat was revealed a forgery, the man who'd shifted hundreds of thousands of dollars to his seven-month-old to sidestep a prenup, the man who'd lost three million in Macau, the client who needed cash to pay one of the New York Yankees to bless his son's bar mitzvah. His stories were about money, not men; money awe-inspiring and irrational and almost all-powerful. George thought money could explain what was happening to them, and that time would tell if money would save them from it. If these people did leave the next day, he'd have to remember to give them a thousand dollars for their trouble. G. H. wasn't sure if he thought they would leave, though.

Dessert, why not? There was an air of finality, at least for Clay. The now-clean clothes tumbled about in the hot embrace of the four-thousand-dollar dryer. He thought Archie's fever would break, thought he'd ask G. H. for directions, a pencil sketch, safe deliverance. He thought the morning would come and surprise them with its beauty and they'd drive home.

They sliced Rose's cake. Ruth put cardboard pints of ice cream onto the table. The well-stocked kitchen had two stainless steel ice cream scoops. There were enough dishes to fill the washer.

Amanda said it: "Well, the electricity is still on." You stopped noticing a thing like the flow of power, a thing you couldn't see but derived some comfort from, rather like God. The water was slowly, very slowly, draining from the tub in the children's bath, but she didn't know that.

The conversation turned to places they'd traveled. G. H., sardonic, said, "You must have had more enjoyable vacations than this one."

Amanda thought of those places where nights never grew dark:

Helsinki, St. Petersburg, small towns in Alaska built for men paid to do things to the earth. She feared the return of that noise, unfathomable in the dark. They already knew nothing. "Disney?" She laughed. She'd hated it at the time but cherished the memory.

"Archie threw up then too," Clay said. He wanted to think of it like that—that vacation meant kids naturally capitulated to virus. Archie, always with the throwing up! Archie, cut it out! This was more enjoyable than believing Archie ill.

Ruth talked about Paris. She and Maya had teatime at the George V, tried on shoes at the Galeries Lafayette, rode the carousel in the Tuileries, though at thirteen Maya considered it beneath her. "A city as gorgeous as you've always been told it is."

"We should do that for winter break. Paris is so beautiful you don't even care if it's cold." Clay saw his kids on the deck of the Eiffel Tower, puffs of frosty breath as they surveyed the world at their feet. He remembered footage of Paris flooding—when was that? The Louvre had moved thirty-five thousand works of art so the Seine wouldn't destroy them. "We'll see *The Lady and the Unicorn*."

"Sounds expensive." Idle promises scared Amanda. What if it was a war, big enough to ensnare the entire world, and national borders became like castle walls? She didn't know that it was worse, that war could not describe it. Those planes had been sent from Rome, New York, to meet another, approaching from western Africa. Bad intelligence: they ended up killing four hundred odd souls before they got near enough our borders to have to fill out their immigration paperwork. The pace of things used to be slower. Now a nut didn't have to shoot an archduke; every day was a jumble of near-simultaneous oddity.

The cardboard cartons emptied. Everyone admired the cake made from a box. Smudges of chocolate hardened on plates. When the true dark set in, the night's winged creatures would beat softly against the glass, the outside lights would click on, illuminating the boughs overhead. A silence settled, one of those natural intervals sometimes experienced in restaurants or at parties when talk relaxes and the assembled company lean forward, straining as though to hear something barely discernible. There were no eggs left in the refrigerator, but perhaps they could serve cereal for breakfast.

They decided, without discussing, to simply sit and feel satisfied. G. H. fiddled with his glass. Clay twitched with that delirious urge to smoke a cigarette, so powerful it was a little frightening. He had to confront the fact that he was weak. Ruth looked toward the window and saw mostly her own reflection. Amanda retrieved the bottle of vodka she'd bought the day they arrived.

G. H. sliced lemons into rounds, yellow coins, fat with flavor.

When Amanda got to the bottom of the first drink, she dug her fingers through the ice and set the citrus on her tongue like the Catholics did with the body of Christ. Transubstantiated into someone new. She was drunk. The tell was the volume of her voice. "I'll have another." This was a command more than a request.

G. H. poured. "My pleasure."

Clay smelled of the cigarette he'd just returned from enjoying, though enjoyment wasn't much a part of it. The crickets conspiring. The possibility of something out there. He'd hoped to see headlights, maybe a plane crossing the sky. There were studies about solitary confinement making you mad. He missed the presence of other humans, and he was putting on a brave front because that was his job as a man. "George, will you make us a map? Tomorrow? You'll show us the way. Clearly I can't be trusted."

"I'll drive into town. You can follow me."

Ruth did not say anything.

Amanda was afraid of slurring and seeming more drunk than she knew she was. She was a woman in control of things. "Are you going to come back . . . here?"

"Yes, we are." Ruth would go with him. She wouldn't stay there alone. She wanted them to leave and to stay. She could not be indifferent, even though she wanted to be. She did not want to feel guilt.

"I wish I knew the roads to Northampton." G. H. was reserved. "It's far. We'll just hope that the phones . . ." He didn't bother concluding.

"We need to take care of Archie—" Amanda's falter said what needed to be said. The boy was sick. It didn't matter what caused it, only what they did about it. All those years fretting about the expensive epinephrine autoinjector, at the boy's side like the president and the nuclear codes, and Archie was undone by a noise. Parenthood was never knowing what was going to hurt your kids, but knowing only that something, inevitably, would.

"Before you go, I'll give you your cash back." G. H. was fair, or a deal was a deal. He was drinking the vodka too. The four of them were united in their search for the temporary peace of oblivion. It almost worked; he almost forgot why they were together in the first place.

"I'm not going to forget that, I can assure you." Clay tried to make a joke of it. Maybe they needed that money to pay the medical bills. Maybe they needed that money to replace a refrigerator full of rotting food. Maybe his editor at the *New York Times Book Review* would so love his essay she'd offer him a contract. Anything, anything, was possible. He put a hand on his wife's to tell her that he thought they were making the right choice.

"We're all going to be fine." Amanda was not addressing him alone, drunk enough not to care that these people were involved. They were family now, or something.

"If it's your last night of vacation, you should enjoy it." Ruth stacked soiled plates one atop the other, leaving aside the fact that she enjoyed restoring order. These people had become their friends, their guests, and Ruth the host, and she just needed to clear the table.

"To enjoyment. To the enjoyment of vacations. To the enjoyment of any moment in life, I guess. Enjoying a moment is a victory. I think we need to hold on to those." G. H. raised his glass. The gesture was sincere.

"I'll enjoy, I'll enjoy." Amanda felt defensive. Like saying: I am having a good time, I am a good time. Optimists believed they could change the world. They thought if you looked on the bright side, the less bright side would no longer exist.

"It's not an order, it's an invitation." G. H. felt at ease. He couldn't wait to see the markets. He couldn't wait to figure out who had got rich, because in such moments, someone brave or just lucky always did. He hoped the night would grow cold. He wanted to stand outside and shiver, then sink into the hot tub and look at the black limbs of the trees.

Amanda refilled her drink. She wanted more ice cream, the lavish sweetness in her mouth. There was no more, but there were doughnuts, there was a package of cookies, she had options. She knew before they went to bed that night she'd steal into the kitchen, tear through whatever she found, palms full of salty Goldfish crackers, limp American cheese, a finger in the hummus. As she stood, the room moved, a little. The table under her fingertips steadied her.

"I think I'll have another." Ruth closed the dishwasher door, satisfied.

"I should fold the laundry. Maybe pack us up." Amanda stood.

"I can help you. Fold. We can fold. Pack—let's go one step at a time."

"I think we should be prepared," Amanda said.

"Perhaps we'll have a nightcap later?" Clay felt it was good manners. Maybe this was their last night together. It seemed they'd been together for weeks. It had been one day.

In the bedroom, they worked in silence. The clothes, still warm, were sorted into tidy piles, dropped to the bottom of the rolling duffel. "I have to remember to go outside and get everyone's flip-flops."

"Let's just be cautious."

"I'm packing. We're not coming back here. We're going home."

Clay understood her insistence. If they thought it, it would be so. He took clean underpants from the chest of drawers and placed them atop the bed. "It's been a strange day. I need reality."

Amanda sat on the bed. "A day that felt like a week."

"Could it be that we're addicted to our phones? Like an actual addiction? Because I feel unwell." Clay was charging his, wanted to be sure it was ready when the network came back online.

Amanda fretted. "What if that noise made us sick?"

"It might be possible." What if the hair fell from his head, as it did for chemotherapy patients on television shows, what if his rubbery fingernails peeled back to reveal the softest part of the body, what if his bones hollowed and weakened, what if his blood ran with poison, what if tumors lurked in the space behind his eyeballs, grew slowly as Amanda's lungs had filled that inflatable pool toy, one breath, then the next, until the thing was a softball pressing into his eye socket?

"And those people." She whispered this. She was betraying them. She hated George Washington (what sort of name was that?) and she hated Ruth and she blamed them for bringing the world into this house. Amanda wanted to be safely buckled into the front seat, her left hand straying unconsciously to squeeze Clay's right arm, recumbent atop the gearshift. She wanted to drive away from this place and these people.

Fear was private. It was primal. It was something you guarded because you thought you could defuse it that way. How could they continue to love each other, having realized that they could not save each other? No one person could stop a determined terrorist or the gradual change in the oceans' pH. The world was lost, and there was nothing that Clay or Amanda could do about it, so why discuss?

In other words: The world was over, so why not dance? The

morning would come, so why not sleep? An end was inevitable, so why not drink, eat, enjoy the moment, whatever it contained? "You know what I feel like doing?" Clay pulled his shirt over his head and tossed it to Amanda for the pile of dirty things, grinning and tumescent.

29

———

MAYBE AMANDA WAS GREEDY. SOMETIMES, NOT KNOWING
what else to do, you had sex. Clay could make her feel better not
psychically but physically. She let him carry her away from herself.
In the body she was far from the mind. She opened herself to it,
though maybe the vodka helped. She consented. More than. She
wanted it. She pushed off her humid underwear. She lay back on
the bright white duvet. The clothes she was packing up fell to the
wood floor.

The shirt Clay wore remembered the sudden sweat, a fear response to that noise. She buried her nose in his armpit and closed
her eyes. She traced the inside of his thigh and tasted salt. The
sounds they made were close to screams. It didn't seem to matter,
nothing did. She let them rise from somewhere deep in her chest,
like she imagined opera singers did. The clap of flesh against flesh.
Hair lacquered to skin with spit. The opportunity to forget.

Amanda thought of the best worst things, that's what sexual fantasy was. One dick, two dicks, three dicks, four! She thought of
G. H. leering at her from the threshold, then coming into the room
to offer some pointers, to encourage Clay in his fucking, to—sure
why not—fuck her himself. Fuck, fuck, forget. She came once,
twice. What was left on her stomach was enough to fill a shot glass,

was the work of a younger man. It was enough to make a baby. You needed so little for that. They could make two, three, ten, an army of them, alternate versions of the children they already had, pink and clean and healthy and strong, a new world order because the old world was so out of order. Amanda propped herself up on her elbows. The stuff slid down her like a snail on a sedge, onto that beautiful white duvet.

Clay was out of breath. Fucking her like that was like inflating fifty pool floats. Sometimes he could picture a tumor blossoming in his lungs, black and terrible. Still, you couldn't live without risk. He lay on his stomach, then rolled onto his back. The sweat on his skin had its intended, cooling effect. "I love you." His voice emerged hoarse after all those exhalations and exhortations. He did not feel cowed by what they'd just done. He felt restored. He thought of Ruth and vowed that when they got back to their apartment, he would listen to *Swan Lake*. And he did love Amanda, he loved her, he *loved*. You endured as long as that was the case.

It felt insincere, to return a declaration of love. An echo was just a trick of physics. She felt free. "I'm worried about Archie."

It was maybe the best sex they'd had, though of course pleasure, like pain, was so soon forgotten. "He'll be okay. We'll get home, we'll see Dr. Wilcox."

She prodded at the stain on the bedspread, worried.

"Who cares about that?" He dipped a finger into his semen like a quill into ink. He wrote phantom letters on her belly.

She'd strip this bed, too, leave the linens on the floor of the laundry room. "Maybe when we're back we can do something special. It's still our vacation. We could drive out to Hoboken and check into a hotel with a rooftop pool. I bet that would be cheap."

"I want to stop at a diner on the way home." Clay was hungry right then. "One of those old-fashioned places. Chrome. Jukeboxes. Corned beef hash." The only things a person ever wanted were food and home.

"A staycation. The movies. Go to the Met. Dinner at a sit-down Chinese restaurant, with those silver pots of tea and orange slices when they bring the bill." The life they had was perfect.

Clay imagined the end of summer city: the shimmer of heat, the drip from window units overhead, the chorus of ice cream trucks, office buildings leaking air-conditioning onto the humid sidewalks where fat tourists were wandering dumbstruck. It would be enough for him. Marble countertops and this perfect swimming pool and the touch-responsive light switches were all well and good, but be it ever so humble, etc.

"You don't think anything's wrong with Rose, do you?" A briefer moment of surrender than orgasm.

Clay began reflexively to say that everything was fine, but he did not believe it, and anyway, in matters of fact, belief was not salient. "She seemed okay to me. Did you notice something?"

"No." Amanda swallowed, a hand at her throat. Was something wrong with *her*? "Do you feel okay?"

"I feel normal. I feel like myself." Clay had never been the most observant of men.

Amanda stood. She wiped her stomach with a pair of his folded boxer shorts. Her arms, her legs, her waist—they showed her forty-three years. There was that sway, the gentle ripple of the excess flesh, the subtle give, though it felt nice in your hand, soft to the touch. Naturally, there were days she rounded her shoulders, wanted not to be seen. Mostly she was the kind of woman interested in blending in. The way she wore her hair, the kinds of clothes she favored. Amanda was a type. She was not ashamed of that. But there were moments—this was one—where she felt individual and perfect. Maybe it was just the barely perceptible reverberations of the orgasm. She was a thing beautiful to behold. Stained and sweaty and sagging, also smooth and ripe and desired. Humans were monsters but also perfect creations. She felt what is termed sexy but is really just an animal's satisfaction in being an animal. Had she been a deer, she'd have leaped over a branch. Had she been a bird, she'd have lifted into the sky. Had she been a house cat, she'd have run her own tongue over herself. She was a woman, so she stretched and shifted the weight from one leg to the other like a statue from antiquity.

"Let's go smoke." Clay, adolescent, was proud of his performance, like he'd heaved a shot put or sunk a basketball. She'd soiled his underwear, so he stalked to the door naked. There was no grace to it; his dick disrupted symmetry, an insult to beauty.

"Put on your clothes."

"What's wrong with sitting naked in the night air and smoking?"

"Well . . . Ruth and G. H."

"Who cares?"

Clay pulled open the door, but it was Amanda who noticed: interruption in the pane of glass. A crack that was more than a flaw. It was thin but deep, stretched for inches, a slash, a rent. "Look at that."

Clay peered at the glass. He put his hand in hers.

"This wasn't here before." She dropped her voice, not wanting to be overheard.

"You're sure?" A mumble, lips puckered around the cigarette.

Amanda traced the crack with her finger. It was from the noise. A noise big enough to crack glass. Noise as a tangible thing. She shivered from the cool air and the reminder too. She closed the door behind her, stood naked in the chill air, unprotected by clothes, a dare to the night and whatever else was out there.

30

STILL NAKED, NEANDERTHAL, ESSENTIAL, CLAY WENT TO FIX them drinks. They'd finish packing later. They'd finish packing in the morning. They'd skip packing, go directly to Target for new toothbrushes and bathing suits and books and lotion and pajamas and earbuds and socks. Or they wouldn't! They didn't need things. Things would not keep them safe from power outages or sudden noises loud enough to crack glass or any other unexplained phenomena. They were extraneous; things did not matter.

Amanda flipped open the heavy cover of the hot tub. The steam was waiting for her, vanished into the dark. There was light illuminating the trees, which made the view more satisfying. You could feel you owned them, though no one could ever claim to own a tree. She couldn't see. She pressed where she knew buttons were, kept at it until the machine whirred into life. The thing bubbled like the Weird Sisters' cauldron. If only it had been. Amanda would have bargained for the health of her poor feverish son, of both her children, of course, even though she had nothing to offer a witch, just the same desire as every human alive. She should, she realized, get up, pull on a robe, tiptoe into the dark room and gauge Archie's temperature with a touch of her hand.

It was G. H., answering the dare of her nudity. He wore his

swimsuit, trim and conservative, the kind of thing white sons named for their great-grandfathers wore in Nantucket. There was not a trace of anything untoward in his smile, as though it were precisely what he expected, to find this woman he barely knew nude and obviously postcoital on his deck. "I see we both had the same idea."

It would have been disingenuous to feign shame. She was released from that. Didn't even blush. "Turned out to be a nice night, I guess."

He gestured toward the tub. "After you, please. If you don't mind the company." Nothing felt strange to him anymore. "We had the same idea. Ruth didn't want to join me, but I'm glad not to be alone out here." As close as he could come to admitting fear.

The water was very hot, but the bubbles the tub was frantic with were cold, popped against her skin, staccato relief. G. H. sat across from her, a decorous enough distance, though what did that matter? She might have been his daughter. They were nothing to each other, naked strangers. "There's a crack in the door." She gestured toward it. "I noticed it just now. I think it must be—"

He had done his own investigation. "There's one in the door downstairs. They call that a hairline crack, right? A nice turn of phrase. The shape of the letter Y. If I push, really push, I bet I can break the thing." He would not push on the glass. He would not break it. He needed it, though glass provided only the illusion of safety.

"Do you think it was from—"

He let his face say it. Why were they still debating this? "I have always thought of myself as a sophisticated man. Someone who had seen the world as it was. But I have never seen anything like this, so now I wonder if this thing I have always thought about myself was a delusion."

Their silence was not unfriendly. They had said everything there was to be said. It was like a love affair ended amicably. They needed only to wait for the sun to rise and the whole thing would be over, relief and regret. In the house, Ruth lay on the bed, thinking of her daughter, and Archie slept dreamless, and Rose slept dreamful, and Clay filled glasses with ice, thinking of nothing.

"I just want everything to be okay."

G. H. looked up at the stars. It was dark enough there that you could truly see them. It never made him feel any which way. He liked being in the country, but not because it was good for his soul. Did the stars make him feel small? They did not. He already knew he was small. That's how he'd got rich. He just said her name, nothing more.

"I didn't believe you. I was wrong. Something is happening, something bad is happening." She could not stand it.

"The quiet is so noisy. That was one of the first things I noticed, when we started spending nights out here. I found it hard to sleep. At home, we can't hear anything. We're high up. Sometimes a siren, but even then, the wind kind of carries that away." The world from their apartment looked like a silent film.

"We still have power." She could see the steam, a veil over the dark.

"I was telling you, earlier, that with information anything is possible. I owe my fortune, humble as it is, to information." He paused. The tub burbled. "I saw it, you know. Before the lights went out. I looked at the market and knew something was coming."

"How is that possible?" This sounded not financial but spiritual.

Clay opened the door. "Are you okay?"

"We're just talking." G. H. waved at Clay.

He walked toward the tub as though it were not odd, to be seen naked like this, to find his wife naked with a stranger. Clay would pretend.

"You learn how to read the curve. You spend as long as I have doing it, and you understand. It tells you the future. It holds steady and promises harmony. It inches up or down, and you know that means something. You look more closely, and try to understand just what it means. If you're good at it, you get rich. If you're not, you lose everything."

"And you're good at it?" Amanda took the glass her husband was offering her.

Clay slipped into the water, making too big a splash. "What are you talking about?"

"Information." G. H. said it like it was simple.

"He says he knew something was coming—," Amanda explained. She believed him. She needed to believe something.

"You saw—what? What's happened, anyway? The power went out. Amanda got some push notifications from the *New York Times*. We heard a loud noise." Hearing himself enumerate it, Clay realized it was enough.

"Did you see the end of the world?" Could numbers really predict that? The glass in her hand was cold and perfect.

"It's not the end of the world," G. H. said. "It's a market event."

"What are you talking about?" Clay thought G. H. sounded like a madman with a placard marching around the financial district. You saw that, often, on Wall Street, the actual street, which was closed off by bombproof bollards.

"I think I know so much." G. H. was apologetic. "Maybe not everything can be known." The steam clouded his glasses. He could neither see nor be seen. Every day was a gamble.

"Maybe everything is fine," Clay said. They were getting carried away. They were saying things they shouldn't say.

"I hope for our sake that it is." G. H. didn't like to have nothing but hope. That was something he'd disliked in Obama; the nebulous, almost religious promise. He preferred a plan.

There was, below them, a loud splash.

Amanda was afraid, immediately. She sat up in the center of the tub, turned to the yard behind them. "What was that?"

G. H. reached out of the tub to silence the jets. The machine responded immediately, a low hum instead of that laundry churn.

The silence made it seem more dark, somehow. There was a splash, a definite, deliberate splash in the pool. Yards away, but it could not be seen.

It was one of the children, sleepwalking to their drowning. It was a watcher from the woods come to kill them. It was a zombie, it was an animal, it was a monster, it was a ghost, it was an alien. "What was—"

George shushed her. He was still capable of fear.

"What is that?" She was not whispering, and she was panicking. "Maybe it's a deer." She remembered the fence. What would a deer in distress sound like, what would a deer's tears sound like?

"A frog." Clay thought this was obvious. "A squirrel. They can swim."

G. H. pushed up out of the tub and walked toward the house, where there was a switch to light the pool from within. It was a nice touch when they had a party. The abstraction of light through water dancing in the treetops. They both saw, there in the pool below them, a flamingo, pink and absurd, elegantly splashing. It beat its wings, impatient, on the surface of the pool.

"That's a flamingo." She said it even though it was obvious. A pink bird was a flamingo. It was so specific—the comma of its beak, the forte mark of its illogical neck—that a toddler would know it. "That's a flamingo?"

"That's a flamingo." With his fingertips, G. H. rubbed the steam from his glasses. They did not know what was happening in the world, but they knew that.

The flamingo beat its wings more. They let their eyes adjust, and they could see another flamingo, no, two, no, three, no, four, no, five, no, six. Strutting on the lawn with their backward gait. Bobbing and sinewy. Two of the birds took flight as birds do: balletic. Lift over the fence, touch down in the water. They dipped their heads below the surface. Did they imagine it held food? There was a disarming intelligence in their eyes. Their wings were wider than you'd think. At rest, they held those so close to the sack of their bodies. Unfurled, though: they were majestic. Their beauty was astonishing. Logic fell away.

"Why—" *Why* didn't matter. Did *how* or did *is this real* or anything else matter? Amanda could see that George Washington could see these birds too, but there was documented evidence that delusion could be shared. She got out of the tub, rubbery with the absorbed heat. She stood naked as the day she appeared on this planet. She watched three flamingos cavorting happily in the swimming pool, their compatriots on the grass beyond. "Just tell me you see this."

George nodded. He didn't know this woman at all. But he knew his mind and his eyes. "I see it."

Clay went cold, deep inside himself. Tomorrow they'd set sail in their car, and here was an omen. Their trip would displease the gods. They were being given a sign. Whisky sloshed into the tub as he stood. The birds started.

Three flamingos lifted out off the pool's surface with a masculine flaunting of wings. Any flamingo, seeing this, would have wanted to incubate their issue. These were flamingos, the best of flamingos, hale and powerful. They rose into the air, a simple trick, and above the trees. The flamingos on the grass followed, seven human-sized pink birds, twisty and strange, ascending into the Long Island night, beautiful and terrifying in equal measure.

They were silent for a while. Good old-fashioned awe. Religious feeling. The stars above didn't cow them, but these strange birds did. Amanda shivered. George blinked behind his glasses. Clay held on to the glass in his hand because it was cold and reminded him that he was alive.

31

G. H.'S FAMILIAR OLD FRIDGE YIELDED NOTHING BUT SUR-
prise. He'd not have filled it with such things: cold cuts in folded
paper, the curls of leftover grilled zucchini, hard white cheese in
greasy cellophane, a Pyrex mixing bowl of strawberries someone
had thoughtfully hulled. He felt insane with hunger, or maybe only
insane. He found a box of crackers, an open bag of chips, a cardboard tube of cookies. He put everything on the counter. Someone
else would have arranged this bounty, complementary items together, but he didn't bother.

Clay did not ask if he wanted a drink. He pressed one into the
man's black hands: "George." He'd found his swim trunks, drying on the railing. He'd found Archie's hacked-at T-shirt, and it
revealed his subdued middle-aged muscles.

"We all saw that." Amanda had put on a robe. She had no idea
whose it was, and forgot to pull the thing closed over her lap.

George thanked him through a mouthful of gummy cheese. He
coughed a little. "I saw it."

"We're all hallucinating?" It was appealing to pretend that you
were exempt from what was happening.

"They're from a zoo. The electrical grid failed and couldn't keep
them in captivity." George hacked at the cheese with a steak knife.

"They must be tagged, you know, like those invisible fences that keep dogs on your property."

"Zoos clip wings, don't they?" Amanda had read this in *The Trumpet of the Swan*. She wasn't sure it was true. "Those birds could fly. Those birds were *wild*."

Clay took up George's steak knife and sliced into the salami. "There has to be a logical explanation."

"They weren't wearing bands or anything." Amanda closed her eyes to return to the scene. "I looked. I looked for them."

George thought it hardly needed saying. "There are no wild flamingos in New York."

"We all just saw it. What the fuck is actually happening?" The vulgarity didn't possess the power she wanted. She wanted to run into the yard screaming at the birds to come back, to show themselves, to explain.

Ruth had showered and changed into the shapeless, expensive things she wore at home, freshly laundered. She emerged from downstairs and didn't even feel undefended, as she would have if she'd encountered the doorman while dressed thus. She was at peace with these people. They knew one another now. Downstairs, she had tried to use her phone to be sure. Yes, she had flipped through the pictures in her album, out-of-focus shots because toddlers never stopped darting, giggling, squirming. She noticed that Amanda's robe was parted so you could see her mons.

George had turned on all the lights, prophylactic against fear. "We're having a midnight snack."

"You missed something." Amanda was not being sardonic but sincere.

"Sit down, darling." G. H. was filled with affection for Ruth. G. H. was reportorial. He stuck to the facts. He mentioned even Amanda's nakedness. Seven flamingos. If he'd been asked to draw a flamingo, he'd have come up with a triangle for the bill, and he'd have been wrong.

"I thought flamingos were flightless," Ruth said. "I assumed. Maybe I never gave it a thought before."

"They were the same size as Rose." Amanda could see them, ascending like Christ was said to have.

"I knew they were pink, but I didn't know they were pink like that. It doesn't seem like a natural color." G. H. made his wife a drink.

"You're sure." Ruth didn't doubt them, though. There was nothing they might have mistaken for a flamingo. She'd abandoned her expectations.

"A flamingo is a flamingo." Amanda wanted to be clear. "The question isn't if we're sure, but why—"

"You've got rich people out here." Clay was inspired. "They're someone's private collection. A miniature zoo. Some Hamptons estate that's actually an ark. Those billionaires are survivalists. They all have compounds in New Zealand where they plan to go when the shit hits the fan."

"Is there something sweet?" Ruth sipped the drink. She didn't really want it.

Amanda pushed the cookies across the island to her. "Maybe the noise we heard *was* thunder. Some kind of mega storm. I've heard of birds being blown off their migratory paths. There was that hurricane in the Atlantic, and the birds got lost."

Clay tried to remember what he had never known. "Are they migratory birds? And if so, do they cross the ocean? Maybe that's possible."

"Don't they congregate in lakes? Don't they eat some kind of shrimp, hence their pink feathers? I think that's true," Ruth said.

"We're just a bunch of adults who don't know anything about birds," said George. He was used to being able to explain everything. Could the curve explain the birds? There was a relationship, but he'd need days to work it out. He'd need a pencil, a newspaper, some quiet. "We don't know anything about noises loud enough to crack glass. We don't know anything about a blackout in New York City. We're four adults who don't know how to get a cell-phone signal or make the television work or do much of anything at all."

The room filled with chewing, ice running up against glass.

"Funny how I was telling you about *Swan Lake*." Ruth smiled. "Swans, flamingos. The same, but not."

"I need it to be tomorrow." Clay consulted the digital clock on the microwave's face. "We should sleep."

"You want to go home," G. H. said. "We're lucky to be already home."

"Unless." Ruth had no interest in dispensing platitude and comfort. She could not see a bright side. "This was a sign. You shouldn't go. We can't go with you."

"You said you'd show us the way," Amanda said.

"It's not safe. Out there," Ruth said. What if Rosa didn't come on Thursday? What if something out there was coming for them?

"We have to take Archie to the doctor!" Amanda felt it in her body like a bird's urge to migrate.

"What do you think is going to happen to us?" Clay wasn't looking for reassurance, just an honest guess. "We're leaving—you said you'd help us find the way."

George had never believed in unknowns. Algebra showed that they were easy to figure out. Math didn't pertain anymore, or it was a math he could barely work. "Nothing will happen to us if we just drive down the road," he told his wife.

"You think traffic will flow. That there's food. Water? I don't trust people. I don't trust the system." Ruth was sure. "Maybe Archie will get better if we stay put. Maybe tomorrow he'll wake up, fever gone, and want to eat everything in the house."

"Maybe he just needs antibiotics or something?" Clay didn't want to go now. He was terrified.

"I feel safe here." Ruth knew that this family's safety was not truly her problem. "All I want is to feel safe."

"You could stay," George said.

"We can't do that." Amanda was decisive.

Could they not, though? Clay was not so sure. "We could—we could go downstairs. You could have your bedroom."

They were quiet, like they knew it was coming. It came. The same noise? Sure. Yes. Probably. Why not. Who knew. Once, twice, three times. The window over the sink cracked. The pendant light over the counter did too. The electricity probably should have turned off, but it didn't. No one would ever be able to answer precisely why. The noises overlapped, but were discrete, the sound—they didn't know this—of American planes, in the American sky, speeding toward the American future. A plane most people didn't know existed. A plane designed to do unspeakable things, heading off to do them. Every action had an equal and opposite reaction, and there were more actions and reactions than could be counted on the party's eight hands. What their government was up to, what other governments were up to; just an abstract way of talking about the choices of a handful of men. Lemmings were not suicidal, they were driven to migrate and overconfident about their ability. The leader of the pack was not to blame. They all plunged into the sea, thinking it easy to traverse as a puddle; so human an instinct in a bunch of rodents. Millions of Americans huddled at home in the dark, but only thousands of them heard these noises, and comforted children and one another, and wondered just what they were. Some people got sick, because that was just their constitution. Others listened and realized how little they understood about the world.

Ruth did not cry out. There was no sense in that. Tears welled, but she blinked them back. Hands on the edge of the countertop, she crouched down, as maybe, decades ago, she'd been taught to, in case of nuclear annihilation. She just hovered there in a half squat, the pull of her muscles not an unpleasant thing.

Amanda screamed. Clay screamed. G. H. screamed. Rose screamed. The children threw themselves from their beds and found the adults, and it was their mother they ran to—always was, in these situations—and they pressed their faces against the foreign robe that covered her nakedness and she held them tight to her body, trying to cover their ears with her hands, but they had four ears between them and she had only two hands. She was not enough.

That noise again. It was the final one. It was one of the last planes. The insects outside fell silent, baffled. The bats that hadn't succumbed to white-nose syndrome fell from the sky. The flamingos barely paid it mind. They had enough to worry about.

32

THEY DID THE SENSIBLE THING. THEY HUDDLED TOGETHER in that big king. Family bed—Amanda hated the idea. Thought it was for antivaxxers and mothers who breastfed their five-year-olds, but she couldn't bear Archie and Rose being away from her. They turned the lights off because the children were exhausted, but privately wished to leave them burning to keep the night away.

"You can—" Clay wanted to invite Ruth and G. H. to bed with them! It almost made sense.

"Try to sleep." G. H. held his wife's hand, and they descended the kitchen steps once more.

Neither adult could sleep. Soon, though, the children began to snore. The curve of Rose's body made Clay think of those natural bridges on the California coast, hollowed out by the ocean over millennia. Eventually, though, those collapsed. They said the ocean was coming for them all. He appreciated the persistence of her lungs. It was incredible that you didn't need to tell yourself to breathe or walk or think or swallow. They had asked themselves questions when they decided to have children—do we have the money, do we have the space, do we have what it takes—but they didn't ask what the world would be when their children grew. Clay felt blameless. It was George Washington and the men of his generation, their mania for plastic and petroleum and money. It was a hell of a thing to not be able to keep your kid safe. Was this how everyone felt? Was this, finally, what it was to be a human?

He kissed the worn cotton on Rose's shoulder and regretted that he did not believe in prayer. God, she looked like her mother. Nature was fond of repetition. Did one flamingo know another from yet another?

Amanda kept reaching for Archie's arm. He flinched a little, each time, but did not wake. She wanted to ask her husband something but couldn't think of the right words. Was this it? Was this the end? Was she supposed to be valiant?

Clay couldn't see his son in the dark. He thought of how he still sometimes crept into the children's rooms. They never woke during these nocturnal visits. You told yourself there was an end to the worry. You told yourself it was sleeping through the night, then weaning from the breast, then walking then shoelaces then reading then algebra then sex then college admissions then you would be liberated, but this was a lie. Worry was infinite. A parent's only task was to protect his child.

He couldn't imagine his own mother anymore; she'd been dead most of his life. His father must have performed this office. It did not square with what he knew of the man, but that was how a parent loved.

Amanda touched the boy's cheek and found it was hot. She tried to distinguish between fever and summer, mammalian adolescence and illness. She touched the boy's forehead, throat, his shoulder, pushed away blankets to cool his body. She touched his chest, the steady drumbeat. Archie's skin was soft and dry, warm like a machine left on too long. She knew that fever was the body's distress signal, a pulse from its emergency broadcast system. But the boy was sick. Maybe they were all sick. Maybe this was a plague. He was her *baby*. He was their *baby*. She couldn't imagine a world indifferent to that.

Theirs was a failure of imagination, though, two overlapping but private delusions. G. H. would have pointed out that the information had always been there waiting for them, in the gradual death of Lebanon's cedars, in the disappearance of the river dolphin, in the renaissance of cold-war hatred, in the discovery of fission, in the capsizing vessels crowded with Africans. No one could plead ignorance that was not willful. You didn't have to scrutinize the curve to know; you didn't even have to read the papers, because our phones reminded us many times daily precisely how bad things had got. How easy to pretend otherwise. Amanda whispered her husband's name.

"I'm awake." He could not see her, then he could. He needed only to look more closely.

"Should we still go?"

He pretended to be thinking this over, but the dilemma was already plain to him: no, they shouldn't, yes, they must. "I don't know."

"We have to get Archie to a doctor."

"We do."

"And Rosie. What if the same thing—" To say it would have been to risk it. She didn't bother. Rose would have loved the flamingos. Maybe they should feel only awe at life's mysteries, as children did.

"She's fine. She seems okay." She did; same old Rose. Reliable, implacable, really, that strength of the second-born. He wasn't even thinking wishfully. Clay had faith in his daughter.

"She seems okay. I seem okay. Everything seems okay. But it also seems like a disaster. It also seems like the end of the world. We need a plan. We need to know what we're going to do. We can't just stay here forever."

"We can stay here for now. They said so." Clay had heard the offer.

"You want to stay here?" Amanda wanted him to say it first.

He tried to think how many cigarettes he had left. He did want to stay. Despite the sick teen, despite the nicotine withdrawal, despite the fact that this was not their beautiful house. Clay was afraid, but maybe they could pool courage between all of them and find enough to do something, anything, whatever that was. "It's safe here. We have power. We have water."

"I told you to fill the bathtub."

"We have food, and a roof, and G. H. has some money, and we have one another. We're not alone."

They both were and were not alone. Fate was collective but the rest of it was always individual, a thing impossible to escape. They lay that way for a long time. They didn't talk because there was nothing to discuss. The sounds of their sleeping children were relentless as the ocean.

33

A DRY HEAVINESS ON THE TONGUE AND IN THE THROAT, A wince that made it hard to see, the brute stupidity of hangover, and God they were too old for this. When would they learn not to be this way? Amanda hurried from the bed to drink at the bathroom sink, accidentally licking the metal faucet. She knew she'd vomit, in that way you always do. Sometimes you just need to admit to yourself what you know. Salt on the tongue. She bent at the waist like a yogi contemplating the toilet, then something that felt like a belch but burned in the back of the throat, and the release. The vomit was thin and pink as a flamingo (get it?). She let it leave her. Her eyes watered, but she did not look away from it. Her stomach contracted once, twice, three times, and the vomit leaped from stomach to throat to water, and once that was done she flushed it down and rinsed her mouth and felt ashamed. That was how all people the world over ought to have felt that morning.

Clay heard her terrible retch. You couldn't just doze through something like that. The room was too warm from too many bodies. At some point in the night, the air-conditioning had switched off. The kind of hangover where you yearn to throw open windows, strip the beds, clean your way back into virtue. A noisy, wet revolution inside his stomach. It would not be pretty.

Archie sat up and looked at his dad. He mumbled like his mouth was full of something. "What's happening?"

"I'm going to get us some water." Did he notice that Rose was not there? It seemed to make sense in that moment.

Clay filled glasses. He sipped his, relieved, then refilled it. "Rosie." He called out to the empty house. There was no answer. The refrigerator's icemaker made its periodic whirr. There was a trick to carrying three, but he managed it.

Pallid Amanda sat on the edge of the bed. Archie had pulled a pillow over his head. "Drink up." Clay put the glasses on the table. Whenever you were sick with something undetermined, you were supposed to drink water. Water was the first line of defense. If there was something in the air—if the storm had blown in more than just tropical birds—and that something was in the water, the whole system a closed loop, he didn't know it.

"Thanks, honey," his wife said.

Clay moved urgently, trot down the hall, quick slam of the door. The bathroom redolent of Amanda's vomit and his own shit, that postmidnight binge pouring out of him in seconds. He stood in the shower as penance, asshole burning, rinsing his mouth over and over again, spitting the water against the tile wall, angry. Did he know if this was hangover or a symptom of something worse? He did not.

On the other side of the wall, Amanda opened the door to the backyard—ugh, the smell of their bodies—where the sweet air was alive with light. She wanted to undo the bed, but her boy still lazed. "How are you feeling, baby?" She thought he looked more himself.

Archie tried to come up with the right answer. He felt strange or weird or sleepy or whatever, but that was how he felt whenever he woke up before noon or so. He was mad or something in that moment, turned away from his mother and pulled the covers over his head.

"I should check your temperature. We were so worried, I was

planning on taking you to see Dr. Wilcox this afternoon, after we get back, but maybe we don't need to."

Archie made an irritated little groan. "We're going back?"

"Come on. I know you're sleepy, but sit up, let Mom look at you." Amanda sat on the bed beside her son.

He pulled himself up to sitting, but slowly, his way of protest and his way of showing off the elastic efficiency of his adolescent body, an angled line morphing gradually from obtuse to acute.

The back of her hand against his forehead, Amanda looked in her son's eyes, bottomlessly beautiful to she who had made them, even when crusted and shrunken by sleep. "You don't feel so warm anymore." She put her palm against his forehead, his neck, his shoulder, his chest. "Does your throat hurt?"

He didn't know if his throat hurt. He hadn't thought about it. His mother would not leave him to sleep until he cooperated, so he did, opening his mouth wide as though to yawn as a way of gauging the health of his throat. Seemed fine. "No."

Good mother, she ignored the boy's sour breath. She looked into the pink recesses of his body as though she knew what she was looking for, or as though what was in there could be seen.

Archie closed his mouth and then his tongue tapped a tooth, a tic, a test, and the salt of blood flowed over his taste buds. Familiar, but you remembered that, no matter what, the taste of blood. Curious, he ran his tongue over enamel again and the tooth yielded to that gentlest nudge. His mouth filled with saliva.

Archie opened his mouth wider, and it spilled out, now, onto his neck, dribbled down his chest, saliva, drool, like a baby's, cut with crimson that didn't quite mix into it, like salad dressing insufficiently shaken. Blood was usually a surprise. His mouth continued to water, and to bleed. He put a finger to it, probing into the problem, and touched the tooth, and it fell over with a fleshy pop, down like a domino, onto his tongue and then, horribly, back into his mouth like a cherry pit almost swallowed. He spit it out, and the tooth landed in his palm. He stared at it. It was bigger than he'd have guessed.

"Archie!" Amanda thought at first the boy was vomiting. That would have made more sense. But this was so controlled, so understated. He'd just leaned forward over his hand and dripped blood onto his bare chest.

"Mom?" He was confused.

"Are you going to be sick, honey? Get out of the bed!"

Archie stood up and walked to mirror. "I'm not sick!" He held the tooth out in his palm, sticky and pink with blood.

She did not understand.

Archie looked at himself in the mirror. He opened his mouth and willed himself to confront the wet dark of it. He swooned a little, because it was disgusting. With his finger, he touched another tooth, a bottom one, and it, too, gave, then he grabbed onto it and pulled it right out of his gums, now near black with blood. Then another. Then another. Four teeth, tapered at the root, solid and white, four little pieces of evidence, four little proofs of life. Was he meant to scream? He closed his mouth and let the liquid gather there for a second, then spit it out onto the ground, not caring if he soiled the rug because what did that matter, really? Another of his teeth fell out and dropped onto the ground, where of course it did not make a sound. In the vast universe, it was too small to matter.

"Archie!" Amanda did not know what was happening. Of course she didn't.

He crouched to the ground to pick up his tooth. It was bigger than the hollow little shells that he'd left under his pillow until he turned ten. It tapered at the root, animal and menacing. He held them in his palm like a diver proud of his pearls. "My teeth!"

Amanda looked at her boy, slender and pathetic in his ticking-stripe boxer shorts. "What is it?"

The boy did not weep because he was too baffled to. "Mom. Mom. My teeth." He held his hand out for them to see.

"Clay!" She didn't know what to do but appeal to a second opinion. "My god, your teeth!"

"What's happening to me?" His voice was ridiculous because he couldn't talk properly without the percussion of tongue against tooth.

Amanda took the boy by the shoulders, steered him back to the bed. He was too tall otherwise. She pressed palm, then back of hand, to his forehead. "You're not hot? I don't understand—"

Clay came as beckoned, towel at his waist, irritation on his face. "What's happening?"

"There's something wrong with Archie!" Amanda thought it was evident.

"What is it?"

The boy held his hand out toward his father.

Clay did not understand. Who would? "Honey, what happened?"

"I was just—my tooth felt weird, and I touched it, and it fell out."

This was the moment. This was the ravine. Clay was going to lay his body down. "How is this—does he still have a fever?" Clay reached out to touch the boy's arm, his neck, his back. "You're warm—does he feel warm?"

"I don't know. I thought it wasn't so bad, but I don't know." Amanda could not remember having said those words so many times. She didn't know, she didn't know, she didn't know anything.

Clay looked from the child to his wife, baffled. Maybe the boy was sick, maybe he was contagious? "It's okay. You're okay."

"I don't feel okay!" But this wasn't true. Archie felt . . . fine? As normal as possible. His body was working to keep it together. It would shed what was extraneous to preserve the whole.

In some private part of himself, Clay stopped to see if all was well with his body. He did not know that it was not. Then he came awake, more truly, and looked at his son, bloody and toothless, and tried to think of what to do next.

"Did you fill the bathtub?" Amanda was doing what she was able to. "It's an emergency! We'll need water!"

34

IT WAS CLAY'S INSTINCT TO CONSULT THE WASHINGTONS.
Put four heads together. A conference, strength in numbers, the
wisdom of their more advanced age, but none of them had ever
seen anything like this. They huddled and inspected like Caravag-
gio's Thomas and friends. Incredulity was about right.

"You're feeling all right, though?" Ruth didn't see how that was
possible.

Archie just shrugged. He'd said it over and over again already.

"Well. This is something. We need to think about getting him
to the doctor." G. H. felt this clear. "Not back in Brooklyn. Here."

"We have that pediatrician's number." Ruth had done her research for when Maya and Clara and the boys came to visit. They'd
never had to use the information, but they had it.

"He needs the emergency room," G. H. said.

Clay nodded, grave. Been there, done that, like any parent worth
his salt. A glob of peanut butter lurking in a berry smoothie. An
overconfident leap from the jungle gym. Labored breath one terrible
winter night. "You're right. This shouldn't wait." How he wished it
could.

"Where's the hospital?" Amanda was unsure what to do with

her body. She walked in circles, she stood and sat like a dog that can't get comfortable. "Is it far?"

"Maybe fifteen minutes—" G. H. looked to his wife for confirmation.

"Farther, I think. You know these roads—it's probably closer to twenty, maybe longer? I think it depends on if you take Abbott or cut over to the highway—" Ruth didn't want to care. She didn't want what it would entail. She couldn't help herself. She was human. "Do you want some water or something?"

Archie shook his head. "I don't need to go to the hospital. I feel okay, I really do."

"We just need to be certain, honey." Amanda actually wrung her hands like an amateur character actor. "You'll give us directions? Unless someone's phone has suddenly started working? No?"

"I can give you directions," G. H. said.

"You'll draw us a map. The GPS is no good. You'll make us a map. And we'll go." Amanda went to the desk. Of course Ruth kept a cup of sharpened pencils, a pad of blank paper.

"I can draw you a map. But it's very simple once you get back to the main road—"

"I got lost." Clay put a hand on his son's shoulder. He could barely look at them. "I got lost. Before."

"What do you mean?" Amanda asked. "Lost?"

"It's not simple at all! I went out. To go and find out what was happening. To get to the bottom of—whatever. And I drove down the lane and I passed that egg stand and I thought I knew where I was going, and I was wrong. I drove around, then I turned around, then I was really lost. I don't know how I found my way back. I heard that noise and I thought I was going to lose my mind and then there it was, the turn I had been looking for, the road up to the lane up to the house. It was just right there."

"So you didn't see anyone. Or anything. You didn't go anywhere." Amanda sounded accusatory, but this was a relief: he hadn't even had the chance to look! They were all overreacting. There was nothing. An industrial accident, those noises four consecutive controlled explosions, the power loss easily explained. Not great! But not the worst.

"I could show you the way. We'll go too. All of us."

"No." Ruth was firm. Her whole body shook. "We're not leaving. We're not doing that. We're waiting here. Until we hear something. Until we know something." She would let them stay, but she wasn't risking her life for them.

"There's nothing to worry about. We'll drive them. We'll talk to someone, find out what people know, maybe we'll fill up the car, come right back here."

"You can stay. All of you. You can stay here, in this house, with us." This was as far as Ruth could go. "Just stay here."

"Stay here." Clay thought about it. He'd been thinking about it. "Until—until what?"

"But George, you can't leave. You can't leave me here, and I can't leave, and that's where we are," Ruth said.

"What if it's forever?" Amanda could not wait. Her son was sick. "What if the cell phones never come back—I mean, they barely worked out here before, when everything was normal. What if the power goes out, what if Archie is truly sick, what if we're all sick, what if that noise made us sick?"

"I'm not sick, Mom." Why wasn't anyone listening to him? He felt fine! Yes, it was weird his teeth had fallen out. But what was the doctor going to do—glue them back in? Something (his own instinct? some other very quiet voice?) told him to stay where they were.

Ruth wondered what Maya was doing. She wondered why it seemed perfectly viable to her that her grandsons had heard that noise in Amherst, Massachusetts. They had only milk teeth, barely held in place at all. Maybe the noise had knocked those loose, and reduced their mothers to hysterics. If you couldn't save your child, what were you doing? She knew they could not choose to stay with her, not when their child was sick. "I don't think I can go out there."

"It will be fine." G. H. couldn't promise that. They'd all been waiting for some decisive moment. Some corner being turned. Perhaps this was it, the gradual descent into illogic, the frog finding that the water is at last too much to bear. The hottest year in recorded history, hadn't he read that once? But the boy was sick, or something was wrong with him, and that was the only information they had. "You can wait here."

"I can't stay here alone."

"We'll pack up, we'll go to the hospital, and then we'll go back to Brooklyn," Clay thought aloud. "You don't need to drive us there. A map should be fine."

G. H. began to draw.

"Or we could come back. We could leave Rose here with Ruth, and we can come back for her." Amanda didn't want the girl to have to see what was happening to her brother. She thought this might be less worrisome.

"I can stay with Rose. I can even pack your things, you can go right now." Ruth liked a project.

"Fine." Clay stood. That made more sense. Let the adults do what was needed. They'd come back for Rose.

It was Amanda who realized, or Amanda who said it. The five of them had been so preoccupied by the situation. A shame: the perfect day. The light playing prettily across the pool, its reflection dancing across the back of the house, the green more lush from the rain, and not a cloud to be seen. "Where's Rose?"

35

SHE WAS WATCHING THAT ONE MOVIE SHE'D FORGOTTEN she'd downloaded. Amanda looked in the girl's bedroom, but the girl was not there. She was in the bathroom. Amanda went to look, but the girl was not there. Back to the living room. "I can't find Rose?"

They all agreed this made no sense. Clay went back to the master bedroom, which was empty. Amanda looked out the back door at the perfect day then in progress. Amanda looked into the laundry room, then went back to the master bedroom herself, not trusting Clay to be thorough. She looked in the walk-in closet, she looked under the bed, as though Rose were a house cat. She looked in the master bathroom, which still smelled of the violent rejections of their bodies.

Clay found his wife in the hallway. "I don't understand. Where is she?"

Amanda returned to the girl's room and peeled back the covers to see the foot of the bed, not sure, exactly, what she expected to find there. She hesitated before the bedroom closet like someone in a movie. Did the director intend a feint (Rose curled up with a book), or a shock (a stranger wielding a knife), or a puzzle (nothing at all)? There was just the smell of the cedar balls left to dissuade moths with a taste for cashmere. Now, then: panic, and at last, a concrete target upon which it could fix.

Back to the living room, where Rose was not watching television or sitting with a book, to the kitchen, where Rose was not eating or working the too-hard Oriental-rug jigsaw puzzle, to the door overlooking the pool, but no, Rose had been forbidden to swim alone (just sensible). Amanda opened the front door as though she'd find the girl there, *Trick or treat!* Nope, just the grass, darkened by the fallen rain, and the chatter of birds.

The girl was downstairs in the part of the house that most belonged to the Washingtons. She'd gone out to the garage to see what diversions it might hold. She was sitting in the car's back seat, obedient as a certain kind of dog, ready for the trip home. Okay, louder: "Rosie!"

"Rosie, Rosie." Amanda said it to herself. She went back into the bathroom. Once the girl had loved to hide and surprise them. Amanda pulled back the shower curtain to find only the tub full of an inch of water. She'd told Clay to fill the tub, and this was what he'd come up with? She went back to the living room. "I can't find Rose."

Clay wanted another glass of water. "Well, she has to be here somewhere." He gestured toward the bedrooms.

"She's not there—" Why wasn't he listening?

"She's taking a shower?"

"She's not—" She was not stupid!

"She's in the—" He didn't know what he meant any longer.

"She's not, she's not, I looked, she's not anywhere, where is she?" Amanda was not yelling, but she was not whispering.

"Did you look downstairs?" Archie's tone was withering.

"I'll look downstairs." G. H. stood. "She's probably just exploring the house."

"I can't find her?" Amanda put it as a question because it seemed so silly—*I can't find her! I can't find my child!* Like saying you couldn't find your earlobes or your clitoris.

Amanda went and stood in the kitchen, unsure what to do next. Ruth followed because she was moved to reassure her. That damnable instinct. She had to help. They were colleagues not as mothers but humans. This—all this—was a problem to be shared. "She must be outside." Ruth could picture the girl, watching monarchs flex their wings on the milkweed. "She's gone to play."

"I looked out front."

"Let's go outside."

Clay sat beside his son again. "Amanda. Calm down. Let's think. She could be in the garage, or out past the hedge, let's just go find her—"

"What the fuck do you think I'm doing, Clay? I'm going to get my shoes to go *find* her." Amanda rushed toward the bedroom.

"Archie, do you know where your sister went?" Clay was patient.

Archie spoke softly. Did he? He had an instinct, but it didn't make sense. "No."

Amanda came back in her slip-on Keds. She didn't even have tears in her anymore. "I feel insane. Where is Rose?"

"I'm sure she's just outside." Ruth wasn't all that sure of anything.

Amanda should have screamed, but there was no scream. The fact that she was so quiet was somehow more unsettling. "Get your shoes on and help me fucking look for her."

Through the door, Clay could see his rubber thongs by the hot tub. "I'll go out front, by the herb garden. I'll look past the hedge."

"She's just wandered somewhere." Ruth tried to convince. "There's no television, so she's playing the way we used to, just wandering about. There's nothing to worry about here." She meant: there was no traffic, there were no kidnappers. There were no bears or mountain lions. There were no rapists or perverts, no people at all. They were equipped to handle certain fears. This was something else. It was hard to remind yourself to be rational in a world where that seemed not to matter as much, but maybe it never had.

Downstairs, G. H. found his closet, packed with supplies, his bed, tidily made, his bathroom, the mute and useless television, the broken back door, his cell phone plugged into its optimistic white cables. He put the phone into his pocket.

In the living room, Archie stuffed his feet into his Vans and used his tongue to contemplate the tender empty pockets in his gums. They were soft and pleasant, like the recesses of the human body his own was designed to fit into, something he'd never know first-hand. Could he forgive the universe that denial of his own particular purpose? He wouldn't get the chance. He opened the back door and went to join his father, went to find his sister.

"There's nothing to worry about?" Amanda's imagination, exhausted, had given up. She went outside with the rest of her family, into that beautiful day, too distracted to notice if it was different from the thousands of other days of her life thus far. Her "Rose! Rose!" was loud and impassioned enough to startle animals she couldn't see and would never know were there.

Amanda had theories. A mother always did. An errant step into an unused well, a hundred feet deep, disguised by the fulsome St. Augustine grass. A bough, sundered by that noise, falling from overhead. A snake bite, a twisted ankle, a bee sting, maybe she simply got turned around. They couldn't call 911! Who would save them?

G. H. took the downstairs door, closed it gingerly. The grass was damp and thick.

"I'm going up front." Clay did just that.

Ruth was afraid; once you had a kid, you knew to be afraid. "We should look in the garage." Ruth led the way.

Amanda followed her.

Archie walked past the yard to the little shed. He knew his sister wasn't in there, but he had to look. The door stood open, and

Archie leaned against the structure, looked back at the house. *Stupid little kid.* He knew she'd gone back into the woods. Why wasn't he able to say this out loud? And how did he know it? It didn't matter. Archie shivered the way you might when you walk into a spiderweb, the way you might if you saw a spider dart from beneath your pillow and lose itself in your mosaic-printed bedsheets, the way you might if a spider crept from your shoulder up your neck and nestled into the comforting cave of your ear, the way you might if a spider dropped from the ceiling and landed on your hair and then picked its way forward carefully down the slope of your nose so you could barely see it with your wide-set eyes, the way you might if a spider started and bit you and its poison dripped into your bloodstream and then became a part of you, inextricable as your DNA, the thing that made you. His left knee felt funny, then gave out beneath him, and Archie doubled over, and he started to vomit but it wasn't vomit, just water, a bit of blood. Guess what? It was pink like—

36

CLAY COULD FEEL THE GRAVEL THROUGH HIS FLIP-FLOPS.
They were almost worn out, at the end of their life. If you wanted
to mitigate your guilt over making garbage, you could mail them
back to the manufacturer, gratis, who would dump them in Ec-
uador, Guatemala, Colombia, some place like that where NGOs
taught people to snip them into pieces and stitch them into rubber mats for white people to buy. There was nothing out front,
there was nothing past the hedge, just the very same view that
had taunted him the day before. Was that only yesterday? "Rose!"
His voice didn't carry. It didn't go anywhere. It fell to the verdant
ground.

In the garage Ruth pointed out the ladder up to the loft. A girl
might want to play up there! Ruth had half-plans to someday turn
it into a guest apartment. Amanda scooted up the ladder, but there
was nothing up there.

The women came out of the garage as Clay rounded the corner and G. H. completed a circuit of the house. The four of them
looked at one another.

"She's gone?" Amanda didn't know what else to say.

"She can't be gone—" Ruth meant gone, finality, disappearance.
Whatever this was, it wasn't the rapture. Rose definitely would

have been saved, but Clay knew they couldn't yield to pure myth. "She must have just—gone somewhere."

"She was so curious about other houses. And the eggs! Maybe she went to the egg stand." Ruth had her doubts.

"Where's Archie?" Clay looked toward the backyard.

"He was right there." Amanda could hold only one thing in her head at that moment.

"He seems better." Such optimism! It only worked if he excused the fact of the boy's missing teeth, but parenthood meant occasional magical flights of fancy.

Ruth nodded. "One of us should go down to the egg stand."

Amanda strode away, impatient. "I'll go. Clay, go to the back. Look in the woods. But don't go far—"

"I'll look inside again." Ruth dismissed the two men. "You go out back."

He and G. H. cut through the front door, and from the back deck Clay saw his son, prone, in the grass. He called his name. He ran toward him. He could no longer remember what he was supposed to be doing.

The boy was on his knees and his chest like a Muslim in prayer. Clay slipped a hand into his armpit and pulled him back.

"Dad." Archie looked at him, then leaned forward and vomited once more, a beautiful plash of liquid onto earth.

"What's happened?" G. H. was demanding an explanation. "You're all right, you're all right."

Ruth saw this from the deck. She hurried, knowing she was needed. They braced the boy's body between theirs and walked at the deliberate pace of the elderly. The boy kept choking, or seizing, but there was nothing left in him to escape his mouth. His eyes were almost but not exactly closed, fluttering like the eyes of a kind of now-antiquated camera, but did they see? Did they capture anything?

Ruth was cataloging. They had old antibiotics. They had a hot water bottle. They had that powdered drink for when you were down with flu. You dissolved it in hot water and slept for hours. They had sea salt and olive oil and basil and laundry detergent and Band-Aids and a huge package of those little travel packages of tissues that were so handy to have in your purse. George had ten thousand dollars in cash tucked away for emergencies. They were rich! Would any of that be a salve to whatever this was?

"Let's get him inside." G. H. captained this endeavor. They proceeded, awkward, up the wide wooden steps. The pool's filtration system began its scheduled cycle, which told him that it was 10:00 a.m. It whirred and gurgled joyfully.

They laid the boy's body on the sofa. "Archie, honey are you okay? Can you tell me?"

Archie looked up at the trio. "I don't know."

Clay looked at the other adults. "Where's Rose?"

"I think she's probably playing down the road. She borrowed one of the bikes. I know she's been bored. She's just having—she's playing." G. H. tried to make this sound inevitable. "Let's get Archie some water. We can't have him dehydrating."

Clay did know that Rose loved to *do*. She was always with a book, and in her books, girls her age had big hearts and appetites for adventure. They did unlikely, brave things, facing down private fears, then chastely held hands with boys with beautiful eyelashes. These books had given her a sense of the world as something to be conquered with derring-do. Books ruined everyone—wasn't that what his academic work was meant to show? "Water. Right."

Ruth had already filled another glass. "Drink this up."

"Sit up, easy now." Clay's body remembered the pose of early parenthood, ready to leap and right your toddler's toppling body.

"We have to go to the hospital." George had decided. "We have to go now."

"You can't leave me." Ruth unfolded the blanket on the sofa's back and draped it over the boy's body.

"He's sick. You see that."

"We can't go without my daughter—"

"We'll go. You and me. We'll take Archie."

"No. You can't, George, you can't leave."

"Ruth. You find Amanda. You two find Rose. You stay here."

Did she have it in her to do this? Wasn't she bored with having to be strong and noble and competent, best supporting actress? Wasn't she allowed to be hysterical and afraid? "George, please."

He looked into his wife's eyes. "We'll come back. We'll come right back."

"You'll never come back. Don't you see that something is happening? It's happening right now. Whatever it is, it's happening to Archie, it's happening to all of us, we can't leave." Ruth was not crying or hysterical, which made what she said more unsettling.

Clay did not notice the tingle in his knees, his elbows, or he did and took it for fear. "Ruth, please. We need help."

This was his moment. Men of his generation made decisions, they waged wars, they made fortunes, they acted with conviction. "We're going. Clay, take Archie to the car. Bring that blanket. Ruth, get him a bottle of water. Archie, you lie down in the back seat."

"George. I won't let you do this. I can't let you do this. I can't."

"This is the only thing we can do. This is the thing that I have to do." George held the keys in his hand. He didn't spell it out for her because he knew Ruth and knew she'd understand: if they weren't human, in this moment, then they were nothing.

Ruth didn't know how to enumerate the things she could not do. She could not do any of this. "You're coming back to me. You're coming back for us."

"Set a timer. Get your phone. Set the alarm. One hour." G. H. was sure he could do this.

"You can't make promises you can't keep!" Ruth fumbled with her phone.

"It will take one hour. Less. I'll drive to the hospital. I'll leave them and turn around and come back for you and Amanda and Rose. You'll find Rose. Do you understand? I'll set a timer too."

"It won't work. It won't work out."

"It will. There is no choice. Look." He pressed the digital display, and the seconds began counting down. "I'm going to leave Clay and Archie there, and then I'll be back for the three of you by the time this goes off."

"How do you know the hospital will be—" Clay faltered.

"Clay." George did not think it worth discussing. He knew what was supposed to happen. "We're going. Get him into the car."

"Come on, honey." Clay helped his son to his feet and remembered his hands at the toddler's waist. So skinny he could circle it, fingertips touching.

Ruth draped the blanket around Archie's shoulders again. "One hour." She pressed the button on her phone, and the seconds started ticking. "That's what you get. You've promised."

"It's nothing to worry about." George gripped his keys, heavy to connote luxury. Was he lying? Was he hopeful?

Ruth didn't believe in prayer, so she thought of nothing.

37

G. H. KNEW THEY WOULD FIND ROSE. THAT WAS WHAT MOTH-
ers did. Some secret sonar, like those birds that hide a hundred
thousand seeds in October and stay fat all winter. The car came to
life like the reliable, expensive machine that it was.

Archie shivered on the leather back seat.

"You tell me if you need to stop and be sick." The way he said
it, it sounded like George was thinking of his car, but a parent was
versed in vomit and worse, baptized in it, able, for the rest of life, to
find not horror but pity. Seven-year-old Maya on the corner of Lex
and Seventy-Fourth, vomiting whole flakes of white fish into his
outstretched hands. Just another memory, just another moment,
but he'd do it again if it had been his adult daughter in the back
seat, toothless and in the grip of some ailment for which they had
no noun. You were a father forever.

Clay shifted to the left to retrieve his wallet from his right back
pocket. Incredible he'd remembered it, some secret instinct. He
thumbed through plastic chits in search of their insurance card.
They used Amanda's plan; it was better than the one at the college.
An exhale upon finding it, the relief of something, finally, going
right.

"We're going to get you to a doctor." Clay turned around to

look at his son. Was he thinner, was he paler, was he frailer, was he smaller? "You're okay. You're okay."

"I'm okay." Obedient Archie was determined to take this like a man. Archie was a man now.

The car turned from driveway to access road to main road. George drove more slowly than normal, despite the quickened heartbeat, the sense of rush, the seconds accruing on the timer. None of the men in the car noticed the little egg shack, none of them knew that Amanda was inside it, finding, instead of Rosie, only the goodly scent of farm labor. The Mudds, whose land that was, would never again bring fresh-laid eggs back to that little shed.

It all swam before Clay, green, green, rich, wet, thick, menacing, useless, impotent, angry, indifferent green. "I saw someone. When I went out before."

George did not mark this. "You said you got lost. Pay attention. There's pencil and paper in the glove box. Draw a map. We turned right from the driveway, and I turned left back there. We go over this hill and make another right." He was planning for contingencies. What if they were separated? What if—there were endless scenarios.

Clay opened the glove box, where there was a pad and a pencil, the owner's manual, the insurance and registration information, a package of tissues, a slender first aid kit. Order, preparation, tidiness. Everything about G. H. and Ruth's life was orderly, prepared, tidy. Rich people were so lucky. "There was a woman. On the road. She flagged me down. She was speaking Spanish."

"You saw someone—yesterday, when you went out?" Absurd that was yesterday! G. H. tried but could not answer what day of the week it was. "Why didn't you say?"

"She was—she was standing on the side of the road. She flagged me down. I talked to her. Well, I tried to." He knew his son was listening. It was terrible to be ashamed in front of your own child.

"We asked you what you had seen." George was irritated. He needed all the information before he could decide what to do next.

"She was dressed like a maid. I guess? In a polo shirt. A white polo shirt. I thought—I don't know. I couldn't understand her. She was speaking in Spanish, and I don't know what she was saying, and I would have used Google Translate but I couldn't and then I just—" He didn't know if he could say it in front of Archie.

G. H. thought of Rosa, who kept their own house in order, whose husband sculpted and tended the hedge, whose children played quietly, sometimes, as their parents worked in the summer heat, pretending not to see the swimming pool, though Ruth had once told Rosa the children were welcome to swim. They never would. It was not in them. Had it been her? "A Hispanic woman?"

Archie was listening, but Archie understood. He didn't know what he would have done; he knew that it was foolishness to pretend that anyone would know what they might do in such a moment.

"I left her there. I didn't know what else to do. I didn't know what was happening. I didn't know *something* was happening." Clay could never have imagined anything so specific as the unexplained birds, the lost teeth. What if Rose, right then, was wandering on the side of the road, and sought help from some passing motorist? Why would she? He had no idea what she thought, his daughter.

"Never mind." G. H. didn't think morality was a test. It was an ever-shifting set of concerns. "Pay attention. Draw a map that you'll be able to read. Write down what we do."

"I left her. She needed help. We need help." It was karma, was that it? Clay thought the universe didn't care. He was probably right. But maybe it did; maybe it was math.

"We're going for help. You see this bend in the road? There's a farm just past there, McKinnon Farms. It's a landmark." It was odd to try to see the whole thing with fresh eyes. G. H. never thought about these roads. He possessed them without having to see them.

This was their place, but it was also not their place. He didn't know who the McKinnons were, if they still had anything to do with the farm that bore their name. He and Ruth hadn't gone round to shake hands when they closed on the house. How would the locals take that, the black strangers in the eighty-thousand-dollar car? They holed up. They didn't even like to stop at the grocery or the gas station, conspicuous and tense. Would he need a gun, in the days to come? G. H. had never believed in the things. Would the cash in the safe in the master bedroom closet do anything to help them?

Clay drew some lines on the paper. They were inscrutable the second he removed the pencil. His heart was not in it. His heart was in the back seat; his heart was wherever Rose was. "You don't understand." The sight lines were unobstructed, and the fields rolled away in their irritating and persistent way. "I didn't know what to do. I can't do anything without my phone. I'm a useless man. My son is sick and my daughter is missing and I don't know what I'm supposed to do right now in this moment right here, I have no idea what to do." His eyes horribly damp, Clay tried for composure. He swallowed the sob like it was a burp. He was so small.

George did not trust the place. If he'd had a cardiac event, he'd have paid the three thousand dollars for a helicopter lift back to Manhattan, where people took on faith the humanity of black people. This place was not good enough for him, beautiful as it was. Here, people were suspicious, resentful of and beholden to the rich, the outsiders. Here, people prayed that Mike Pence was an agent of the godly in the imminent end. All that research that doctors and nurses thought black people could *take it*, and withheld the palliative opioids. "I know what to do."

Clay couldn't say out loud that he didn't think the doctor would have anything for them. He had put the child's teeth into a Ziploc bag. It was in his left pocket, and he worried it like some gruesome rosary. "Maybe they'll be able to explain everything at the hospital."

"Before that. We need to stop. We're going to Danny's house."

"Whose house?"

George couldn't explain his faith that Danny, of all people, would understand what was happening, and have, if not a solution, a strategy. That's the kind of man he was. They could go to Danny and say the girl was missing or the boy was sick or they were all afraid of the noises in the night, and Danny, like the Wizard of Oz, could grant good health and safe passage. "Danny was our contractor. He's a neighbor. He's a friend."

The day outside seemed so normal. "We have to get Archie to the hospital."

"We will. Ten minutes. We'll stop for ten minutes. I'm telling you, Danny will help, he'll have an idea."

Clay was supposed to fight, he felt sure, but he only shrugged. "If you think so."

"I do." George had made his life this way. Problems had solutions, and Danny would have information and also might lead by example. He and Clay could come back, roll up the sleeves of a chambray shirt, and protect the people they loved.

"There's no one around." Clay wondered if they'd see that woman again. He'd huddled with his family in the comfort of the king-size bed with its lovely semen-stained sheets, and that Mexican woman—but maybe she wasn't Mexican—had passed the night . . . he had no idea where.

"Too far from the beach to be a beach house. Not actually on a farm, so not a farmhouse. Not especially old, so not an historic house. Not brand-new and tricked out, so not a luxury house. Just a quiet place, the ends of the earth, somewhere to be alone and quiet and comfortable." Hadn't they earned the luxury of a little remove from the poor, the ignorant, the worse? "But it's an illusion, really. It's just a few minutes. A couple of miles this way. Stores, a movie theater, the highway, people. A movie theater, a mall. The ocean."

"We went there."

"A Starbucks."

"We stopped there."

"The conveniences. Alone but not really alone. It's just the idea. It's the best of both worlds."

"No cars. Have you heard a plane?" Clay stopped expecting to recognize the trees, the bends, the turns, the rises. "A helicopter? A siren?"

It was clear they'd have to learn a new way through a new world. "I haven't heard anything."

From the back seat, Archie listened. He watched out of the window, but he could only see the sky. He thought of Rose, and the deer she'd seen, but didn't know that they'd all got quite far away, in the night.

There was meaning in G. H.'s exhalation. Age made you more patient. "Everything is different. Are you writing this down?"

Clay looked at the map he'd made. It was illegible, useless. So he'd failed as a cartographer too. You told yourself you'd be attuned to a holocaust unfolding a world away, but you weren't. It was immaterial, thanks to distance. People weren't that connected to one another. Terrible things happened constantly and never prevented you from going out for ice cream or celebrating birthdays or going to the movies or paying your taxes or fucking your wife or worrying about the mortgage. "I'm writing it down."

G. H. was sure of it. "Danny will know something."

38

RUTH PULLED OPEN THE DOOR TO THE LITTLE SHED. THE hinge complained, but Amanda did not respond.

"Come on, now." Ruth didn't want to be this person. The help-meet; the supporting player. Her daughter was also lost to her. Who would help her find her grandsons? Who would hold her up?

"Where's Rose, where's Rosie. What are we going to do?" Amanda was sitting on an upturned bucket.

"Come on. Stand up. Come out of here. Into the light." The little building smelled.

The women went outside. The sun asserted itself. Ruth checked the timer on the phone. It had been eleven minutes. George would be back in forty-nine. This was not so long. You could reduce it down to seconds and keep vigil, count it out loud. She'd hear the approach of the car on the gravel. She'd see him again. "That's better," she said, and it was. The fresh air made some kind of promise. "They took Archie. He was sick again."

Amanda couldn't think about this too.

"We made a plan. One hour. They'll take him. George will be back for you and me and Rose."

"Should we go to the woods in the back? Should we walk to the road? How far is it? Is it this way?" Amanda pointed, but she wasn't sure where.

"The road is down that way. Would she go down there?" This didn't make any sense to Ruth. She couldn't imagine why the girl would forsake the safety of the little brick house.

"I don't know! I don't know why she'd leave. I don't know where she'd go." Amanda couldn't say it, but what if the girl hadn't left at all, was already dead, somewhere in the house? That thing with JonBenét Ramsey had begun as the search for a missing child, but her corpse had been in the basement all the while. Who killed Jon-Benét Ramsey, anyway? Amanda couldn't remember.

"Let's go back inside. Let's walk through the house once more." Ruth had a terrible vision—the girl in the powder room by the side entrance, toothless and faint?

"Rose!" Amanda screamed it. The day was silent in response. There was nothing out there for them.

"Let's look inside. Let's be methodical." Ruth needed them to make sense of things.

They hurried up the driveway, the gravel shifting under their steps. Amanda could feel every rock through the thin rubber soles of her shoes. Ruth could not move quite as fast as the younger woman, but she did. There was an urgent matter to attend to. "Let's go inside." Amanda said it like it had been her idea. "Maybe she's hiding." There was no reason for the girl to hide, but maybe she was? She was jealous of the attention her brother had earned. She was lost in a book. She didn't want to go home. "Do you think they've got to the hospital yet?"

"It's too soon. But they're on their way." Ruth went into the house by the side door. She opened the little closet where they had some waterproof boots, the chemical ice melt for the steps, one of the two broad plastic snow shovels, an old canvas tote bag stuffed with other canvas tote bags. No Rose.

"They're going. They'll be safe." Amanda was convincing herself.

"George will leave Clay and Archie. They can see the doctor. Then he'll come right back for us."

"I'm not leaving without Rosie!" Amanda opened the powder room door. Nothing.

"Of course. That's the plan. He'll come back for the three of us." It was just sensible.

"And what? We'll leave? We didn't finish packing!" They needed their things.

"We'll go back. We'll see to Clay and Archie. Then I don't know what." Ruth wanted to say: You don't need your things. You have us. We have one another.

"Rose!" The name just fell into the empty house. There was only the exhalation of all those appliances, but neither woman heard that anymore. "Then what? What's the doctor going to say? What's the doctor going to do? Did Clay even take the teeth with him?" They'd put them into a plastic baggie. Macabre. Would a doctor screw them back into his head?

"I don't know then what."

"We'll go home? We'll come back here?" Neither made any sense.

Ruth opened the pantry door. No thirteen-year-old girl would hide there. "I don't know!" She was, in fact, yelling. Ruth was mad too. "I don't know what we'll do, don't ask me as though I have some answer at my disposal that you don't. I don't know what we'll do."

"I just want to know what the fuck is going to happen. What the fuck is the plan. I want to know that we're going to find my kid and all three of us are going to get in your fucking expensive car and drive to the hospital and the doctor is going to tell me that my baby is okay, and that we're all okay, and that we can all go back to our house."

"I know that. But what if that's not possible?"

"I just want to get the fuck away from here and you and whatever is happening—" Amanda hated her.

"It's happening to all of us!" Ruth was furious.

"I know that it's happening to all of us!"

"You don't care, do you, that I'm here and my daughter is in Massachusetts—" She could feel the ghost embrace, her grandsons' four sweet hands.

"I care, I don't know what I'm supposed to do about it. My daughter is in— I don't know where my daughter is!"

"Stop yelling at me." Ruth sat down at the kitchen island. Ruth looked up at the glass globe of the pendant light, the one that had shattered when the planes—she didn't know those were planes— had flown overhead. Why did this woman not understand that however unlucky they were, they were also lucky? Ruth wanted to sleep in her own bed. But she wanted these people to stay.

"I'm sorry." Did she mean it? It didn't matter. "Rose!" Amanda looked at the woman and understood. They could not leave this house. They could not go back to Brooklyn. They could see the doctor and maybe stop at the store and come back here and hide and wait for whatever was coming. This woman was not a stranger at all; she was their salvation. "I'm sorry. I just want my daughter."

"I want my daughter too." Ruth could hear Maya's voice, the sweet register of her girlhood. Ruth could not make peace with whatever was required. She wanted to know that her child and her grandchildren were safe, but of course, Ruth would never know that. You never know that. You demanded answers, but the universe refused. Comfort and safety were just an illusion. Money meant nothing. All that meant anything was this—people, in the same place, together. This was what was left to them.

"Rose!" Amanda did not sit because she could not. She went back through the living room, into the bedroom that was Archie's, through the bathroom where the tub was now empty, to the bedroom that had been Rose's. Amanda knelt on the floor and looked under the bed, where there was nothing, not even dust. She went back to the bathroom and plugged the drain properly and began filling the tub with water.

She emerged into the living room. "I'm sorry. I'm sorry I yelled. I'm sorry I'm terrible. I want my daughter, I don't know why I yelled at you. I know you understand, but I want my daughter. She was just right here. I don't understand what's happening." She wanted to hug Ruth, but she could not.

Ruth did understand. Everyone understood. This was what everyone wanted, to be safe. This was the thing that eluded every single one of them. Ruth stood up. So, she'd look for the girl, or her corpse, if she was dead. She'd do what was required, she'd do what was human.

Amanda pushed open the doors to the back porch and looked down at the pool. She screamed her daughter's name at the woods. The trees moved a little in the wind, but that was the only thing that happened.

39

IT DIDN'T EVEN LOOK LIKE A DRIVEWAY, BUT THROUGH A little copse, the way widened, and then was paved. There was a lawn that seemed manicured from a distance but was actually wild, feverish. From afar the green was so dazzling, you assumed it had to be the work of man. There was a fence, and there was the house, colonial, an ersatz echo of the original American ideal, with seven bedrooms, whirlpool tubs, granite countertops, central air.

George saw the silver Range Rover and was reassured. Danny was in residence. They'd been right to come. He'd only begun to say "Let's go," but Clay's need was as urgent as his, because he was already out of the car. "Archie. You stay there. You lie down."

The boy looked up at the older man. He could see that the sky was more blue now, that it would be a perfect day for lunch outside, though what he could eat with his toothless mouth he wasn't sure. "Okay. I'll wait."

The front door was a slick and jolly yellow, something Danny's wife, Karen, had seen in a magazine. G. H. rang the doorbell. He almost knocked and then told himself to be more patient. It wouldn't do to turn up like a lunatic. The world might have gone mad, but they had not.

Danny and Karen had passed the night as uneasily as the rest of them. The family bed, four-year-old Emma between them as the boom died out overhead. Karen almost catatonic, thinking of her son, Henry, at his father's place in Rockville Center. Their phones hadn't worked, and the boy was deeply attached to his mother, and she knew, they both knew, he was probably even then calling out for her, fruitless. Would his father bundle him into the car and drive him home? Karen tried to will it to be so, but among their irreconcilable differences was his inability to understand what she wanted. Danny was in the kitchen, taking stock of what they had on hand, and was irritated by the interruption. This was evident as he opened the door.

"George," he said, recognition but not warmth. Danny was very handsome. This was always the first impression he made. Regular exposure to the sun had rendered his skin golden. Genetic predisposition had salted his brown hair. His stance was wide as his shoulders, his posture confident, because he knew that he was handsome and therefore he stood like he knew it. He offered himself to the world, and the world said its thanks. He was surprised but also not that surprised.

"Danny." G. H. hadn't planned what would happen next. But there was some relief in just seeing another human being. It seemed it had been so long since that night at the concert, shaking hands and praising the performers.

The sight of the man reminded Danny of work. That was just a matter of putting on a smile, reassuring people, barking orders, collecting a check; it had nothing to do with his real life—the woman upstairs reading a book about dragons to a frightened but also indifferent little girl. Once he'd seen the news alert, Danny had gone out for supplies, for news. He'd come home with groceries but little else. "This is a surprise."

G. H. could see he'd miscalculated. He understood the man's posture. He should have known that what he'd always believed of people was true; that social order had allowed most of them to believe themselves not social animals. "I'm sorry to bother you at home like this."

Danny looked from George to the stranger beside him. Had he ever liked George? Not really. It didn't matter; that was not the question. There was nothing to it. So he didn't like Obama, either. It had to do only with the presumption of it, the fist bumping, the joviality. It insulted him, a mockery of the world as he understood it. "What—what can I do for you?" He made it clear that he was off the clock, not interested in doing anything for the many.

G. H. felt the beginning of a smile, a salesman's tactic. "Well, something is happening." He was not stupid. "We were driving by, and I thought I would check in on you. See if you're here. If you're okay. If you'd heard anything."

Danny looked over his shoulder, back into the house, past the curlicue of the banister. He saw motes dancing in the morning light from the living room's double-height windows. He saw everything as it ought to have been, but he didn't trust it. He didn't trust anything. He stepped toward the men and closed the door behind them. "Heard anything? You mean, besides what we heard yesterday?"

"I'm Clay." He didn't know what else to say. Clay wondered if this man would walk the woods with them until they met Rose. Would he have medicine for Archie? Would he have an internet connection? Would he welcome them into this handsome house, the size of a hotel, and would it be like a party, and if so did they have a swimming pool? He imagined the women had recovered Rose, playing in the shade of the woods. He imagined that Archie was feeling better, a temporary stomach bug. Maybe they didn't need anything from this man and all was well, maybe they'd just say hello, commiserate, ask whether the noise—when had that been?—had cracked any of his windows.

Danny went on. "I'm surprised you guys are out."

"What do you mean?" G. H. was trying to get something, anything.

"What do I mean?" Danny's laugh was hard, angry. "There's some real shit going on out there, George. You don't know that? You can't hear it from that nice house of yours? My guys did a good job, but I know you heard that last night."

"My family is renting George's house. We're here from the city." Clay didn't know why he was trying to explain himself; he couldn't understand how little Danny was interested.

"That's a lucky break for your family." Danny knew the man was from the city. It was clear. He did not care. "Can you imagine what a shitshow that must be?"

"What do you know? Have you heard anything?" George asked.

"I know what you probably know." Danny sighed, impatient. "Apple News says there's a blackout. I think, okay, we're safe out here. I've got no service. I've got no cable. But I've got power. So I drive into town for some stuff. I think the store's going to be mobbed, right? Nope. Quiet. Not like before a snowstorm, more like after a foot has fallen. No one knows what's going on. It's just another day. I come home, hear that noise, and think, That's it, we're not leaving. Then last night—the noise again. Three times. Bombs? Missiles? I don't know, but I'm staying put until I hear that I shouldn't."

"You went to the store." George wanted to be clear.

"Stocked up. Came home. It just doesn't feel like out there is the place to be."

"My son is sick." Clay didn't know how to explain that something had knocked the teeth from Archie's sixteen-year-old mouth. It made no sense. "He was vomiting. He seems okay, now." Clay was still hopeful.

G. H. interjected. "He lost his teeth. Five of them. They just fell out. We can't explain it."

"His teeth." Danny was quiet for a while. "You think it had something to do with that noise?" Danny didn't know that the teeth in Karen's mouth were themselves loose, would soon fall out.

"Did your windows crack?" George asked.

"The shower door. The master bath." Danny thought it was obvious. "It's something. Had to be a plane. I don't think there's any information getting out, so I assume it's a war. The beginning of a war."

"War?" Somehow this had not occurred to Clay. This seemed almost disappointing, a letdown.

"Has to be an attack I think? They were talking about the super hurricane on CNN. The Iranians or whoever—they planned it right. The perfect shitshow." Danny had seen a broadcast of a local Washington anchor in a boat to show the water standing inside the Jefferson Memorial.

"You think we're under attack?" G. H. didn't, but he wanted to hear.

"They've been saying there was chatter, this has to be what they were chattering about." Danny pitied anyone who couldn't see how obvious it was.

This man was a conspiracy theorist. He was crazy. Clay was a professor. "Chatter? What happened at the store? We need to go to the hospital."

"You've got to read the papers. Deeper than page one. The Russians recalled their staff from Washington, did you notice that? That was in bold print, that got a 'breaking.' Something's afoot, man." Danny coughed and put his hands in his pockets.

"We're going to the hospital." Clay said it again, but he was less certain.

"What you do is your business. What I'm doing is staying right here." Danny wanted them gone.

"This is what you think, Danny?" G. H. turned it around on him.

"Nothing is making a whole lot of sense at the moment. If the world doesn't make sense, I can still do what's rational. It's not safe out there." Danny nodded toward the expanse of nothing, which did not look any different, but he wasn't fooled.

"Archie is sick." Clay needed an answer.

George understood why Danny had closed the door at his back. George had expected human communion, but he forgot what humans were actually like. "I thought it was the right thing to do. Seek medical attention."

Danny was not smiling. "That's the old way, George. You're not thinking clearly."

"My daughter is missing. We woke up this morning, and she was gone. She was in the woods with her brother, playing, when we heard that noise. Then last night, his teeth." Clay didn't know how to finish so absurd a story. "I don't know what to do." It came out of him as a confession.

It wasn't that Danny didn't feel bad. There was only so much he could think about. "He's your son. You have a difficult choice."

"He's sixteen." Help us, Clay was saying, in his way.

There is no help, Danny was saying. They had misunderstood what kind of person he was. They had misunderstood people. "I don't know what you're going to do. I'd do anything I had to for my daughter. So that's what I'm doing. I'm locking the doors. I'm getting out my gun. I'm waiting. I'm watching."

Was the mention of a gun a threat? G. H. understood it as one. "We shouldn't go to the hospital."

"I don't have any answers for you guys. I'm sorry." This apology was mostly a remembered instinct. But Danny was sorry, for all of them. He shared what information he had. "Yesterday, I saw deer from the kitchen."

G. H. nodded. Deer were everywhere out there.

Danny clarified. "Not deer, not a *family of* deer. A migration. I've never seen so many in my life. A hundred? Two hundred? I couldn't even guess." There were more than that. The eye couldn't take them all in, couldn't find them in the shadows of the trees. Only the people who knew such things knew there were around thirty-six thousand deer in the county. They were not the deer Rose had seen but were on their way to join those. A mass migration. A disaster response. A disaster indicator. A disaster unfolding.

Clay wanted to tell him that the night before they'd seen a flock of flamingos, but it would have seemed like one-upmanship.

"The animals," Danny continued. "They know something. They're spooked. I don't know what's happening, and I don't know when we're going to figure out what is. Maybe this is it. Maybe this is as much as we'll ever know. Maybe we just need to sit tight and be safe and pray or whatever works for you." They were animals too. This was their animal response.

Clay felt they'd been talking for an hour. "You told Ruth you'd be back."

"We have time." G. H. would keep his promise.

Danny felt there was little point going on like this. "Guys, I'm going to go inside now. I'm going to say goodbye and good luck." He meant that last bit. They'd all require it. "If you go back out. If you—well, you can stop by. But I can't offer you much more than just conversation. You understand."

George felt foolish. Of course this was how Danny would be. All business. They were not friends, and even if they had been, these were extraordinary circumstances. "I guess that's it then."

Danny offered some advice. "I think you should get back in your car and drive to your house." Leave, also leave me alone. "That's the only thing I've got for you. Hunker down, lock the door, and—" He didn't have a plan beyond that. "Fill the bathtub. Store water. Take stock of your food. See what supplies you have."

"I think we'll do that." G. H. wanted to be back among his things.

Danny nodded, kind of tossing his chin forward, authoritative. He extended a handshake. His grip was firm as it always was. He didn't say anything more, went back inside. He didn't lock the door. But he stood just inside to listen to the men walk away.

In the car, Archie sat up. He looked better or the same. He seemed weak or strong. That moment was what counted the most.

They sat in the idling car for a minute. Maybe two. Maybe three. It was Clay who broke the silence. "George. What are we doing?"

G. H. had been foolish. People disappointed. He would do better. They would still be good, kind, human, decent, together, safe. "I don't think we can go to the hospital, gentlemen. Do we agree? I don't think we can go."

Archie understood. Archie had been listening. "I'll be fine. I don't think we should go."

Clay said it. "I want to go home. Can we go home? Let's go home. It's not far. We're so close. Let's go." He meant George's house, of course, and so they went, were back well before the alarm on Ruth's phone told them that it had been an hour. Less than an hour, and everything was changed.

40

ROSE HAD WOKEN WITH CONVICTION. THAT'S WHAT IT WAS
to be a kid, but also she had a mission. Her eyes sharpened their
focus: bedside table, green porcelain lamp, a framed photo she
hadn't even bothered looking at yet, her own pale foot poking out
of the bed linens, sherbet light melting onto the wall. Slack, damp
mouths, pink shoulders, tangled hair. Another day, and those were
a gift. Rose scooted free of her family and onto the carpet. The
youngest child was used to not being noticed.

She left the suite because she didn't want to wake them. No
one took her seriously because she was a kid, but Rose was not an
idiot. That noise last night was the answer her parents had been
pretending not to wait for. But Rose had read books, Rose had
seen movies, Rose knew how this story would end, and Rose knew
they shouldn't panic, but prepare. In the bath off her bedroom,
she peed, and it took a long time. Rose washed her hands and
face. Though Rose wasn't particularly quiet—letting the toilet seat
bang, running the water, closing the door more noisily than was
necessary—this all felt furtive.

Shoes tied, a spritz of Off! on the ankle where the mosquitoes
were most merciless, water. She pushed her refillable plastic bottle
into the refrigerator's built-in dispenser. Rose unwrapped a banana

and listened to the wet sound of her own chewing. The garbage was overflowing: crinkled cellophane, stained paper towels, used-up hunks of lemon no one had thought to compost. They had almost nothing left to eat. Rose knew they needed things, but more than that, they needed people. She would find both, in the house in the woods. Rose put a nectarine into her bag, where it would knock around in the cheap nylon, be bruised and leaking by the time she got around to it. She packed a book, as you never knew when you'd need a book.

Rose remembered. Into the woods and just in that direction, over there, that way, right there, kind of to the left, straight, under trees and over that little hill. She had an instinct that city living hadn't dulled. An animal, damp on canvas toes, her steps barely registered on the leaves, just the tiniest protest amid birdsong and breeze. Her body knew there was no predator nearby.

Rose and Archie had only been improvising, but maybe they hadn't. Kids knew something, and the knowledge that they had was tacit or unspeakable. Rose recognized every marker: the swell of the earth, the moldering log, certain fallen limbs. If she had looked back, Lot's wife, Rose might have seen a flamingo, pink and furious, flying through the air. The truth: they'd blown in on the winds. One of evolution's old tricks. Stowaway lizards on a log, swept to sea like Noah and Emzara, might make landfall on some new shore, and get busy getting busy, their descendants devastating native foliage. The flamingos were as angry as the humans to find themselves there. But they'd have to make do. They'd have to suss out some algae. They nested once a year, but that was all it took, and maybe a thousand generations from then they'd be inbred and some other crazy color (antifreeze blue from sipping from swimming pools?), some new species. Maybe they'd be all that was left.

Rose sang to herself, in her head first, and then she felt bold, or different, or fine, or happy, and sang out loud, a One Direction song, the kind of thing Archie would have mocked her for liking but secretly enjoyed. Rose felt a clarity that was hers by rights. She understood. Once she got to that other house, she'd be able to answer the questions that seemed to matter to everyone. There would be people there and they would have an answer, or at least her family would not feel so alone.

The morning was cool, but you could tell the day would be hot. The leaves underfoot were barely damp: the tops of the trees were that thick. A time zone away, it was still dark, but then it was dark in so many places. Some people were committing suicide. Some people were packing things up in cars and hoping they'd be able to get a mile or two or ten or whatever it would take to reach wherever safety endured. Some people thought they'd cross the border, not realizing that such lines were imaginary. Some people didn't know anything was amiss. There were towns in New Mexico and Idaho where nothing had happened yet, though it was odd how no one could seem to talk to the satellites overhead. People still went to jobs that in time they would see were wholly useless, selling potted plants or making up hotel beds. Governors declared states of emergency but couldn't figure out how to tell anyone. Stay-at-home mothers were irritated that Daniel Tiger was not available. Some people started to realize they'd had a naive faith in the system. Some people tried to maintain that system. Some people were vindicated that they'd stockpiled guns and those filter straws that made any water safe to drink. However much had happened, so much more would happen. The leader of the free world was sequestered beneath the White House, but no one cared about him, certainly not a little girl tripping through the woods and thinking about Harry Styles.

Rose wasn't brave. Kids were merely too young to know to look away from the inexplicable. Kids stared at the raving schizophrenic on the subway while adults cast eyes down and thought about podcasts. Kids asked questions they didn't know were deemed impolite: why do you have that bump on your neck, is there a baby growing in your tummy, did you always have no hair, why are your teeth silver, will there still be elephants when I'm all grown up? Rose knew what the noise was, but no one had asked her. It was the sound of fact. It was the change they'd pretended not to know was coming. It was the end of one kind of life, but it was also the beginning of another kind of life. Rose kept walking.

Rose was a survivor and would survive. She knew, by some instinct (maybe just the human connection), that she was in the minority. Somewhere south, levees had ceded to the river. Waters rose into second-story bedrooms and people made their way to attics and rooftops. In Philadelphia, a woman delivering for the third time—a son, to be named for her brother, killed while deployed in Tehran—felt the baby on her chest just as the hospital lost power, so it was like the blackout was due to the shock of his skin on hers. All the babies in the neonatal intensive care unit died within hours. Christians gathered in their churches, but so did nonbelievers, thinking their devout neighbors might be better prepared. (Not so, alas.) In some places people were panicking about food, in others they were pretending not to. The staff at a Salvadoran restaurant in Harlem grilled food in the street, handing it out for free. Only twenty-four hours in, most people stopped listening to archaic radios and expecting to understand. Was this a test of faith? It affirmed only their faith in their ignorance. People locked doors and windows and played board games with their families, though a mother in St. Charles, Maryland, drowned her two daughters in the bathtub, which struck her as far more sensible than a round of Chutes and Ladders. That game required neither skill nor strategy; all it had to teach was that life was mostly unearned advantage or devastating fall. It took unimaginable courage to kill your children. Few people could manage it.

Damp at her neck, her forehead, her upper lip with its nascent mustache, Rose marched on. A few miles away, the herd of deer that Danny had seen had found another, strength in numbers, and were walking in the direction that instinct told them, an astonishing sight, like the buffalo on the plains before white people killed them all. People in nearby houses couldn't exactly believe it, but were more credulous than they'd been a week ago. The next generation of these deer would be born white as the unicorn in those Flemish tapestries that Rose and her family would never see. Not albinism, the one geneticist who worked it out would discover, but intergenerational trauma. Life was like that; life was about change.

Some of the nearby locals got into their cars and drove toward the city. There were no police, so they sped. Brooklyn smelled: spoilage in refrigerated cases gone warm, garbage accreting on corners or wherever, plus the trapped commuters—the bipolar homeless man, the press secretary to the mayor, the optimists who'd been heading to job interviews at Google—slowly becoming unclaimed corpses.

There, in the woods, the air was sweet and rotten, as summer air tended to be. Rose wondered: Would they be a mother and father and one or two children? Would they be white like her family, or black like the Washingtons, or Indian like Sabeena's family, or from Saudi Arabia or Taipei or the Maldives? Did they know, in Saudi Arabia and Taipei and the Maldives, what was happening in Waycross, Georgia, where the staff of forty jailers had left fifteen hundred men to the elements? Unexpected liberty: the sodden ceiling yielding, trapping bodies in the rubble, forever behind bars, but maybe their souls got out? None of those forty believed wind and rain could undo the work of man. None of those forty mourned those dead even one bit. They were bad men, they told themselves, not knowing how little it mattered whether you'd spent your life being good or bad.

Rose had been walking for an hour or her entire life. She unzipped her bag and bit into the bruised nectarine. Some flying insect, sensing the sweetness, hovered nearby. She ate the white flesh in one, two, seven, fourteen bites. The fruit pulled away so neatly from the stone at its center. A fruit's stone was something like a miracle, rutted and rough. She let it fall to the ground, hoping that, years from now, it might yield a tree.

She was not dumb. She did not expect salvation. She understood that alone, they had nothing. Now they would have something, and it would be thanks to Rose. She saw the roof through the woods, just where she knew it was going to be.

But the house was just like theirs! That seemed to mean something, even if, in a way, all houses looked the same. Rose was heartened by this, the echo of the Washingtons' house, the way a baby's babble sounds like reassuring speech. Brave, she made her way around to the front door. Rose walked right up the brick path meant for visitors. She knocked firmly, fist tight and confident.

Careful not to crush the plantings, she stood in the mulch and pressed her face against the windows. A field of flowery wallpaper, an oil painting of a brown horse, a brass sconce, a closed door, a mirror reflecting back only her own face—her face, resolute and optimistic. She couldn't know, would never know, that the Thornes, the family who lived there, were at the airport in San Diego, unable to make arrangements since there were no flights operating domestically because of a nationwide emergency without precedent, as though precedent were required. The Thornes would never see this house again in their lives, though Nadine, the matriarch, would sometimes dream of it before she succumbed to cancer in one of the tent camps the army managed to erect outside the airport. They'd burn her body, before they stopped bothering with that, as the bodies outnumbered the people left to do the burning.

Rose walked to the back of the house and knocked on the sliding glass door. The room was different from the Washington's: the furniture heavier, the walls darker. The house was not made to welcome vacationers but appointed according to the tastes of the people who lived there. Maybe those people were huddled in the basement, waiting with guns; maybe those people had heard the sound and got into their car and driven as fast as possible. Rose went to the detached garage and found cardboard boxes and pegboards hung with tools but no car. There was, though, a boat, sheathed in dirty canvas.

"You're not home." She said it out loud, but was talking to herself. She rang the doorbell, and heard the tinkle of it through the cheap, hollow door. She was not going back without what she had come for.

There were ornamental stones marking the flower bed alongside the house. Rose weighed tossing one against the back door, then noticed that the panes bedside the front door were already cracked. She stood back and threw it. The glass spilled into the house, the stone fell back at her feet. The noise was brief; there was just the sound of nothing. Rose pulled the sleeve of her hoodie over her hand, held a smaller rock like it was a hot pan, and banged into the points of glass that clung to the frame. She reached inside, and the dead bolt was right there. It was that simple.

The house smelled of cat. She'd find the cat food and the litter box, but never the animal itself, which had gone off to do whatever the animals were doing. She turned on the lights as a concession to her own fear. Rose knew, in that way you do, that she was alone. But she went into every room, opened every closet, pulled back the shower curtains, knelt to look beneath the beds. There was a pink-carpeted bedroom, the wooden bed with its floral spread angled to catch the full view of the treetops. There was a den, cabinets full of board games and puzzles, wide sectional in a standoff with the biggest television Rose had ever seen. There was a dining room, the vacuum cleaner's path marked on the immaculate blue carpet, the table polished and lustrous.

The refrigerator was a cacophony of magnets and notes and recipes and holiday cards, smiling families barefoot at the shore or posed against autumn foliage. Rose opened the door, and there was more there than at the Washingtons': salad dressings, ketchup, a glass jar of cornichons, soy sauce, one of those cardboard cans you pop to reveal biscuit dough. There were little plastic bottles of some medicine, an open stick of butter, some white cranberry juice. There were clean glasses in the dish rack, and she helped herself.

Sitting at the kitchen island, Rose saw the telephone, the fruit bowl with two lemons in it, the jumble of papers and mail. She opened a drawer in the kitchen, and it was that drawer: rubber bands, dimes, an old battery, a pair of scissors, some coupons, a wrench. In the powder room off the hallway, Rose admired the little dish of soaps molded to look like seashells.

She went back to the den and switched on the television. The screen was blue. Rose opened the cabinet beneath it and found the PlayStation, the dozens of plastic boxes holding the various games, and dozens of DVDs. They didn't have a player at their house, but there was one in the classroom, and she was not stupid. She decided on *Friends*; they had the whole box set. It was the episode where Ross fantasized about Princess Leia.

The sound of the television made her feel so much better. She turned the volume loud to keep her company as she ransacked. Band-Aids, Advil, a package of batteries. These were treasure but meant as proof. There was a blue-walled bedroom, sparsely filled; clearly its teenage inhabitant had left home. This, Rose thought, this could be Archie's. She wouldn't mind the guest room, its staid oval rug, its fussy, frilly curtains. Home was just where you were, in the end. It was just the place where you found yourself.

She didn't know that her mother was, at that moment, sitting in quiet in the empty, bird-smelling egg shack. When Amanda saw her son again, it would take her some time to find her voice. A shock. Then, later, she'd see her daughter again, and still be unable to speak. She'd just shiver.

Rose knew the way back—over that rise, then down it, carefully, correcting for gravity—past this familiar tree and that familiar tree and the little clearing with its sacred beam of light. She'd seen once, on the internet, that trees knew not to grow into one another, held themselves at some remove from their neighbors. Trees knew to occupy only their given patch of earth and sky. Trees were generous and careful, and maybe that would be their salvation.

She'd go back. She'd probably been missed, already, and felt a little guilty over not leaving a note. But she'd show them her bag, the things she'd found, tell them about the house in the woods with the DVD player and the three nice bedrooms and the camping supplies in the basement and the pantry lined with cans. She was only a girl, but the world still held something, and that mattered. Maybe her parents would cry over what they didn't know and what they did, which was that they were together. Maybe Ruth would empty the dishwasher and G. H. would take out the garbage, and maybe the day would truly begin, and if the rest of it—something for lunch, a relaxing swim, those pool floats, catching up on a magazine, attempting that jigsaw puzzle?—was unclear, so be it. If they didn't know how it would end—with night, with more terrible noise from the top of Olympus, with bombs, with disease, with blood, with happiness, with deer or something else watching them from the darkened woods—well, wasn't that true of every day?

ACKNOWLEDGMENTS

I'm deeply indebted to this book's editors—Helen Atsma, Sara Birmingham, and Megan Lynch—as well as to all their colleagues at Ecco, and, as always, to Julie Barer and Nicole Cunningham. I am very thankful for the generosity of Laura Lippman, Dan Chaon, Jessica Winter, Meaghan O'Connell, and Lynn Steger Strong. It is not an exaggeration to say this book would not exist without David Land; David, I hope for many more years of vacations (crumb-topped doughnuts, swimming pools, cake from a box on rainy days) with you.

A Conversation with

Rumaan Alam

BARNES & NOBLE EXCLUSIVE

You've written about female friendship; you've written about motherhood—this book seems like a departure.

This book is different from my first two; I wanted to push myself to try something new. At the same time, this is the work of the same sensibility and the same interests. As with my first two books, this one looks at the relationships between people, and how those relationships are shaped by differences in class and race. As before, I'm looking at domestic life. I have two kids, and maybe that's why I'm so curious about the question of what it is to be a parent, or how labor and emotion are divided between parents within a family unit. I'm very interested in domestic life—its comforts, like food, and its traps and complications. So yes, this book is different, and yes, it's the same.

This new book moves almost like a thriller. Was it a challenge to work in that form?

This novel is indebted to works of suspense, even horror. I wanted to capture the languor of summer vacation, then disrupt that, and that is a real convention—the idyll that shatters to become something else altogether. So I was thinking about certain kinds of books and movies, trying to figure out how they work on their audience, why they are structured in a certain way. I think it's a mistake when people are dismissive of certain genres—horror or romance or what have you. It's remarkable how books can adhere to the conventions of a genre and make their readers swoon with romantic feeling, or feel afraid, or breathless. I wanted to write a story that had that kind of effect on the reader—something that felt soothing, then addictive, then frightening, then moving.

Leave the World Behind tells the story of a family vacation gone horribly wrong. What inspired you?

In a way, this is my most transparently autobiographical work. The house depicted in this book is, in my mind anyway, the very Long Island house my family and I rented for our summer holiday a couple years ago. I studied the Airbnb listing as I started writing, reminding myself of how the rooms fit together. And I borrowed from life: we took a trip to the beach on a strange and windy day, we had warm afternoons in the beautiful swimming pool. I love the summer and have always had very fond memories of the various summertime trips we've taken. I wanted to capture those times. That said, this is a book that tries to conjure the fear and anxiety of being alive at this particular moment. So my favorite times are depicted here because they're in contrast to what unfolds.

In this book, a family has rented an Airbnb; the owners arrive with news of an emergency. No one knows what's happening. Beyond what inspired the setting, where did you come up with this story?

There is another convention: the unexpected visitors whose arrival upends all order. And another: the people who have arrived are different from the other people we've met, and we understand some friction will occur. It's easy to see why this would be a common starting point for movies or books—you want to know what's going to happen! That desire to know is very human. Especially now. My phone pings when there's news; it buzzes if the weather changes. It notifies me if I receive an email, tells me the definition of a new word every day, reminds me that I ought to work out. We're acclimated—maybe *addicted* is the word—to our phones and all they bring us. When we're separated from our phones (for the duration of a plane trip, or even a movie), we almost feel withdrawal symptoms.

So I wrote about characters grappling with an unexpected arrival, facing an inability to know what's happening out in the world. The premise felt like it contained a lot.

QUESTIONS FOR DISCUSSION

1. What were your first impressions of Amanda and Clay? Ruth and G. H.? Did your understanding of them change as the novel progressed, or did they uphold your initial expectations?

2. At the beginning of the novel, Amanda makes a grocery list. How may this list reflect her background and her hopes for the days ahead? Think of a trip or a vacation you've taken in recent years and how you prepared for it. What do you think your approach to planning a trip says about you? How is it similar or different from Amanda's approach?

3. *Leave the World Behind* is a work of fiction, written before the COVID-19 outbreak and the societal uprisings that have shaped 2020. If you had read the novel before 2020, do you think you would have had a different response to it? If so, in what way?

4. For much of the novel, Amanda, Clay, Ruth, and G. H. can't agree on whether or not they are truly in danger. Why do you think they found it so hard to assess their situation? What would you have done if you were in the shoes of Amanda and Clay? Ruth and G. H.?

5. Ruth and G. H. are separated from their daughter and grandsons for the duration of the crisis, while Amanda and Clay have their kids with them. Do you think that changes their responses to the situation they are facing together?

6. How do you think the children, Archie and Rose, see the world in comparison to their parents? Do they share a similar vision of it? If not, how so?

7. In *Leave the World Behind*, the families grapple with the sudden loss of communications technology—cell phone, internet, and satellite services all fail. What is your relationship to technology? Do you embrace it? Do you wish our society handled its role in our lives differently?

8. This novel pairs two couples together who are from different demographic backgrounds in terms of race and wealth. How do those qualities impact the way they interact with one another?

9. What do you think this book says about the role of friends and neighbors? Do you think these characters will have to fend for themselves, or is there hope that they will have others to lean on? What do you think happens to these families after the book ends?